SWORDS
IN THE NORTH

By

PAUL L. ANDERSON

BIBLO and TANNEN
NEW YORK
1 9 6 8

BIBLO AND TANNEN
BOOKSELLERS AND PUBLISHERS, INC.

63 Fourth Avenue, New York 3, N. Y.

Reprinted with the permission of the publisher.

COPYRIGHT, 1935, BY
PAUL L. ANDERSON

Library of Congress Catalog Card No.: 57-9448

Manufactured in The United States of America
by Noble Offset Printers, Inc.

Although a character of fiction, the son of Flava Rufus typifies so well the qualities of courage, high patriotism, inflexibility of purpose, and a noble and lofty ambition—the qualities which not only made Rome great but which have animated the entire Western world in its rise from barbarism—that it seems proper to inscribe this book to one who might well have been the ancestor of any true American,

TIBERIUS CORNELIUS RUFUS

CONTENTS

CHARACTERS OF THE STORY

ROMAN

GAIUS IULIUS CAESAR, Proconsul of Gallia
GAIUS AEMILIUS DURUS, a nobleman, having the rank of *Eques*
LUCIUS AEMILIUS DURUS, father to Gaius Durus
TIBERIUS CORNELIUS RUFUS, a patrician
FLAVA RUFUS, mother to Tiberius
LUCIUS MARO ⎤
MARCUS CELER ⎥ patricians; *homines belli*
AULUS FLAVUS ⎥
DECIMUS VARRO ⎦
PUGNAX, a freedman
POLLA, wife to Pugnax
GAIUS HORTENSIUS, a lawyer
FLACCUS, a banker
MARCUS GANEUM, a trader
DUMNORIX, a trainer of gladiators
QUINCUNX, a farmer
PUBLIUS CLODIUS PULCHER, a gangster
TITUS LABIENUS, Lieutenant-General under Caesar
MAMURRA, Chief Engineer under Caesar
GAIUS VOLUSENUS, Tribune under Caesar
CRASTINUS, First Centurion of the Tenth Legion
LUCIUS FABIUS, a centurion of the Tenth Legion
TITUS, a decurion of the Tenth Legion
QUINTUS, Quartermaster's Clerk of the Tenth Legion
MANIUS CORNUTUS ⎤
  also called BOMBYX ⎥
ARCULARIUS ⎥
PORCULUS ⎬ soldiers of the Tenth Legion
SCAEVOLA ⎥
DECIMUS ⎦
DORIS ⎤
PERICLES ⎬ slaves to Gaius Durus
CARINTHUS ⎦
SLAVES, GLADIATORS, DAGGER-MEN, ETC.

ix

BRITANNIC

ESUS, Chief Druid of Britannia
TANARUS, a Druid
TASCIOVANUS, Chieftain of the Dumnonii
CARTISMANDUA, wife to Tasciovanus
ADMINIUS, also known as BRITANNICUS, son to Tasciovanus
BRIGHDE ⎤
EPONA   ⎬ daughters to Tasciovanus
BOUDICCA ⎦
LUGOS   ⎤
LUGOTORIX ⎮ noblemen of the Dumnonii; tribunes under
CAMULUS   ⎰   Gaius Durus
TOGODUMNUS ⎦
CASSIVELAUNUS, Chieftain of the Catuvellauni
DUBNOREIX, a sea captain
DRUIDS, SLAVES, CLIENTS, TRADESMEN, OUTLAWS, SOLDIERS, ETC.

SWORDS IN THE NORTH

Thine, Roman, is the pilum; Roman, the sword is thine,
The even trench, the bristling mound, the legion's ordered line;
And thine the wheels of triumph, which with their laurelled
    train
Move slowly up the shouting streets to Jove's eternal fane.

MACAULAY, *The Prophecy of Capys*

CHAPTER I

Of the Dinner-Party at Lucius Maro's; and Britannicus the Gladiator

LOOKING back over the affairs of my early life, it is strange to reflect that my adventures with Gaius Caesar in Gallia and Britannia, my marriage with Brighde of the Dumnonii and my adoption into her tribe, together with my later fortunes—that all these things were really due to the facts that Marcus Celer threw the Venus throw of the dice at Lucius Maro's dinner-party and that Tiberius Rufus was a guest at that same party. So deeply involved is the web of life that Lachesis weaves for us mortals!

Know, then, that my name is Gaius Aemilius Durus, that my mother died when I was about three years old, and that my father, Lucius Durus, whose only child I was, was an *eques,* that is, of the second rank of Roman nobility. The patricians owe their standing to birth, but membership in the equestrian order is largely a question of money, and though my family had been noble for four generations, we were distinctly below the Senatorial rank in social position. My father was a banker, of considerable wealth and influence in the Republic, and was not only an able and a good man, respected by all who knew him, but was in addition a generous and an affectionate parent. There was but one flaw in his character, and that a venial one; he desired social position, less, be it said, for himself than for me. Not that he was snobbish to his own class, or servile to those of patrician birth; his self-respect and good sense prevented that; but of choice he invited patricians to his dinners, and was glad to have me bring friends of social standing to our great house on Mons Palatinus. He never stinted my allowance, giving me ample gold to keep my end up with the wealthy young men of Rome, and encouraging me to associate with those gilded idlers.

Also, a marriage had been arranged for me with Terentia Laeca, niece of that Marcus Laeca at whose home in the Street of the Scythe-Makers the conspiracy of Lucius Catilina was born and nurtured. Of patrician blood, she was of decayed fortunes, and the match was altogether one of policy, since her social standing and my money would supplement each other; there was no question of love between us. Indeed, she half despised me for a pushing upstart, and I rather more than half despised her; I have never been able to discern any vast moral gulf between the women of the Subura who sell their charms informally for gold and the patrician dame who does precisely the same thing with a gloss of ceremony and legality. However, the wedding never took place, so let it pass.

It is not seemly to criticize one's parents, but I cannot feel that all this was the best of educations; riches and indulgence are evil things for a youth whose character is forming. To be sure, my father meant well by me, but as I have heard the great Imperator say: "Tartarus is full of those who meant well," and in my eighteenth year I was no better than a *"homo bellus,"* a "pretty man,"— one of the oiled, perfumed, jeweled loungers who spend their days in bathing, in having their hair and beards curled and their togas arranged, in calling on idle ladies of fashion—preferably married ones of easy virtue—and their nights in drinking-bouts or the still less reputable diversions of the Subura. Such was my life until the month of Junius of the year DCLXXXXVI from the Founding of the City,* when the Fates saw fit to weave white threads into the somewhat soiled web of my existence.

One desperately hot and sultry day, when most of the nobles of Rome had fled to their villas at Baiae or Praeneste, and I was meditating the same exodus, I was lounging on a marble slab in the *frigidarium,* the cold room of the public bath. The *unctor* had finished oiling and massaging me, and I was trying to summon up energy to dress and dare the heat of the Forum, when Lucius Maro entered. About two years my senior, he was already jaded and worn by dissipation, as the heavy pouches and purple rings under his eyes testified and his general languor of manner confirmed.

"Ha, Gaius," he greeted me. "The very man! Manius Corbulo has failed me, and I have but eight for my dinner to-night. Will you be the ninth?" It was a sufficiently cavalier invitation, but Lucius was of the great gens of the Cornelii, and carried no small measure of patrician arrogance of birth. Still, he was not devoid of manners, and softened the rudeness of his phrasing by adding: "You shall have the Consul's Seat, on my left. I had intended that honor for Corbulo, but since he has gone to Baiae with that singing-girl he is mad about—. Do not refuse me, Gaius; my cook is preparing Lucrine oysters and roasted peacocks, and there will be old and crusted Falernian to drink. Also, I have a troupe of dancers from Gades, one of whom—a fascinating maiden!—nay, I will tell you no more; you must see with your own eyes. At the ninth hour, then; I may count on you?"

I nodded agreement.

"I will be there."

* June, 58 B. C.

"Good!" said Maro, and passed on to the disrobing room.

The early hour set for the dinner proved that it would be none of those late and stodgy affairs beloved of such men as Cicero, Cato, Atticus, and their friends, but a real *tempestivum convivium,* or early party, which would be wildly hilarious, and would be prolonged far into the night..All one to me; I was used to such riots, and enjoyed them; also, it would help me to forget the heat, and would be something to remember when I was enveloped in the quiet of Baiae. Possibly, too, we would later go on to the house of someone else, or wander in a band through the darkened streets, singing and shouting, to serenade some damsel of our acquaintance. More likely, though, our slaves would carry us home and put us to bed, as they were wont to do. Well, anything for diversion; life was deadly dull with nine-tenths of the better folk gone from the City.

Since this was to be a riot, it might be well to snatch a little rest. Clapping my hands, I summoned a slave and bade him examine the water-clock and let me know the time.

"It lacks a quarter to the seventh hour, *Domine,*" he reported. Two and a quarter hours before I must be at Maro's.

"Call me at the eighth hour," I commanded, and he answered, respectfully:

"Very well, *Domine.*" Whereupon I relaxed for a nap on the cool marble.

Maro's dinner was all that I expected. When I entered his home I found the other guests already there, amusing themselves in various ways. Marcus Celer and Aulus Flavus were casting dice, Aulus cursing furiously when he lost, as one always did who played with Celer, though none had ever actually caught the latter cheating. Of course no one in Rome ever paid the slightest attention to the laws against gambling. Maro and several others were admiring a new mosaic which bordered the rain basin in the center of the room; the picture had just that day been completed by a Pompeian artist, and was a cleverly suggestive portrayal of the many loves of Jupiter. In one corner Tiberius Rufus was examining a wall decoration of arms, and I was surprised to see him there, for he did not usually attend such parties. Still, he was of the Cornelian gens, a distant relative of our host, and some obligation of blood might account for his presence.

This Tiberius Rufus, though but a few years older than myself, had known one of the most eventful careers imaginable, and was the only patrician in the Republic who could show the pierced ears and scourge-marked back of slavery. Shipwrecked and counted lost in early childhood, he was rescued and brought up by a fisherman, being later kidnaped by pirates and sold for a slave. Bought by Dumnorix the *lanista*, he was trained as a gladiator, and fought many times in the arena. Purchased from Dumnorix, he aided Marcus Tullius Cicero to break up the conspiracy of Lucius Catilina, and afterward, recognized by his mother, he took his rightful place in Roman society. Since then he had married Aurelia of the Tullian gens, who left him a widower after a year of wedded life. Also, he had been successively quaestor, aedile, and praetor, and was mentioned for the consulship. For the rest, he was left-handed, red-haired, conspicuously handsome, a magnificent athlete and a deadly swordsman, and a patrician of the patricians. No, he certainly did not belong in this dissolute company.

The dinner was served in the open air, in the shaded *peristylium*, where the beautiful marble colonnade, the grass, trees, flowers, and fountain all added their share to our enjoyment, and it more than fulfilled Maro's promise. Nine of us lay down on the couches, I having the consular place, with Tiberius in the next most honorable, on my left. Oysters, onions, and other appetizers were served, and the character of the party was indicated thus early by the fact that the diluted honey which accompanied them was not fresh, but fermented, and spiced with thyme and sage. Broiled fish, cold ham, small roasted birds, and vegetables followed, wine being served with these and later courses, and then came a whole roast peacock stuffed with savory herbs for each guest, and a dessert of pastry, nuts, fruit, sweets, and so on.

While we ate we were entertained by singers, acrobats, and gymnasts, and by the Hispanian dancers, who, most scantily clad, proved as graceful, skilled, beautiful, and debauched as anyone could desire. Then the table was cleared, a libation of wine was poured, flowers and perfumes were scattered to retard intoxication, each diner was crowned with a garland of flowers, and we settled to the serious business of the evening.

First it was necessary to choose a Master of Drinking, and for this the dice were brought. We threw with varying fortunes until they reached Marcus Celer, who breathed on them, murmured: "Be propitious, oh Fates!" and threw. Lifting the dice-box, he exclaimed:

"Ha, three sixes! The Venus throw."

"As ever, when you throw," sneered Decimus Varro.

Celer raised his head and stared at Varro.

"And what does that mean?" he asked, coldly.

Varro had thrown the *caniculi*,* and was in a bad humor.

---

* "The puppies"—the lowest throw.

"Merely that you have the dice well trained; they know their master's touch."

Celer slammed the dice-box on the table and half rose.

"Per Deos Immortales—" he began, but we others interposed with soothing words and calmed him down.

Finally he said:

"If I am to be Master of Drinking, I proclaim my first rule—no water in the wine."

A chorus of protest went up, and Flavus objected:

"Be merciful, oh Master! You will have us drunk too soon."

"It is not possible to be drunk too soon," rejoined Celer. "And, Aulus, you are fined six *cyathi*—half a pint—for rebellion. Slaves, fill his goblet."

The slaves obeyed, and Aulus, saying: "I accept the sentence," tossed off the wine, adding: "I propose a health to our host—a *cyathus* for each letter of his praenomen."

"Accepted!" answered Celer. "Slaves, six *cyathi* to each guest."

The goblets were filled and emptied, then Maro said:

"A health to the guest of honor."

Five *cyathi* were drunk to me, and I proposed a toast to the principal dancer of the evening.

"What is her name?" demanded the Master, and I was forced to admit that I did not know.

"You are fined six *cyathi* for proposing a health to an unknown name," he sentenced me, but I protested.

"Justice, oh Master!" I cried. "Make it a toast to the land whence she comes—Hispania."

"The emendation is accepted and the sentence remitted," gravely acknowledged Celer. "Eight *cyathi* to each guest."

By this time the party was growing hilarious, faces were

flushed, voices raised, and the slaves were scattering flowers in profusion. Varro had a suggestion to offer.

"Lucius," he said, "why not have the dancers in to sit
with us and share our wine? There are nine of them, one
for each, and all young and beautiful. Youth and wine and
love go together; Bacchus and Venus were ever friends."

"Ask the Master," said our host, and Varro turned to
Celer.

"An excellent idea," pronounced the latter. "Slaves,
summon the dancers."

While the dancers were sought, I felt a hand laid on
my shoulder, and looked around to meet the eyes of
Tiberius Rufus.

"Gaius," he said, "come with me for a moment."

Wondering, I rose from the couch, as did Tiberius also.
Celer lifted his voice to warn us.

"You may not leave until the Master grants permission;
it is strictly forbidden, and there is a heavy fine."

Tiberius made a placating gesture and smiled, a singularly sweet and compelling smile.

"Surely," he asked, "you cannot think that we are leaving so distinguished a drinking-bout permanently? We
crave your indulgence to retire."

"Oh, well," granted Celer, "if it is but a brief absence—"

Tiberius smiled again, and led me to the *atrium*. There
he looked me over, and said, on a note of seriousness:

"Gaius Aemilius, you are too good a man, there is too
good stuff in you, for you to be wasting your youth and
health in such foul, disgusting revels. What do you say
we leave this pig-sty and seek some cleaner diversion?"

I was amazed at the suggestion, and for a moment
hardly knew what reply to make: I had never suspected
that Rufus owned any such feeling toward me as his words

indicated. It would be discourteous to our host to leave his party, but, to tell the truth, deep down in my heart I was a trifle sick of such doings, and went to these affairs mainly from habit and because I did not know how else to occupy my time. And for one in my position to have such a man as Tiberius Rufus seek my company was no light compliment. Further, there may have been some touch of vanity in my thoughts; to walk out of Maro's party arm in arm with Tiberius Rufus would be a slap to my host's arrogance. Tiberius saw my doubt, and added:

"You need not hesitate on Maro's account; in half an hour they will all be too drunk to know or care whether we are on Palatinus or standing before Pluto's throne." This was unquestionably true.

"I am with you," I said, and called my slaves, as he called his.

The slaves put on our sandals and we started out, I conscious that I walked a trifle unsteadily; wine always affected my legs before my head. I noted with surprise that Rufus had but two men with him.

"You must have expected to return home after night-fall," I remarked. "And indeed I see that your slaves carry torches. Do you not fear to walk the streets of Rome after dark with so few attendants?"

He laughed, and opening the folds of his toga showed me a long, straight, double-edged dagger girt to his side.

"My hand can keep my head," he answered. "Do you think any dagger-man would care to attack Tiberius Rufus?"

"*Mehercle*, no!" I acknowledged. "Not if he was in his right mind and knew your reputation. But not knowing—"

"He would learn."

"True. Well, where do we go?"

"I am taking you to call on a friend of mine. To-night, my Gaius, I mean to show you a different side of life from that we have just left—a home which, although it is that of a Gallic-born freedman, yet maintains the simple virtues of the older Republic. You have heard of Pugnax the armorer?"

"Who has not? I have often been in his shop in the Argiletum, though never in his home."

"We are going there now; it is on Aventinus. Pugnax was my friend when we were both in the school of Dumnorix, and after Catilina's death he married my sister—"

"Your sister! A freedman marrying a patrician?"

"My foster-sister, I should say. Polla is so dear to me that I forget, at times, that we are not of the same blood. I often visit there, when weary of the somewhat formal mode of life to which circumstances compel me—much as one seeks the freedom of his country villa after a season at Rome. Have you ever been in a freedman's house, Gaius?"

"Never. Are there *insulae*—tenements—on Aventinus? It is news to me."

I caught a flicker of mirth in my companion's voice as he replied:

"Hardly. I think there may be a surprise in store for you."

He spoke the truth; there was. The home of Pugnax, though small and simply furnished and decorated, was no filthy Suburan tenement, but was modeled after the typical patrician house, and was exquisitely neat and well appointed. Pugnax received us with grave courtesy but with evident pleasure, and his wife, though not lacking in dignity, was a bright and merry soul whom one could not help liking. Tiberius introduced me and I shook hands with the pair, though even now I blush to recall the patronizing manner I used. But Pugnax and Polla seemed not to notice it, and invited us to share their dinner. Their manner to me was frank, straightforward, and properly respectful, with no faintest hint of servility; the freedom they used toward Rufus was amply justified by the relation existing between him and them.

The family was indeed a revelation to me. Of course I knew plenty of the solid citizens, such men as Gaius Caesar, Pompeius Magnus, Flaccus the banker, Marcus Cato, and others, with their wives and children, but these were of the patrician or equestrian orders; of course, too, we had three or four hundred slaves in our City home and many more on the farm; in my capacity of "pretty man" I had known many gladiators; and naturally, I had dealt with many freedmen in their shops about the City. But though I had known the highest and the lowest classes of society, my dealings with the middle class lacked intimacy, and when I thought of the matter at all—which was seldom —I scornfully assumed that they all lived in plebeian fashion—huddled in squalid tenements or at best in the contemptible shacks of Mons Esquilinus. So it was with no little astonishment that I found here a dwelling which bore the same relation to my own that Pompeii or Ravenna bears to Rome—identical in type though smaller in size— and a family in which the ancient Roman virtues of simplicity, sobriety, courtesy, industry, hospitality, and reverence for the Gods and for one's superiors were apparent on every hand. And this was the home of a Gallic-born freedman! It showed how far we Romans had wandered from the teachings of our forefathers when a foreigner could instruct us anew in those principles which had made Rome great. Though I must admit that this thought did not occur to me at the time.

On the whole, I had much to do to conceal my amaze-

ment, and more than once caught Rufus watching me
with veiled amusement in his glance.

"We are about to lie down to dinner," said Pugnax.
"Will you do honor to our house by joining us?"

"We have dined," Tiberius answered, "but we will take
a cup of wine while you eat."

Rufus was given the place of honor, and the second
was assigned to me, while Polla, who had been about to
recline, sent for a chair now that guests were present.
The fresh air and the walk had cleared the fumes of wine
from my brain, and while Tiberius and Pugnax spoke of
politics I found myself conversing with my hostess, whose
feminine curiosity made her eager for details of the circle
in which I moved. Pugnax's wine was a fairly good vintage
from Beneventum—of course not equal to Maro's priceless Falernian—and the food, I observed, was good, wholesome, and attractively prepared, though plain and without
ostentation.

So while Polla ate and I sipped my thrice-watered wine
I gave her details of formal banquets, with a summary
of various menus; described the interiors of sundry great
houses; characterized some of the patrician women whom
I knew; and retailed bits of scandalous gossip such as
delight all women—how Julia had taken a new lover, how
Varro's wife Sempronia was planning to divorce her husband that she might take a richer one, and whence Gaia
had her new necklace of pearls. Polla had been hand-maid
to Fulvia, who was mistress to Quintus Curius, one of the
Catalinarians, but Fulvia, though of patrician birth, was
not received by the better citizens, and Polla had seen
just enough of that life to make her thirst for more. I
tried to make my talk bright, and more than once I succeeded in drawing a gurgling chuckle from Polla, who,
indeed, was not hard to amuse.

At length Tiberius turned to me, saying:

"Gaius, Pugnax has been telling me of a young gladiator of promise, a compatriot of his—"

"Not a compatriot," Pugnax interrupted. "I am from Gallia Transalpina, whereas he is from Britannia; he is of the tribe of the Dumnonii, who inhabit Belerium, in the southwest corner of the land."

"Well, well, at any rate he is a barbarian, like yourself." A friendly grin softened the insult, and Pugnax affectionately answered:

"Pluto seize you!"

Though it was nearing the end of the eleventh hour, and the heat was much abated, still the prospect of another walk was not alluring; my tunic was even yet soaked with perspiration and stuck to me unpleasantly. Maro's party being a formal one, we had worn our togas, and fifteen pounds of woollen cloth wrapped about the body and limbs offer no incentive to exercise on a muggy June day. But there seemed no limit to the energy of Tiberius Rufus, and I had read his mind correctly, for he added:

"According to Pugnax, this young Britannicus, as they call him, shows much promise, and should go far in the arena. Suppose we look him over? There are still some hours of daylight."

Reluctant to confess my vitality less than his—though I knew very well that it was—I agreed, and, Pugnax' slaves having brought water to wash our hands, we resumed our sandals, bade farewell to Polla and the children, and set out.

The school of Dumnorix the *lanista* was a rectangular group of buildings set in the angle formed by Tiber and the City wall, hard by the Porta Flumentana, and comprised sleeping quarters, mess hall, kitchen, baths, armory, and exercise ground. The gate was, of course, locked, and the keeper was chained to the wall, that he might not escape when he opened the door. He inspected us through a small grille, then flung the door wide, and bowing low, invited us in.

"Enter, most noble sirs," he begged. "A day to be marked in white, that brings such distinguished visitors! Marcipor—" this to a slave who stood near "—run and inform Dumnorix of the honor done us. Speed, whip-scoundrel!"

The slave ran off, and presently the *lanista* came hurrying across the quadrangle, to bow low before me, lower yet before Tiberius, and not quite so low before Pugnax— a greeting carefully adjusted to our relative social importance. It was amusing to see this burly ruffian cringing before two of his old-time slaves.

"Welcome, noble sirs!" he said. "Thrice welcome! How may I serve your pleasure? You wish to inspect my bully boys? They and I are at your command. Will you be seated? I will have wine brought."

We refused the wine, but sat down on a bench at one side of the exercise ground, while Dumnorix stood before us, bowing continuously as though his back worked on a well-oiled hinge.

"Leave off that bobbing up and down," commanded Rufus. He glanced at Pugnax. "Did you ever think, in the old days, to see Dumnorix bowing thus to you and me?"

"Never," laughed Pugnax, shaking his head. "When I recall how he used to curse us in the name of all the Gods, and order us to the stocks and the lash—"

"Oh, *Patrone!*" broke in the *lanista*. "I beg you will not mention that. My forehead is in the dust when I think of it! That ever I—had I but known—"

"Enough!" Rufus checked him. "What is past is past. Not even the Cumaean Sibyl could have foretold what the

Fates had in store for us. To business! You have here a youth who goes by the name of Britannicus? How does he fight?"

"As a Samnite, *Patrone*," replied Dumnorix. "Heavy armed, with helmet, shield, and short sword."

"Yes, we know the Samnite's arms," answered Rufus, dryly, and we all laughed, for in the old days Rufus had fought as a *retiarius*, a net-man, who invariably opposes a Samnite, and Pugnax had taken the latter part. Dumnorix grinned in an obvious effort to be ingratiating, and sent Marcipor running to fetch Britannicus.

The gladiator proved to be a youth of my own age and weight, though some three inches taller. His eyes were deep blue, his hair was flaxen, and his features and smile were pleasant enough, but wearing a suggestion of arrogance, or perhaps I should rather say bland self-confidence, as of one who knew his own worth. He had not been long enough in the school and on the sands for the life to have its customary brutalizing effect, and I was favorably impressed by his aspect, for not only had he the slim, firm muscles and easy grace of the good athlete, but there was about him a high-bred, courageous look which promised well.

"You are a Samnite?" asked Rufus.

"Yes, *Domine*."

"A good one?"

"With deference, *Domine*, I am. Not to seem boastful, next week will show better than words; I am to fight in the games given by the aedile Curio."

"You have not fought in Rome?"

"Not yet, *Domine;* at Ravenna and Pompeii, but not at Rome."

"He slew Aulus Corvus at Ravenna," put in Dumnorix, and Rufus nodded.

"Whom do you fight next week?"

"Taranis, from Gallia, and Dax the Thracian, *Domine*."

"Not a *retiarius?*"

"No, *Domine*."

"H'm! Well, let us see how good you are. Dumnorix, will you send for practice swords?"

"At once, *Patrone*. Shields and helmets also?"

"No, I wish to see what Britannicus knows of his weapon, that I may judge how to place my bets."

A slave was sent scurrying, and a number of gladiators who had been lounging around now came drifting toward us, scenting the prospect of amusement. They were a hard and brutal lot, coarse and savage, and their jests were for the most part too foul for repetition. Although Tiberius was known to them by reputation, Dumnorix and Pugnax were the only ones there who had ever seen him fight, most of his former associates having long since passed out through the Porta Libitinensis, the fatal door through which dead gladiators are dragged from the arena. Therefore the audience saw only an amateur fighter confronting a professional.

"Cut his liver out, Britannicus," suggested one.

"And eat it," added another.

"Carve him neatly," offered a third. "Even as old Coquus carves a goose."

Britannicus answered nothing, merely smiling a confident smile, and Tiberius took no notice whatever. Dumnorix saw fit to interfere.

"Be silent, you!" he roared. "Louse-bitten whelps of Tartarus! More respect to your betters—would you taste the stocks and the lash?"

Evidently the *lanista* ruled his men with iron hand, for the comments ceased abruptly.

I might say that I was no little amazed and shocked at

such condescension on the part of Tiberius—a patrician to fight in public—or semi-public—with a gladiator, even a practice bout! Still, it was Tiberius' affair, and I kept silent.

Wooden swords were brought, and choosing one, Tiberius motioned Britannicus to take the other, then rose from the bench.

"Ten *denarii* for each time you touch me, fifty for each time you draw blood, and two *sestertia* * if you lay me unconscious," he said. "Well, what are you waiting for?"

"Will you not remove your toga?" asked Britannicus. The gladiator wore only loin-cloth and sandals.

"No. It will not hamper me unduly."

"I was not thinking of that," was the naive reply. "But the woollen folds make it difficult to draw blood."

"It is for that reason that I offer fifty *denarii*. I want you to play for my head and arm. Are you ready?"

"Ready."

And the combat started.

The swords used in practice are of olive or cornel wood —sometimes of ash—and are a palm in breadth and a cubit in length, like the weapon of the legionaries. Also, they are weighted and balanced so as to be a perfect imitation of the fighting sword save that, lacking point and edge, they cannot inflict a dangerous wound. In the end of each is fixed a sharp metal spur about a quarter of an inch in length, which can readily deliver a superficial cut, and can even rake and tear the skin for several inches; further, a blow with the edge can bruise and stun, so that even with practice swords it is a rough game. The spur, of course, is to encourage thrusting, since the Roman style of swordplay favors point rather than edge.

All knew that when a gladiator, Tiberius fought with

* $1.70, $8.50, and $86 respectively.

net and trident, and a *retiarius* is hardly ever skilled with
the sword; besides, an amateur can rarely match a professional, whose life hangs on his skill, and though Tiberius
had fought professionally, it was not for some years, and
his repute was dimmed. All in all, Britannicus looked for
an easy victory, and attacked with confidence. I noticed,
however, that Dumnorix was chuckling to himself, and
Pugnax wore a look of repressed amusement.

No swordsman myself, I could not follow what happened; the blades flickered in and out too fast for my un-
trained eye. Still, anyone could see two things; first, that
Britannicus was trying hard, whereas Tiberius was not
extending himself; and second, that Tiberius remained
unmarked, but the gladiator's forearm, upper arm, chest,
thigh, and face showed an increasing number of red spots,
with here and there a streak and trickle of blood where
Tiberius' point had slid along the skin. A third thing, too,
I noted; that the faces of the watching gladiators lost their
amused expression, took on an air of wonderment, and
from that passed again to mirth as the tale of spots on
their comrade's skin grew and grew.

As for myself, though I could not appreciate the fine
points of the fencing as did the laughing, applauding
gladiators, none the less I felt my admiration for Tiberius
grow apace; it seemed to me an admirable, a glorious,
thing that a man of rank and wealth should so cherish
the stern ability which from olden times had been the
foundation of the Republic's greatness. And therewith I
knew an unaccustomed—and, as it seemed, a futile—
wish that I might be like him.

For perhaps fifteen minutes the two fought, and the
gladiator was beginning to breathe hard, when Tiberius
stepped back and raised his point.

"Enough," he said, and handed the blade to Dumnorix,

who by now was slapping his thighs and laughing openly, his huge, coarse face screwed up with mirth. "He has the makings of a good swordsman," was Rufus' comment. "He knows the feints, attacks, and parries; a little more practice, to develop his speed and accuracy, and he should do you credit. Do not let him be overmatched and slain. Above all, do not match him with a *retiarius;* a good net-and-trident man, such as Orontes, who taught me—"

"Or such as yourself, *Patrone,*" interjected Dumnorix, ingratiatingly.

"—would make sausage-meat of him," Rufus concluded, not noticing the interruption.

The young foreigner, meanwhile, had stood with eyes fixed on the ground, a rather sullen look on his face. Tiberius stepped toward him and extended his hand, which the other took without glancing up.

"Be not discouraged, Britannicus," said the patrician, kindly. "Practice, practice, and still more practice, and you will be an admirable swordsman. And rub your scratches well with turpentine and salt while yet they are fresh, that they may not fester."

The youth dropped Rufus' hand, choked, flung his sword from him, burst into tears, and strode hastily away.

"You certainly trimmed that young cockerel's comb for him, *Patrone,*" remarked the *lanista,* and Tiberius smiled faintly.

"He is a good boy," was his answer. "Watch over him carefully, Dumnorix; he should go far on the sands."

"I will, *Patrone,* I will," came the obsequious assurance. "Would you see some of my others?"

"No, I think not; we came for a special purpose, and must be starting homeward. You say Britannicus is matched with Taranis and Dax, for next week?"

"Yes, *Patrone.*"

"How are the odds?"

"Five to four on Taranis; even money on Dax."

"H'm! I must place a few wagers; he will slay them both."

"With your word to that effect," grinned the *lanista,* "I will get down a few bets, myself."

We said good-night and left, Pugnax turning off to his home on Aventinus, while Tiberius and I continued on up the Vicus Tuscus and the Via Nova. When we halted at the parting of the ways, the freedman thanked Tiberius heartily, and the latter, noting my puzzled look, explained.

"You were doubtless shocked, my Gaius," he remarked, "to see me lowering myself to a passage of arms with a gladiator."

I had been, yes; but would not admit it.

"Not at all," I denied. "It is your affair; you know your own business best."

"Your face betrayed you," he chuckled. "And I grant that I would not ordinarily do it. But Pugnax is interested in this young barbarian, and tells me that though he is a good youth, he will not practice as he should. Scourging and the stocks have proved vain to make him study, and Pugnax thought that a public humiliation might avail; mentally, the lad is above the dull and stupid brutes who are his companions, and Pugnax felt that a shock to his pride might rouse him."

"But why did not Pugnax—"

"Do his own dirty work?" interjected the freedman. "Because this red-headed scoundrel is ten times the swordsman that I am."

"So you say," retorted Tiberius.

"So I know!"

"Personally," continued Rufus, "I think it was either

sheer laziness or a fear for his precious skin; he has grown soft with marriage and parenthood."

"Pluto seize you! You know you are lying."

Again I was astonished at the freedom between them; I could not imagine even a patrician, a man of his own class, much less a freedman, using such language to Tiberius without grave consequences. But ancient friendship excuses much.

"At all events," Tiberius resumed, "Pugnax asked me to give the boy a lesson. We will see what effect it has on his resolution when he is beaten so badly by a mere amateur, an oiled and scented patrician."

"You could hardly be counted an amateur," I offered, but he corrected me.

"For present purposes I am," he pointed out.

We had no more conversation until my home was reached, then as we halted to say farewell I took my resolution in both hands.

"Tiberius," I said, then hesitated.

"Well?" he prompted me.

"Tiberius, I am sick of the life I lead—sick to death of it—a folly of gossip, baths, idling, gambling, and lecherous, drunken parties—a futile round! And I am sick of the 'pretty men' who are my companions—idlers, gluttons, sots, utterly worthless. I . . . I . . . ."

"Yes?" he prompted me again.

"I . . . well, Tiberius, you have chosen the better part. To-night you have shown me, as you promised, another side of life; a cleaner side. Pugnax and Polla . . . their home . . . I . . . would you take me under instruction? Teach me swordsmanship—and other things? I ask it humbly." I do not know why I specifically mentioned swordsmanship, except that in some vague way it seemed to typify the older, sturdier Roman virtues.

Tiberius put his arm around my shoulders.

"Frankly, my Gaius," he said, "I hoped for some such words from you. I make no secret of it; I have watched you for some time, with regret, and sought an opportunity for this; I asked Maro to invite me to his party in the hope that a chance might offer. I thought to discern in you seeds of worth beyond that of Maro, Celer, Varro, Corbulo, and the others of your set."

Here was new food for amazement—that Tiberius Rufus had noticed me and singled me out beyond my companions.

"Day after to-morrow," he went on, "I leave for my villa at Praeneste. Can you spend the summer with me there?"

"My father is at Baiae, and expects me—still, I can send him a letter explaining matters. He will not object."

Object to my visiting Tiberius Rufus for three months —I should think not!

"Do so, and meet me at the Porta Praenestina at noon two days hence. We will divide the summer between Praeneste and Baiae, and will study swordsmanship—and, as you say, other things. Now farewell, my Gaius; the Gods keep you!"

"And you also, Tiberius. Farewell."

He waved his hand, and with his two bodyguards disappeared into the gathering dusk, while I turned in and sought my couch, more comfortable in mind than I had been at any time during the past two years, and wondering not a little what the coming months would have to offer.

CHAPTER II

Of My Summer at Praeneste; and What I Learned from Tiberius Rufus

KNOWING Tiberius Rufus but slightly, I had never realized what a delightful companion he could be; he had always impressed me as being high-bred, yes, but reserved and cold. But that summer showed him to me in the light of a most charming, well-educated, and thoughtful—instructor, I was about to say, though the word is hardly apposite; he was no mere *grammaticus* or *literator*. No, his instruction was administered with such skill, and he led me along from one point to another with such effortless smoothness, that he seemed more like Plato or Socrates, or some other of the old Greek philosophic guides, than a teacher. Later in life I came to marvel at the consummate artistry of his method; at the time, my astonishment was chiefly at the extent of his knowledge and at his caring to devote so much time and thought to me. I once expressed myself to that effect, and asked him —but I will tell of that conversation in its proper place.

Praeneste being only about twenty-five miles from Rome, I had a feeling that Rufus would think me effeminate if I ordered out my traveling carriage, or even a litter, for so short a journey. Also, since I was to be his guest, I took no slaves, but placed the entire *familia* in charge of Carinthus, a Greek slave who had been ours since birth, and had risen to be steward of the town house. I sent off a letter to my father, then, though unused to horseback riding, ordered a steed to be bridled and held in readiness at the Porta Praenestina, where at the appointed time I waited only a few minutes for Rufus. I noted with satisfaction the glance of approval which he gave my horse.

"You are prompt, my Gaius," he remarked. "Have you been here long?"

"Less than quarter of an hour."

"A client came to ask aid, and I could not leave sooner. Shall we be riding?"

"At your service."

Slaves held the bridles of our horses while we mounted, then, dismissing our attendants, we set out.

Though the air was dryer and fresher than it had been, it was still hot, so we did not urge our horses unduly, sparing them for the climb into the Alban Hills. We conversed idly of unimportant matters as we rode, and halfway to our destination we halted for a few minutes in the ancient town of Gabii to let the animals rest and drink; then on again, and so as the sun was dipping toward the horizon we came to Rufus' villa. I was rather weary and sore from the unwonted exercise, but Rufus was entirely fresh.

The villa was a lovely home, with white buildings of marble from snowy Paros set on the western face of a hill, where now in the low sun they shone cream-colored, with shadows of intense blue. All about were glorious groves of cypress, ilex, elm, and olive trees, between whose trunks we could, as we climbed, catch glimpses of the town below, and of the magnificent Temple of Fortuna which is the pride and boast of the citizens. The trees were perfectly trimmed, the lawns beautifully tended, and a brook which tumbled and brawled down the slope to cross and re-cross our path had been landscaped and bridged with the art that conceals art. The air, at twelve or fifteen hundred feet above the sea, was cool and fresh, the slaves were deft, silent, and efficient, and altogether I received an impression of quiet luxury and refinement far different from the ostentation of Maro's home or, in less degree, my father's.

"Are there guests to-night, Cleon?" Tiberius asked one of the slaves who received us.

"No, *Domine*," was the answer. "Nuntius arrived yesterday with word that you were bringing a guest, and your lady mother judged that you would prefer not to have company this first evening. She is at present in the upper gardens, inspecting her roses," he added. "The tables are set in the *peristylium*, according to custom." I noted with passing interest that he spoke in the clipped dialect of the Praenesteans, so I judged that he was permanently attached to the villa.

Rufus nodded.

"We will wait on her as soon as we have removed the dust of travel," he said. "See that she is informed."

"Yes, *Domine*," the slave acknowledged. Then, with the freedom of a privileged servitor, he added, in gossiping fashion: "Olinthus was whipped to-day. A foolish hare wandered into the gardens, and Olinthus loosed the dogs on it. The hare fled through the roses, the dogs followed, and your lady mother had Olinthus beaten."

Again Rufus nodded.

"Quite right. If Olinthus does not get sense, I will sell him or send him to the quarries. Was the hare caught?"

The slave grinned.

"Olinthus had it for supper. He said such a tidbit was worth a beating."

Tiberius laughed outright.

"I suspect my mother did not have him very seriously lashed," was his amused comment.

He gave an order, and three or four slaves escorted me to the bath, where they removed my clothes and bathed and oiled me, the *unctor* apologizing for giving me so hasty a massage.

"I would not have you think me ignorant or careless, *Domine*," he said, "and to-morrow I hope to prove my skill. But the hour advances, and dining by lamplight you would be annoyed by insects." The man's pride in his ability was, I discovered later, a common trait among Rufus' slaves, and was fostered by an occasional quiet word of commendation from Tiberius or his mother. These bits of approval were so highly esteemed that more than once I saw a slave flush with pleasure at receiving one, and be almost unable to speak for emotion.

I held the *unctor* excused, and when he had finished, fresh garments were waiting me; I had sent them ahead by a slave, the day before. So, bathed and cleanly dressed in my best tunic and sandals—of course we wore no togas in the country—I was escorted to the colonnaded garden, where Tiberius, also refreshed, presented me to his mother.

Flava Rufus was a tall, handsome woman of about forty-five, and, as her name implied, a blonde; she wore a magnificent coronet of golden yellow hair such as no other woman in Rome, and few in Gallia or Britannia, could show. She greeted me courteously, saying:

"My son's friend is mine also. Beyond which, I know and admire your father. I bid you welcome, Gaius."

I bowed low over her hand in acknowledgment, and felt her fingertips give mine a little pressure of reassurance—for which I was more than grateful, since I knew myself sadly out of my depth from a social point of view. To one who has not experienced it, the gulf between Romans of Senatorial rank and all other classes is difficult to realize; like some tremendous chasm in the Apennines, it may be bridged but it still exists, and though I had been on terms of more or less intimacy with a number of the profligate young aristocrats, Tiberius and his mother were of a different sort.

It was easy to see whence Tiberius had his patrician dignity, for Flava was the very personification thereof, though not in the least stiff or stilted; on the contrary, she owned a natural, easy grace of manner which ere long dispelled my embarrassment and made me feel at home. Departing from the custom of most Roman women, she wore no cosmetics whatever—not so much as a touch of rouge—nor any jewelry save a princely emerald ring on the thumb of her left hand; in truth, her beauty needed no adornment. Nor did she recline at table; even in the intimacy of the villa she sat in a chair so long as men were present—quite other than the loose women of Maro's and Celer's feasts, the Sempronias and Fulvias, and the dancers and singers!

Flava's husband had died in the shipwreck in which Tiberius was lost, and she had never remarried, so there were but three of us at table. The dinner was as simple as that of Pugnax, but cooked and served with the most exquisite perfection of skill and deftness, and the wine was a Caecuban which far surpassed even Maro's boasted Falernian—so rich, indeed, that it was diluted with eight parts of water instead of the usual three.

Unlike that of a City home, the *peristylium* was not enclosed by a wall, so as we ate and chatted we could look between the columns, out over the beautiful Alban Hills, and watch the changing lights of sunset; watch the rosy color fade and the purple twilight sweep up from the lowlands, while in the sky the afterglow changed to palest green and one by one the stars came twinkling out. Then, when the meal was ended and the dusk had fallen, there ensued no such vicious entertainment as Maro's; instead, a lamp was brought, and a young slave girl with a lovely contralto voice recited to us from the mighty works of the blind bard, the sixth and seventh books of the wanderings of great Odysseus, telling how he landed in Phaeacia and met the white-armed princess Nausicaä, and of the welcome given him by King Alcinoüs. And as she spoke, a great, round, honey-colored moon came sliding up above the eastern hilltops to flood the valley with light, and a cool breeze drifted down from the upper gardens, enveloping us in a rich and heady scent of roses so deep and luscious that my brain swam from it as from a draught of unwatered wine.

The recitation over, Tiberius suggested bed, and as we said good-night, Flava remarked in courtesy:

"I trust, my Gaius, that your first evening with us has been a pleasant one?"

"Domina mea," I answered fervently, "I can truthfully say that it has been the most pleasant of my life. Were it not that I feel myself a living man, I could easily imagine myself in the Elysian Fields." Mother and son chuckled softly, and I continued: "May I prefer one request?"

"Certainly," Flava told me. "What is it?"

"That to-morrow you will show me your roses. The roses of Praeneste are famed throughout Italia, and I have heard yours spoken of as the finest of them all. And, indeed, their perfume foretells their beauty."

"Flatterer!" she laughed, though clearly not offended. "I fear, my Gaius, that you were born with a silver tongue. Still, you shall see them. Sleep well."

"And you also, *Domina mea.* Have no fear that I shall not."

As we went to our sleeping-chambers, Tiberius said to me:

"You have made a friend of my mother already; admire her roses, and she will give you her heart; they are her chief pride in life. After me, that is," he smiled. "And by the way, did you speak the truth, or were you merely being courteous?"

"Nay, I spoke sincerely. If she was pleased, so much the better."

"She was," he responded, dryly. "And one other thing, if I may offer a suggestion. Do not call her *'Domina.'* I know you mean it simply in courtesy, but it sounds a trifle . . . not obsequious, exactly, but . . . well, a trifle . . . after all, it is a slave's word. Best say merely 'Flava.' "

"That seems unduly familiar," I objected. "In the circumstances—"

"No, she would prefer it. And now, the Gods keep you, my Gaius. Have a good rest, for to-morrow we start sweating fat off you—both mind and body."

Many a time, in some stern camp of the far North, or on Afric's burning sands, as I rested from a hard-fought, bloody battle, the memory of that Praenestean evening has risen before me, and I needed only close my eyes to see again the lovely garden in the Alban Hills, to hear the music of the slave-girl's voice, to catch in my nostrils the exquisite scent of Flava's roses. So do these pictures live forever in our minds.

Tiberius was a vigorous, though not a harsh, taskmaster, and he possessed the wonderful faculty of making every lesson interesting. Rising with the dawn, he worked me for two hours each morning, then after the midday meal and siesta, for two more in the afternoon. He taught me swordplay in the Roman fashion, with the rectangular curved shield and short sword of the legionary, and in the Gallic, which uses a small, round buckler and which depends on the edge rather than the point of the weapon. Also, he taught me to oppose one style with the other, and showed the superiority of the Roman.

"A thrust ever beats a cut," he told me. "It is quicker, and does more damage when it gets home. Further, when your enemy lifts his arm for a downward blow, he lays himself open to a stop-thrust in the forearm, which disables him so that you can slay him at leisure. And with the short ,sword you can get inside the sweep of a longer blade."

"But," I asked, "if he used a long sword and was trained to use the point, he would have the longer reach. Then would not the advantage lie with him?"

"By no means. Leaving out of the question your use of the shield, the greater leverage of your short blade makes it easy to put his aside, when by closing you are again within his point. Here, let me demonstrate." And he did so, proving his contention to the full.

He taught me, too, the use of the *pilum*, the deadly six-foot, four-pound javelin of the legions, nor was he satisfied until I could pierce a Gallic shield with every cast, at ten full paces.* And he pressed into service one Quincunx, a scarred old veteran of Marius' wars with the Cimbri and the Teutones, to fence with us; this Quincunx was now a small farmer in the neighborhood, a tenant of Rufus', and it was pure delight to him to use his weapons again, even in mimic war, and during the rest periods to tell us stories of his adventures.

From all this work the flesh literally melted off me, till I grew lean as a Celtic *vertagus*, a coursing hound. But Tiberius and Quincunx laughed when I expressed anxiety.

"It is soft fat you are burning up, my Gaius," the former said. "Presently you will replace it with hard and healthy

* Fifty feet. The Roman pace was a double step.

muscle. And I can see your health improve; already your skin is clearer, your eye brighter."

"I must admit," I rejoined, "that I go to my meals with more zest. And, oddly enough, it is the simple things that my palate craves; elaborate and highly spiced fare no longer appeals to me."

Tiberius laughed again, and Quincunx treated himself to a grim chuckle.

"The sum of it is, my Gaius," said Rufus, "that you are in good condition for the first time in your life, and you do not recognize the unwonted state. Well, we will continue the treatment and see what comes of it."

I might say here that though I never became so wonderful a swordsman as Tiberius, I got so that I could defeat Quincunx quite handily, and was afterward considered nearly or quite the best of Caesar's men.

Usually there were just the three of us at dinner, Tiberius, Flava, and myself, but sometimes guests came in from nearby villas. These guests, intimates of my host and his mother, were as distinguished of manner and of intellect as Tiberius and Flava, and every night, whether in company or by ourselves, after the tables were cleared we men reclined while Flava—the other ladies, too, if any were present—sat with us, listening to the slave girl read aloud from the Odyssey or the Iliad of Homerus; the comedies of Aristophanes or Plautus; or the works of the tragic dramatists, Aeschylus, Sophocles, and Euripides. Sometimes we listened to the lyric poetry of Pindarus or Sappho, but more often to Xenophon's account of the teachings of the divine Socrates, to the philosophy of Plato or Aristotle, or others of the great leaders of thought. Often, too, we discussed the doctrines and beliefs of these giant souls— that is, the others discussed them while for the most part I listened in silence; at least I had wit enough to know that I was in the presence of those who were my superiors in learning as well as in social caste.

One evening about the middle of Quintilis,* overcome by long-pent curiosity, I asked:

"In the name of Pallas Athene, Tiberius, will you tell me where you gained all this wisdom? Unless I have been sadly misled, neither fisher-boy nor gladiator—which were your occupations during your early years—is apt to be deeply versed in the lore of the philosophers."

In the moonlight I saw Flava shiver, and put out her hand to touch his, as though to reassure herself that he was actually there. He patted her fingers, then replied:

"My foster-parents were at all events decent folk, revering their ancestors and the Gods; the altar of the Lares in their home was carefully tended. Still, they were not educated; indeed, they could neither read nor write, and it is owing to the kindness of the priests in the local Temple of Neptunus that I learned to do so, and that I learned the Grecian tongue. As for the gladiators who were my companions in the school of Dumnorix—*Edepol!* save for Pugnax, the less said of them the better; they were mere brutes—ignorant, savage beasts—whose only amusements in their leisure hours were drink and gambling, and the most stupid, brainless conversation." I winced at this; save for some polish of manner, it described accurately enough my own circle.

"Having no taste for such diversions," went on Rufus, "I spent what money I got on books, and my leisure time in studying them. Is it explained?"

"In truth, yes. But it argues a strong natural bent for good literature."

"The Gods so favored me. Hence I pray and sacrifice chiefly to Minerva, who must have been my guide."

* July.

I lay silent for a time, reflecting on this and that; chiefly on the difference between Tiberius and myself. Fisherman, slave, and gladiator, yet he had trained and educated himself till now he was a credit to his caste and respected of all men, and with it all he was modest and unassuming of manner. I, with wealth and teachers, with every opportunity, had wasted my years in idleness, drinking, gambling, and even worse dissipations—the Gods pity me! Deep in my heart I swore a solemn oath by Jupiter Optimus Maximus that from now on things would be different. And that Flava and Tiberius might not see the regret in my face I turned away from them and gazed out across the quiet slopes to where the lovely white buildings of Praeneste glimmered in the cold light of the moon. By now the roses were mostly gone, but still the air was rich with the perfume of other flowers, blending with the scent of field and wood and stream; even after these many years, that woodsy perfume on a moonlit night brings back to me the scene as sharp as any picture ever painted by Zeuxis or Parrhasios.

Presently I asked:

"Tell me this, my Tiberius—why do you take such trouble with me? I am not of your kin, not even of your social class, nor have we ever been intimates; my friends have been—well, you know them. Yet you, a master swordsman, labor to teach me fencing; you labor to instill into me your love for great literature; and, a philosopher, you strive to lead me on the path of knowledge. And your most gracious mother seconds your efforts. Do not deny it; I am no half-wit, and though you seem to make these teachings a matter of entertainment—"

"Do you not enjoy them?" he smiled.

"The Gods know well I do! But I can recognize the guiding hand—can realize that you have a purpose not yet revealed to me. Do not think I am objecting," I added, hastily. "I am only too glad of your interest. But I am not so far gone in conceit as to think it sheer love of my personality. What is the reason?"

He was silent for so long that I almost thought he had not heard, and I wondered if I should repeat my question. At length he moved slightly on his couch, and seemed to consult his mother with a glance. She nodded faintly, and he took a sip of wine, then sent the slaves beyond earshot.

"To answer you, my Gaius, I must talk of politics," he began. "You are right; it is not purely for love of your conversation, though, to tell the truth, I find your company far from dull."

"My thanks," I murmured, and he went on:

"A storm is coming. No—" as I glanced at the sky "—not of Aquilo's brewing: a tempest in the Republic. Like the folk of Pompeii and Herculaneum, we are living on the slopes of an active volcano. You may have seen it?"

I shook my head.

"No," I admitted, with some contrition, "I have lived from day to day."

"Like most Romans," he said, bitterly. "It is coming, though. Conditions in the Republic grow intolerable; the ancient virtues are lost, and greed, dishonesty, knavery of all sorts, the foulest license, run riot in the City, on Palatinus as in the Subura. Not in the provinces; there virtue makes its last stand. But in the City—*per Deos Immortales!* It is an open secret that consulships, quaestorships, proconsulships, and all offices which give the slightest chance of loot are bought and sold like any article of commerce. Graft is rampant, the provinces are robbed to the very marrow of their bones, and Roman society is rotten to the heart.

"Look at Gaius Verres; he differed from the ordinary provincial governor only in the fate which overtook him. Look at Marcus Antonius; of the best blood of Rome, boasting descent from a demi-god, he openly keeps a harem. Look at Sempronia the fascinating, and at Fulvia; women of the highest caste, of ancient lineage, with their many lovers; at the beautiful, charming, and abandoned Clodia; and at countless other patrician dames, with their manifold divorces; wherein are they better than the street women of the Subura?

"I tell you, my Gaius, there is such an explosion in store —unless the Gods avert—as will blow our Roman state, which has stood for seven hundred years, which has grown from a little settlement on Tiber's banks to be the Mistress of the World—an explosion which will blow that state to atoms and give our proud Republic to kite and raven; if the Gods withhold Their mercy, the fox and the wolf shall prowl in the Roman Forum, and bat and owl shall feed their young in the Temple and the Atrium of Vesta!"

I was shocked at the picture, yet could not help thinking it overdrawn, and said so.

"*Per Deos Immortales!*" he burst out, then: "Mother, forgive me for swearing in your presence, but—"

"I understand," said Flava.

"I have not told the half," went on Tiberius. "History repeats itself. Where now is Carthage, whose vessels once ranged the Mare Internum from Sidon to the Pillars of Hercules, and traded even to the far land of the Hyperboreans? Where are ancient Ilium and Gnossus, homes of kings? Where the great cities of the East, Nineveh and Babylon? The lion and the lizard keep their courts, and their degenerate sons cringe beneath the lash in our vineyards and quarries. Luxury destroyed them, and even so shall it be with Rome unless the Gods show mercy, for luxury begets greed, and greed, dishonesty. Wealth brings idleness in its train, and idleness means softness, degeneracy, and a craving for excitement, and the lust for excitement breeds licentiousness as putrid flesh breeds maggots."

This was hitting near home to me!

"Oh, there are some good men," Tiberius admitted. "Caesar, Drusus, Cato, Cicero, and others. And some good women."

"Your wife, Aurelia, was such a one," murmured Flava.

"A pity she could not live; it is such as she and you who give me hope for the future. But these men and women are few. They are lost in a greedy, gold-loving horde that scrambles madly for wealth, obtains this wealth by fraud and oppression, then flings it to the winds for costly palaces, dinners that would shame Sybaris, priceless gems, armies of slaves, the *tesserae* and *duodecim scriptae,* and profligacy fit to make the porticoes of Tanit and the groves of Ashtaroth appear the home of maidenly innocence and matronly virtue.

"Now, Gaius, you know my creed. I believe in the Gods, though frankly admitting that I cannot prove Their existence; for all the priests and augurs tell us, no man has ever seen Them, has ever heard Them speak. But whether They exist or not, I cling most passionately to the belief that unless a man can serve his fellows, can leave this world better than he finds it, he is of less worth than the lowly ox which drags the plow, than the swine which roots for mast under the shade of the beeches.

"Your companions, Corbulo, Celer, Varro, and the rest, are past praying for; they are sunk too deep in the mire of their sty to be lifted out. Of that group, you alone are not too far gone; I discern in you the seeds of worth, and

by Jupiter Capitolinus, I will have you out of that wallow
if I have to tear you out with my hands!"

Flava laid her hand on his arm, and he laughed.

"Very well, Mother," he said. "I will calm down. Well,
my Gaius, are you answered?"

"I do not see," I offered, after some thought, "how I
can aid you to arrest this moral degeneracy—which, now
that you call my attention, I realize exists. What can two
men do? For that, I take it, is your purpose?"

"I do not so far flatter myself, Gaius, as to think I am
equal to that Herculean task; the Twelve Labors were
naught compared to it—child's play. But a leader will
rise—" Then, doubtfully: "Gaius, this is for your private
ear, and not to be breathed elsewhere."

I raised my hand.

"By Jupiter Optimus Maximus I swear it," I responded,
and Tiberius nodded.

"I think a leader is in course of preparation," he said.
"Naught has been told me, for the man I have in mind
confides his thoughts to no one. Still, I have watched him
and studied his path, and I believe he purposes the regeneration of the Republic. And he is the man to do it—a
brain of crystal and a will of steel! There will be a dreadful time, a frightful civil war, and the gutters of Rome
will run with blood, but I think that in the end he will
prevail. The Gods send that he may!"

I thought for a moment, casting over in my mind the
leaders of the Roman state, then nodded agreement.

"I know whom you have in mind. Pompeius Magnus.
He is the greatest man we have." But to my surprise,
Tiberius shook his head. "No? Not the Magnus? Who
then?"

Tiberius hesitated, then replied:

"You have sworn . . . Gaius Iulius Caesar."

"What? The proconsul of Gallia?" I was frankly amazed. "That effeminate lounger? That self-seeking politician and demagogue? Tiberius, you jest!"

Rufus looked at me oddly.

"He is no effeminate lounger—"

"Such is his common reputation."

"Common report is a common liar, and never more so than in this case. And I know that most folk think him at best a clever political leader; ambitious, but of no great depth. But, my Gaius, I watched him through the Conspiracy, and stood at his elbow when Lentulus, Cethegus, and the others were executed in the Tullianum. His bearing at that time set me to studying his life, and I believe I have divined his thought, have guessed the purpose behind his acts.

"I have spoken of this to no living soul save you two, but, my Gaius,—" he reached out his hand to me "—I would have you by my side—and his—when the storm breaks. It is for this that I labor with you."

Convinced by the force of his personality, I took the hand which he extended.

"If you say it, I must believe," I answered. "And I will be there, Tiberius. I swear it. What I can do—"

His fingers pressed mine.

"Good man!" he approved. "I was sure you would see it."

There was little more conversation that night, and we retired early, but from that time on I knew a higher purpose than before. Thinking over Tiberius' words, I saw clearly the degeneracy, the rottenness of which he spoke, and of which, as the greatest of our poets has said, *"magna pars fui."* * So I brought to my studies, both of mind and

* "I was a great part."

of body, a new ardor, a new concentration, that when the
time came I might be fit for the high task laid on me. So
far had I grown from the careless youth who lounged in
Maro's dining-room.

About the middle of the following month, a slave
brought a letter from Pugnax, saying that Britannicus was
to fight in Pompeii, and my host suggested that we ride down
and see the bouts.

"I should like you to watch some swordsmanship which
is neither mine nor that of Quincunx," he explained. "Shall
we take horse to Pompeii?"

"I am agreeable," I returned, and we made our plans
accordingly.

We followed the inland route, the Via Latina, through
Anagnia, Frusino, and Casinum, making the distance in
four days, by easy stages, and spending the nights with
friends, for all Italian inns are too foul for decent habitation and both Tiberius and I had guest-rights in most of
the towns of the Republic. On the fourth day we turned
off a few miles north of Capua, and so through Puteoli to
Baiae, where we passed one night at my father's villa.

My father received us gladly and made us welcome,
though he was clearly overcome by the honor of Tiberius'
presence, and his manner lacked the ease which I had
noted in Flava Rufus. It was not that he was servile—
merely that he tried a shade too hard to be courteous
and entertaining; he was a thought over-eager. A trifle
ashamed, I spoke of this to Tiberius, who brushed it
aside.

"A matter of habit only," he said. "Habit and use. A
venial fault—superficial. And certainly preferable to the
insolent arrogance of many of Senatorial rank; better be
over-anxious to please than indifferent to the feelings of
others. Your father is a fine man, my Gaius; a man of

heart and brain, whom I admire greatly. Equal him, and you will do well."

It is unfortunately the case that young people sometimes tend to look down on their parents if these have not enjoyed the advantages which the children have had, and though I loved my father I had begun to have a feeling that I moved in better society than he did; it was not contempt exactly, but a sense of superiority, a feeling that I condescended in associating with him. Tiberius checked this, and set me back where I belonged; if Tiberius Rufus could admire my father, then, *Edepol!* so could I. Another sound lesson to the credit of my new friend.

Next day we resumed our journey, back through Puteoli, then south by the coast through Neapolis and along the base of Vesuvius, through Herculaneum to Pompeii, where we were welcomed at the house of Lenticulus, the aedile who was giving the games.

Thanks to our host, we had the best possible seats, and I was much interested in the three days' fighting, but even more in the amphitheatre, which, only about sixteen or seventeen years old, was admirably arranged for the viewing of combats. We had but one amphitheatre in Rome, that built during the previous year by Gaius Scribonius Curio, and it was of wood, whereas the Pompeian one was of stone, set chiefly in a great bowl which had been excavated within the southeast angle of the city wall. The gladiatorial shows of Rome were held, up to Curio's time, in the Forum or in the Circus Maximus or the Circus Flaminius, which, being intended for racing, had *spinae* down the middle, these walls shutting off half the gladiators from view. Especially designed, the Pompeian arena had no such barrier; its entire oval of forty-five by twenty-five paces * was unobstructed, so one could watch whatever fight he chose. Of course it was much smaller than the Roman circuses, its thirty-five tiers of seats accommodating only about twenty thousand spectators, but it was beautifully arranged and built, and I admit I envied the folk of Pompeii their arena; such a one in the City would add much to our pleasure.

I observed, too, that the gay and mercurial Pompeians were a trifle less savage than the folk of Rome; a defeated gladiator had a slightly better chance than with us of seeing waving kerchiefs or down-turned thumbs.†

Britannicus won three combats, slaying all his adversaries handily, and since Pompeian pride would not admit that their gladiators could be defeated, I profited to the extent of thirty *sestertia* through betting on my acquaintance. So after the games we looked him up in the barracks to give him, as the custom is, a share of our winnings. I handed him three *sestertia* and Tiberius two, this being ten per centum of our gains, and Dumnorix— again according to custom—promptly pouched half of the gift. Following that, we got into conversation with the young swordsman—he was a courteous and well-bred youth, for a barbarian—and learned something of who he was and whence he came.

"My real name is Adminius," he told us. "And my father Tasciovanus is chief of the Dumnonii, a tribe who inhabit Belerium, in the southwest corner of Britannia. In our country there are large tin mines, from which my father draws his revenue, and the miners take the ingots

* To be exact, 218½ by 115 feet. The outside dimensions of the building itself were 444 by 342 feet.

† Contrary to the popular belief, the thumb turned toward the earth was the signal for mercy; the signal for death was given by turning the thumb toward the spectator's own bosom.

of refined metal to Ictis, an island off the coast; that is, it is an island at high tide, but at low water can be reached by wagon or by horse train.

"Hither come the traders from Massilia * to buy our product, and on one occasion a party of these traders saw an opportunity to snap up me and half a dozen others and sell us into slavery. Having dealt with them before, we suspected no treachery, and were thoughtless enough to give them the chance; I admit the carelessness.

"And there you have the whole matter, briefly told. Could I get word to my father, he would gladly send gold to buy me out of this vile servitude, but as it is—" he shrugged his shoulders "—here I am and here I stay until Fortuna sets me free or I take a handful of steel through my gizzard."

"Your fate is a hard one," Tiberius acknowledged, "yet others have borne the like, and have won through."

"Meaning yourself," smiled Britannicus. "Oh, I do not despair; I have already saved almost half enough to buy my freedom. And the rest will come. Incidentally, I must thank you for the lesson you gave me when last we met." He smiled wryly. "It took effect," he added. "The swelling in my cranium is much abated."

"I can see that something has made a difference," laughed Tiberius. "Well, be not downhearted; Fortuna ever favors the bold. Farewell."

We remained for several days in Pompeii, and I had other talks with the young Briton, learning much of his home, his people, and their mode of life, also some words of their speech; it was almost as though some prescience bade me interest myself in these things, warning me that the day would come when I should visit that remote land. And indeed, I came to hold a better opinion of these for-

* Marseilles.

eigners. Of course, Rome is Rome, and no other place in the world can rival it for beauty and civilization, for wealth and luxury, but I learned from Britannicus that the folk of his country and of Gallia Transalpina were far from being the ignorant savages I had thought them. True, they could not boast a culture equal to ours, or even to that of Graecia, but in their way they were distinctly worthy people.

Then back to Baiae, where, my father having returned to the City on business, we had the estate to ourselves during a fortnight. Of course I do not mean that we were solitary; merely that Tiberius and I were the only free-men, for there were about two hundred slaves on the place. I was not sorry to have Tiberius see our villa, for though it lacked the quiet elegance of his, it far surpassed the Praenestean home in size and costliness, and for the rest was not in actively bad taste. I think there must still have been a good deal of the small boy in me, that I was so delighted to show off before my aristocratic friend.

Tiberius admired the place generously, and I think sincerely, and we enjoyed our visit to the full. I imitated him in having our dinners served outdoors, on the marble terrace overlooking the sea, and in having a slave read to us from my father's library, which was a large and well chosen one, though principally for show; Lucius Durus was no reader.

Twelve happy days we spent there, fencing in the mornings and afternoons, then swimming in the ocean or in our marble pool of fresh water, and in the evenings dining and loafing on the terrace, where, the gayly striped awnings rolled back in the cool of the day, we could enjoy the ocean breezes and could gaze upward at the sky and stars, or out over the incredibly blue waters of the Mare Tyrrhenum, to watch the colors fade and deepen as the sun sank below the water, while the fishing-boats and pleasure-yachts, with variegated sails and white, flashing oars, winged their way, like homing doves, back to port.

Twelve happy days, then on the thirteenth—unpropitious number! *—came a messenger post-haste from Rome, bearing a letter which announced the blow that transformed me from a man of wealth and position to a homeless pauper, and sent me, like great Odysseus, wandering through far lands.

* The supposed unluckiness of the number thirteen long antedates the Christian Era.

CHAPTER III

Of the Wreck of My Fortunes; and How I Enlisted Under Gaius Caesar

THE letter was from my father's secretary, a Greek slave named Pericles; that is, he was in theory Greek, though actually he was three-quarters Roman, and my own half-cousin. His grandmother was sold into slavery at Delos, coming to Rome and to the house of my great-grandfather, where her daughter, Pericles' mother, was born, my grandfather being also grandfather to Pericles. Thus I was born in freedom, whereas the secretary was legally a slave. The blood relationship—not uncommon in such cases—though of course not recognized by law, was a strong bond, and Pericles, brought up like myself and as well educated—better, since he had not wasted his opportunities—loved my father as much as I did. By its very abruptness the letter showed his grief and dismay, for he customarily wrote in polished phrase. Thus it ran:

S.V.B.E.E.V. Your honored father is slain by dagger-men of the band of Publius Clodius Pulcher. Grief overwhelms me. I pray you hasten home at once. Vale. Pericles. To Gaius Aemilius Durus at Baiae. With speed. A. D. III Kal. Oct.

Temporarily dazed by the shock, I could not fully grasp the import of the news until Tiberius recalled me to myself.

"You must go at once," he said. "Play the man now,

Gaius; this is a responsibility laid on you. Order out the horses and we will ride."

"*Vae mihi!*" I wept. "My father is dead—would that I had been a better son to him!"

Tiberius laid his hand on my arm.

"Regret is vain, Gaius," he said. "Live in future so that he who is now with the Gods may be proud of you. And doubt not that he will know."

With this I regained control of my spirit, had horses brought, and while they were being made ready I questioned the messenger. Apparently my father's assassination was a matter of personal enmity; he had refused to lend money to Clodius and had balked him in some of his political machinations, so the schemer had set his daggermen to stab my father from behind. Naturally I swore a most solemn oath, by the ashes of my ancestors, to be revenged on Clodius. I knew him both personally and by repute; though a man of good family and of political influence and ambitions—at that time he was a tribune of the people—he was utterly dissolute and unscrupulous, having even been involved, some years before, in a most disgraceful scandal in connection with the celebration of the rites of the Bona Dea. He had gathered to him a band of hired scoundrels, *homines perditi*—"lost men"—whom he used to further his schemes, and whom on occasion he rented out to the highest bidder, to remove witnesses, intimidate judges, dispose of personal or political enemies, and the like. The Gods did not see fit to grant me my revenge, though at least They repaid Clodius in his own coin, for some four or five years later he was slain by a like band of assassins in the pay of Titus Annius Milo, a rival gangster.

Tiberius accompanied me to Rome, and since I was now hardened to exercise we made the hundred and twenty miles in a trifle over eight hours, changing horses at post-houses. We took the short route by the Via Appia, and went at once to my home on Palatinus, where my father lay in state in the *atrium*. It was the first time I had ever seen the melancholy cypress before our house, and though I knew it must be there, it was a shock to me when we turned the corner from the Via Sacra and I caught sight of the mournful boughs beside the door. Still, they were in some measure a preparation for what awaited me within.

Tiberius was most kind and sympathetic throughout the trying time which followed; he assisted me in making arrangements for the funeral, which took place three days later; in performing the customary rites; and in receiving and acknowledging the many expressions of condolence. Then after my father had been cremated and his ashes laid to rest in our family tomb on the Via Flaminia, Rufus and I set about the administration of his estate.

This we found to be most horribly involved. My father had lent large sums to speculators, on security which was sound but not readily transformed into cash; he was backing a number of trading ventures in Egypt; and he had contracted for the revenues of the Sicilian and Egyptian provinces, for which he had already paid in his bid to the Treasury. Naturally, he was obliged to borrow largely to do all this, and though the ventures were sound, and would have profited him greatly had he lived, the inevitable result followed; at his death his creditors became fearful of their security and settled on the estate like vultures on a corpse, each one seeking to rend his own share from the remains. As nearly as I could determine, my father's debts amounted to about a hundred and twenty thousand *sestertia*,* whereas all his assets and estates would not bring the twentieth part of that sum at forced sale. Altogether,

* $5,160,000.

it was a rather exceptional case of money being lent on the security of character rather than collateral.

Through the influence of Tiberius, and partly, too, through his friendship for my father, Flaccus the banker was brought into consultation, but his report was discouraging.

"It grieves me deeply to say it, my Gaius," he told me, "but there is no blinking the fact that your father died a bankrupt. Had he lived, all would have been well, for his enterprises are sound—he was a man of wholly superior judgment—but such ventures call for the guiding hand of the master."

"Could I not borrow the money to satisfy the creditors, and carry on until I can realize on the speculations?"

Flaccus shook his head definitely.

"Times are hard," he returned, "and money is tight. You do not need me to tell you that the political situation is one of extreme gravity, and that a serious rupture among the Triumvirs is imminent. What the result of that may be, only the Gods know. And this reacts on business. Your father could borrow because of his reputation, but—" He checked himself, but I knew what was in his mind; my own reputation as a "pretty man." "I would gladly take over the debts and the ventures," he resumed, "but I simply cannot do it; I myself am over-extended at present. I am sorry," he added, with evident sincerity.

"I also," offered Tiberius, "would be glad to lend the money, were it not beyond me. It is well known that I am far from rich."

"Is there," asked Flaccus, "none of your kinsmen of the Aemilian gens who could aid you?"

I shook my head.

"None to whom I could appeal; wealth is not characteristic of the clan. My father was by far the richest, and

he was not loved for it. He did much for them, much, but
—well, you know how it is."

"Do I know!" ejaculated the banker. "Do I know! The
more one does for folk, the worse they hate their bene-
factor. The philosopher spoke truly who called gratitude
'a lively sense of favors to be received.'

"Well, I see no help for it," he concluded. "It is un-
fortunate to the last degree, but there it is."

I resolved to appeal for help to my friends—I should
say, rather, to those who had so often expressed the warm-
est feeling for me; three attempts were enough to teach
me my first lesson in worldly friendship. Maro greeted me
coldly and gave a flat refusal, Celer put me off with vague
expressions of sympathy and vaguer promises, and Varro
refused to see me at all. And two days later the three
turned away and would not speak when I greeted them
in the public baths. Tiberius was not surprised; he merely
shrugged his shoulders and remarked: "It is what I expected," but I was amazed, deeply hurt, and not a little
angry. However, the same day an incident occurred which
went far to restore my faith in human nature. It was
this:

Most of the four hundred servants in our City mansion
were *vernae;* that is, they had been born in our household, my father and grandfather preferring to breed rather
than buy their slaves. Although decidedly more expensive
than purchasing from recognized dealers, the custom has
definite advantages; for one thing, *vernae* are better fitted
to stand the heat of our Roman summers than slaves from
cooler climates, and further, they are more apt to feel
loyalty to their owners. This last fact was now proved
when a deputation of a dozen or so begged to speak with
me. On being admitted, their spokesman, who was Carinthus, steward of the household, said:

"Domine, we have all suffered the deepest sorrow at the untimely death of our most honored master, and we have learned with grief of the state of his affairs." I must have looked surprised, for Carinthus hastily added: "It is a liberty, I know, but Pericles . . ." He hesitated, seeming embarrassed, then resumed: "Therefore, we have held a meeting, and have voted to offer you our savings to tide you over until you can realize on your father's estate. We —all of us—most humbly beg that you will accept."

I was overcome, and felt the tears start to my eyes, felt a sob rise in my throat as I compared the conduct of these humble servitors with that of my former associates. Though a slave may not legally own anything whatever, none the less those of a City household receive small gratuities from their master's friends, sell left-over food, get commissions from tradesmen on things purchased, and in various ways pick up trifling amounts, so that a popular City slave can ordinarily put aside enough to buy his freedom within five years. Many of them do not do this; if their positions are good—like that of Pericles—they prefer to remain slaves and spend their money for luxuries, but in general they save with freedom in view. Most masters wink at the practice, for the hope of legal freedom does as much as the lash and the cross to keep slaves contented and to avert the ever-feared slave insurrection, so none but the more grasping deny their slaves this *peculium,* as it is called.

And now my slaves were offering me their little savings, their hope of freedom; to be sure, I could legally have seized the money, but they knew well that no decent man would do that. And I heard Tiberius swear under his breath:

"Mehercle, this passes belief!"

Getting control of myself, I inquired:

"To what do these savings amount?"

"About one thousand *sestertia*, all told," replied Carinthus. "We had been saving for freedom, as do all slaves, but at this juncture—" He broke off, and I answered:

"A drop in the ocean!" I got to my feet. "My friends— for you have shown that I may so call you—I thank you from the bottom of my heart for this most generous offer. Words are vain to express my gratitude. But I cannot accept. To do so would lose your savings without profiting me. There is no help for it; all my estates must go under the spear—must be sold at auction. And if your savings were in my hands they too would be confiscated, for I learn that Clodius—" here I choked on my anger "—that Clodius plans to buy everything in cheaply, using his dagger-men to over-awe other bidders."

A sudden thought struck me, and I turned it over in my mind.

"You also will be sold," I continued. Several of the men swore under their breaths, and one of the girls, a Greek named Doris, my own personal *vestiplica*, broke into stifled sobs. "And if you have any savings, they will unquestionably be seized, for Clodius is greedy beyond words. You had best bring your money to Carinthus, let him make a list of what each has, and give it all to Tiberius Rufus, here. That is, if you are willing to trust him."

"Oh, *Domine!*" breathed Carinthus, reproachfully. "We would as soon doubt Jupiter Optimus Maximus as Tiberius Rufus."

I turned to Rufus.

"And," I pursued, "if you do not fear the wrath of Clodius, and do not mind a slightly illegal act."

He snapped his fingers in contempt.

"That for Clodius and his assassins! He knows very

well that if he laid hands on one of the Cornelian gens
he would be beaten to death with rods as surely as if he
outraged a Vestal. As for the illegality, what is a slight
infraction of law in Rome to-day? Beyond which," he
added, sententiously, "there is a vast gulf between law and
justice. Bring me the money and the lists, Carinthus, then
all of you keep me informed as to your whereabouts after
the sale, and when it is safe to do so I will see that you
have the savings back again."

They thanked him and withdrew, and he turned to me.

"Your slaves," he said, "must have loved your father
dearly. Nor," he added, smiling, "do I think they precisely
hate you."

"We have always treated them well," I returned, "and
they recognize it."

"What is more to the point, and more apt to secure
their loyalty, is the fact that, unless I am vastly mistaken,
you have treated them with justice."

"Oh, that, of course. Besides, most of them were born
in the house. Pericles, for example, is my own cousin, and
we grew up like brothers. Half-cousin, I should say; we
are of different grandmothers."

"Naturally! But in all this there is one thing you have
overlooked."

"That is?"

"The strong probability that you, too, will come under
the spear. Clodius is both vindictive and greedy, and he
hates you. And has reason to fear you, besides."

Per Deos Immortales! Sell *me* into slavery?"

"Even so. Of course a free-born Roman cannot legally
be sold into slavery without his own consent, but a man
of Clodius' wealth and influence can readily suborn or
defy the officers of justice—as we have seen him do."

"I would fall on my sword first!"

"Folly! One can be ransomed from slavery, my Gaius, but not from the tomb. Nevertheless, it would be well to avoid it if possible. Let me think. . . ."

We were silent for a time, no sound being heard in the *atrium* save the rain—for it was a stormy day—splashing musically from the eaves of the *impluvium* into the basin in the floor. At length Tiberius shook his head.

"I am at a loss," he admitted. "I can think of several ways, none of them satisfactory. Would that Marcus Cicero were not in exile; he would advise us. Well, failing him, let us call on Gaius Hortensius; next to Cicero, he is Rome's ablest lawyer."

I ordered out my litter and we went to Hortensius' home, where we had the luck to find him kept indoors by the conjunction of the storm and a trifling illness. He made us welcome, listened to our tale, and drew down the corners of his mouth.

"There is no help for it," he dashed our hopes. "If the creditors insist, Gaius must be sold. It will not be strictly legal, of course, but what is that to such a one as Publius Clodius? You are sure they will, my Tiberius?"

"*Edepol!* Clodius hates the very name of Durus. But suppose I should wait for the sale, then bid in Gaius, or buy him from whoever takes him over, and manumit him? I can at least raise the money for that."

Hortensius nodded.

"It might well be done. But I see two objections. First, if Clodius is moved by hatred, he might refuse to sell, and send Gaius to the quarries or the oar. And second, even should you carry out your plan, Gaius would be a freedman, deprived of his rights as a freeborn *eques,* and it would be a tedious and costly process to have them restored by the Senate, especially if Clodius opposed; you would have to out-bribe him."

"What, then, is your counsel?"

Hortensius stirred slightly in his chair, and a whimsical smile twitched the corners of his mouth.

"In my position I hesitate to advise anything illegal . . . h'm! . . . it seems to me that if I stood in Gaius' boots I would order out my swiftest horse and ride as fast and as far from Rome as he would take me."

"Flight? I had thought of that, but—"

"Flight. It is not likely that Clodius will push his vindictiveness so far as to ask a decree of outlawry, and since the Durus estates are lost, Gaius must in any case be the architect of his own fortunes. I would suggest Alexandria; opportunities are plenty there. Though for obvious reasons I should prefer not to know his destination."

We thanked Hortensius, and returned to Tiberius' home instead of to mine.

"The creditors may place a *quaestor* in charge at any moment," argued Rufus, "and there is no sense in taking chances. I can outfit you and speed you on your way. Have you thought where you will go?"

Remembering what he had told me on a certain evening in Praeneste, I replied:

"Gallia Transalpina."

"To Caesar?" He raised his eyebrows.

"Even so. To Caesar."

"Edepol!" He was delighted. "If only I could go with you! And I would, did not affairs chain me at Rome. You will give my most humble respects to the Imperator; they say he remembers everyone, so he may remember me. And may Fortuna attend your steps. I will sacrifice a white bull in the Temple of Mars for your welfare."

Two hours later, wearing a broad hat and a raincoat of Tiberius', with ten *sestertia* of his providing in a money-belt around my waist, and astride the best mount in his stables, I rode through the deserted, sodden streets and out from the Porta Flumentana. My friend rode with me across Tiber, reining up in Janiculum.

"Here we part, my Gaius," he said, not without regret. "May the Gods have you ever in Their keeping."

"And you also, my Tiberius. I can never forget, nor can I thank you and your mother enough for all you have done for me, for all you have taught me."

He waved his hand.

"Profit by it, is all I ask. We shall meet again. You have chosen a hard path, yet a glorious one. And meanwhile, be not too eager in seeking wealth. Apart from such trifles as honor and decency and the respect of one's fellows, I think I have shown you that excessive greed defeats its own end. Gallia is a rich province, and there will be opportunities, but—oh, well, you understand."

"Trust me! I hope to repair my fortunes, yes, but at the same time I would leave a sweet-smelling name."

"It can be done. And there are other things of more value than gold, though it is hard to convince a Roman of that fact. And now farewell, my Gaius."

"Farewell, Tiberius. My most humble and grateful respects to your gracious mother."

We embraced, kissed each other on both cheeks, and on the Via Aurelia I set my horse's head for the north. Once I looked back, to see Tiberius still sitting where I had left him; we waved our arms in a last farewell, and when next I looked, the gray, shrouding rain concealed him from my view.

And now I entered a new era of my life—in truth, it was even as though I entered a new world. I had been brought up in the extreme of luxury, with an army of slaves to fulfil—nay, to anticipate—my slightest wish, but now I must fend in all things for myself. I had slept soft, dressed well, eaten the best of food, been sheltered from the weather, been waited on hand and foot; I had even had a specially trained slave-girl—Doris—to drape my toga on me. Now I lay on the insect-ridden straw of change-houses and roadside inns, wore coarse garments, ate vile, garlic-soused stews which I would not have given my farm-slaves, and drank thin, sour wine that was little better than vinegar. Also, I took what the Gods sent in the way of burning sun or driving rain or bitter cold. In truth, I had good cause to thank Tiberius Rufus, for without the hardening he had given me during the summer I could not have endured the change, but must have fallen sick or exhausted by the wayside. Oddly enough, the thing I missed worst of all was not shelter, food, wine, or clothing, but the daily massage, and when, years later, that indulgence again was possible, I reveled in it as I have seen cats revel in a bed of the fragrant herb which intoxicates them.

After passing Massilia I found the hardships less; the Gallic inns are in every way a thousand times better than those of Italia—in every way, that is, save in the prevalence of insects. There may have been some diminution of these stinging hordes, but what matters the loss of three million bites if seven million still remain? To be sure, the inn-keepers—shrewd scoundrels!—knew me correctly for a gentleman in misfortune, and as I have since realized, fleeced me right and left; I knew nothing of the value of money. One of them, whose place bore the sign of the Phoenix, was so remorseless that even I saw through his rapacity, but when I protested he called out his grooms and stableboys, who would have beaten me soundly had I not paid the exorbitant charge. I had my revenge, though, for six years later, passing south with the army, I happened to mention the circumstance to some of the lads of my legion, and the four thousand halted long enough to drink twelve casks of his wine, then laughed in his face when he asked for payment. Had this come to Caesar's ears, doubtless they would have been punished, but since the Imperator never heard of it, and since it was done in such a way that I was not obliged to take official cognizance, all was well.

At Massilia I learned that Caesar was expected to pass through that city shortly on his way to spend the winter in Gallia Cisalpina, so I resolved to wait him there. And since he probably would not stay more than twenty-four hours, I presented myself at his quarters, the home of one of the chief men of the city, soon after his arrival.

The house was guarded, of course, by a detail from the legion which accompanied the proconsul, and it took some argument before the decurion in charge would send my name in. Word came back that I was to be admitted, so I was escorted to a large room, very elaborately furnished —over-furnished, it seemed to me—where the Imperator was dictating to two scribes. One of these men was apparently taking down a permanent record, for he wrote in ink on a papyrus scroll, whereas the other used a stylus on wax tablets of the kind employed for letters. Caesar did not notice me at first, and I had a chance to observe him ere he turned his attention my way.

I saw a man between forty and forty-five years of age, above middle height, of slim though muscular build, and informed with the same high-bred dignity that was found in Tiberius and Flava Rufus. His thin brown hair was brushed low over a high, broad forehead, to conceal incipient baldness—a ruse that deceived no one—and his nose was thin and high-arched, his mouth broad and firm, with a hint of humor about it. His chin was well modeled and slightly rounded, his ears were small and close to his head, his teeth white and perfect, and altogether he would have been thought handsome in any company, though far from the Apollo or Narcissus type. Indeed, I think his attractiveness came less from regularity of features than from the sense of power which radiated from him like a visible, tangible aura; he gave the impression of tremendous strength of character controlled by an inflexible will, and when at length he turned his head and bent his large brown eyes on me I felt almost the shock of a physical impact. It was not that there was anything savage or cruel about his look; on the contrary, it was kindly and reassuring, but I felt myself in the presence of an overmastering soul.

"Gaius Aemilius Durus," he repeated my name. "What can I do for you? You are, I take it, the son of Lucius Durus." His voice was amazingly rich and musical, as became a man who was reputed one of Rome's greatest orators, surpassing even the famous Marcus Tullius Cicero.

"The late Lucius Durus," I corrected. "And I wish to enlist with the Eagles, Imperator, if you will have me."

"Why? As I recall it, you are rated a 'pretty man.' Why this sudden urge for the rigors of a soldier's life?"

I was astonished that he knew my reputation, but gave him a brief account of my misfortune, adding:

"I hope to repair my state in military service."

"At present I have no vacancy among my tribunes," he replied, coldly.

"Nor do I desire such office, Imperator," I answered. The tribunes were largely dissipated young men of wealthy families, sent to the frontier to get them out of the City's temptations. "I wish to be enrolled as a legionary," I went on. "If I deserve promotion, let me have it; if not, so be it."

He gazed at me for some time in silence, then:

"I do not believe you realize what you ask. As a legionary you would receive your arms and equipment, a bushel of grain a month, and two hundred and twenty-five *denarii* * a year, plus your pro rata share from the sale of captives and loot from conquered towns. You would grind your own grain and eat it in the form of porridge or bannocks, and you would drink *posca,* a mixture of vinegar and water; no more Lucrine oysters or roasted peacocks, no more Falernian wine. You would be under a sharp, stern discipline, requiring instant and unquestioning obedience, even to death, and you would be working or fighting hard all day and every day, risking wounds and fatigue and death, and when the bugles blew for rest, you would wrap yourself in your cloak and sleep on the ground, or at best on a truss of straw. And you would be among a rough, hard-bit crew who would tolerate no airs and graces—a heavy-handed lot, quick to resent and punish any fancied slight."

"I understand, Imperator."

"And you still desire the service?"

"If you will have me, yes."

"Very well. You shall have a chance to make good your words." Taking a pair of tablets and a stylus from the table, he wrote a few words, tied the cord about the tablets and sealed it with wax and his signet ring, then gave the letters to me, saying: "Hand these to Titus Labienus at Vesontio.† Do you know how to reach that place?"

"No, Imperator, but I can learn."

* About $38.
† Besancon.

He nodded.

"I thank you," I continued. "One thing more, if I may, Imperator. Tiberius Cornelius Rufus asked me to convey his most humble respects to you."

"He who helped break up the conspiracy of Lucius Catilina?"

"The same."

Caesar nodded again.

"A good man," was his comment. "Is he your friend?"

"I think I may so far flatter myself, Imperator."

He raised his eyebrows, but made no further remark beyond:

"My thanks, Gaius."

I bowed and withdrew, even as he returned to his dictation.

Vesontio, I learned by inquiry, lies some three hundred and fifty miles from Massilia, being almost due north from Nemausus,* and on the Dubis River, in the country of the Sequani, whose chief town it is. Five of Caesar's legions were in winter quarters there, under command of Titus Labienus the *legatus,* or lieutenant-general—he who afterward was the only man of all Caesar's forces who deserted to Pompeius during the Civil War. It must be admitted, however, that so long as he served Caesar he served faithfully and well; next to the Imperator he was the ablest man in the whole army.

Inquiry taught me the route and other things also, and I made certain purchases ere setting out from Massilia. A short Roman sword to supplement my dagger; clothing to withstand the Gallic cold; flint and steel and tinder, to kindle fires; dried meat and unleavened bread in case I should be obliged to camp out over night; and a heavy

* Nîmes.

cloak to wrap around me if I slept on the ground. *Edepol!*
I was coming on; the Gaius Durus of four months earlier
would have been in utter consternation at the mere thought
of such a journey—three hundred and fifty miles alone,
in the heart of a barbarous country! I chuckled as I
thought that I was at least beginning to deserve my
cognomen.*

Since the legions were in winter quarters there was no
need for haste, and I took the journey easily, sleeping
when possible in roadside inns or peasant huts, for I passed
through no towns of consequence after leaving Nemausus.
Two nights I slept out, for the first time in my life, and
did so with much trepidation, having been taught that the
night air was unwholesome. Also, I feared prowling beasts,
though none came near me, nor, to my surprise, did I take
any harm from the exposure. But I found it hard to get
to sleep the first night; I lay and listened to the many
noises of the dark, starting up time and again at some
unaccustomed sound, so that dawn was in the east ere
Morpheus laid his fingers on my eyelids. Thereafter it
came easier, and so strange a thing is custom that later,
after a summer's campaign, it always took me three or
four nights to get used to sleeping in a bed.

As I have said, the inns were far better than those of
Italia, but the roads were vastly worse; no construction
whatever had been given them, and instead of being
smooth, level, hard-surfaced highways, they were merely
beaten wagon-tracks, well-nigh impassable for mud when
the frost left the ground in spring-time. Still, they were
good enough at this season of the year, and I had no
trouble in averaging thirty or thirty-five miles a day—it
will be understood that I still rode Tiberius' horse—and I

* "Durus" means "hard."

reached Vesontio on the twelfth day out from Massilia, having had but one adventure by the way. This came about as follows.

On the third day out from Nemausus, about the ninth hour, I was traversing a forest when two coarsely clad, rough-looking men sprang out from a thicket beside the road and bade me stand. That is, they uttered words which were incomprehensible to me, but the idea was clear, for they carried strung bows with arrows drawn, and these arrows pointed accurately at my stomach. Reining up, I looked inquiringly at the men, shaking my head as they spoke. Thereupon they motioned for me to dismount, and I obeyed. The next move was a gesture for me to throw them my purse, and when I looked blank one of them laid down his bow and arrow and stepped toward me to help himself, his companion moving around to my left and keeping his arrow trained on me.

As the first one drew near, I suddenly reached across my body and caught him by the left arm, then jerked him around and stepped behind him, at the same time driving my dagger upward under his left shoulderblade. The other, flurried, loosed the string, and his arrow smote my captive in the chest, driving through far enough to scratch me slightly. Dropping the doubly slain robber, I leaped at the other, who, unable to fit a second arrow in time, snatched out his dagger and made a vicious pass at me. I had not studied under Tiberius and Quincunx for nothing, and I parried the blow, thrust my dagger through his forearm, and when he dropped his weapon I stabbed him through the heart.

All this took but a few seconds, and drawing my sword I stood on guard to meet other assailants. None appeared; save for the two bodies I was alone, and the only sounds to break the stillness were the chirp and flutter of birds,

the sigh of wind in the treetops, and the thudding of my
horse's hoofs, for he had taken alarm at the violent action
and the smell of blood, and was galloping off down the
road. Presently I relaxed, then after some consideration
dragged the corpses into the thicket and concealed them,
scraped some dust over the blood in the road, and set off
to catch my horse. This was the first time I had ever slain
a man, and I was a little surprised to find that I felt no
regret, but rather a definite exultation. Still, why should I
regret it? These men had definitely asked for what they
got. My reason for hiding the bodies was, of course, to
avoid getting the hue and cry out after me, but I might
have spared myself the trouble; as I learned afterward,
dead bodies were too common along the roads of Gallia
Transalpina to call for much attention so long as they
were not those of wealthy or influential men, and the death
of a casual highway robber was of no importance to anyone except himself and his proposed victim.

I had little trouble in coming up with my horse, for he
had run only about a mile, then stopped and fallen to
cropping grass, and this was the sum total of my adventures during the journey. I rode for one day in the company of an itinerant trader named Martus, a small,
oily-tongued, thin-faced, crafty-looking man with only one
eye, who extracted from me all I knew of affairs in the
City, and in return gave me a most amazing lot of information concerning Gallia Transalpina, most of which was
false. I liked him little, and was glad to ride on alone
when he stopped to trade at an insignificant village. I
saw many other travelers, some on foot and some on
horseback, mostly peasants or small merchants, and once
I turned aside to allow a Gallic knight, with his train of
three or four hundred mounted clients, to pass. They
looked at me with no friendly eyes, but did not molest me,

and on the twelfth day, about the sixth hour, I came to Vesontio, where I asked my way to the quarters of Titus Labienus.

The Sequani were one of the principal tribes of Gallia Media, that is, the central portion of the country, and were ever in conflict with the Aedui, their chief rivals, for the rulership of the land, so that, as was to be expected, their largest city was a veritable stronghold. On a sloping peninsula, it was almost encircled by a loop of the Dubis River, the neck of land leading to it being scarcely three hundred paces across. On the land side a wall built after the Gallic fashion, of loose stones alternating with transverse balks of timber, protected the city, which housed perhaps twenty-five thousand souls; and though to my eyes, accustomed to the stately buildings and half million people of Rome, Vesontio appeared small, mean, and dirty, the Sequani were intensely proud of their city. After all, things go by contrast in this world, and Vesontio was one of the best of the towns of Gallia Transalpina.

The Gauls are a nation of craftsmen, and Vesontio was a manufacturing city of some importance, but the streets were narrow and unpaved, overhung by timber houses which jutted forth story by story, and were inexpressibly filthy, for there were no sewers, nor even decent drainage of gutters, and all sewage, garbage, and the like was tossed from the windows, often to the vast discomfort of pedestrians, for the citizens commonly shouted: "Heads below!" after rather than before emptying the refuse. Herds of scavenging hogs grunted and rooted in the trampled mire, not infrequently lying down to sleep on the comparatively dry footpaths, whence no kicks or curses might dislodge them. The citizens walked around these sodden porkers, even stepping into the mud to do so, but the soldiers used to move them by tickling their ribs with a dagger-point, when the great beasts would explode into grunting, squealing action and plunge off across the street, throwing fountains of mud into the air as they went. This was considered a huge joke, even more uproarious when, as often happened, the hogs tripped up some luckless burgher, dumped him in the mud, and careered on over his prostrate form. A sure mirth-provóker, this last. Even in winter, the continual dumping of slops and waste water kept the roadways soggy, and in spring they were utterly beyond description; the Augean stables were nothing by comparison.

About half the houses were of wood, and the other half, in the poorer section, of wattle-and-daub. Perhaps one in fifty, housing some wealthy nobleman and his retinue of slaves and clients, was of stone, and it was in one of these that I found the lieutenant-general.

Titus Labienus was by far, the best, from a military viewpoint, of Caesar's officers, but he did not own the personal attractiveness of the Imperator. A big man, with a hard, cruel, and sensual face, he showed plainly the marks of that greed and avarice which made him so roundly hated, and which caused him to desert Caesar for Pompeius Magnus. In complete confidence of the victory of the Optimates, and with the hope of greater chance for looting Italia, he deserted at the beginning of the Civil War. How the Gods must have laughed when They saw him make that error of judgment—one of the few he ever made, yet that one grave enough to undo all he had labored to accomplish through many years.

When I was ushered into his presence I found him stretched at ease in a deep, soft Gallic chair such as could not be matched in all Rome, where the chairs are stiff and uncomfortable, not fitted for lounging. The neck of his tunic was unpinned, his feet reposed in another chair, and in his right hand he held a goblet of beaten gold, full of imported wine. Facing him lounged, in similar manner, an officer who was as big, as hard-faced, and even more gross of feature. This was Mamurra, Caesar's *praefectus fabrum*, or chief engineer, who was a crony of Labienus and as competent in his own line as the lieutenant-general in his, but who so far outdid the other in sensuality and greed that Formiae, whence he came, was afterward called in contempt "a city of Mamurras." A man may properly enrich himself from a conquered province, it being a settled principle of warfare that to the victor belong the spoils, and Caesar was no niggard in allowing his men the *spolia classium*, the spoils of war; but this precious pair showed no faintest sign of human decency, looting right and left as shamelessly and as atrociously as did Gaius Verres in Sicilia.

I was announced by a decurion, and Labienus, without relinquishing his hold on the goblet, extended his hand for the tablets, which I gave him.

"Cut the seal," he ordered the decurion, who obeyed, and Labienus read what Caesar had written. "H'mph!" he snorted, and tossed the tablets to Mamurra. "Another young sprig of the nobility," he sneered, "who thinks he has a turn for war. You expect a tribuneship, doubtless?"

"No, General," I replied. "I wish to enlist as a private soldier."

The two burst into laughter, and Labienus answered:

"You shall have your wish—and may the Gods pity you! Titus—" this to the decurion "—turn him over to Crastinus; the Imperator says he is to be enrolled in the Tenth."

"The Tenth!" exclaimed Mamurra. "But why?"

Labienus shrugged.

"You ask me? A whim of the Imperator's. At all events, they will soon take the conceit out of him."

He waved his hand, and the decurion said to me: "Come," then led me out. As I went, Labienus growled something to Mamurra, and they laughed again.

For myself, I wondered why Caesar had ordered that I be enrolled in the Tenth, that group of picked and chosen men, who were mostly, so to speak, graduates of other legions; promotion to the Tenth was considered a reward of merit. It could not be on account of my friendship with Tiberius, for he did not know of that until after writing the letters. Perhaps, as Labienus suggested, he thought the Tenth, being so far above me, would sicken me of soldiering quicker than any other legion, so he would easily be quit of me. Or could it be that he liked my looks, and was minded to favor me? Or had some word of me reached him before I presented myself?

Well, doubtless he had some good reason, and it was never Caesar's custom to explain his acts, so I followed my guide without comment or question; after all, if the Imperator saw fit to honor me, who was I to complain?

CHAPTER IV

Of My Life Under the Eagles; and the Maritime Reaping-Hooks

TITUS was a friendly soul, chatting agreeably enough and pointing out various sights of interest as we passed along the streets. We found Crastinus, who was a fine, soldierly man of about thirty, *primipilus,* or standard-bearer and first centurion of the Tenth Legion, and who made a note of my name, then said:

"Take him among your ten, Titus; you are short in your roster."

"Very well." And Titus saluted, then turned to me with: "Follow me, Durus."

He led me first to the office of the quartermaster, where I took the oath of fidelity and service, afterward being outfitted with shield, helmet and crest, greave, corselet, and two javelins; I already had sword and dagger. Also, I received a small trenching spade, a change of underwear, army boots, a different cloak, a stone handmill, a bushel of wheat—unground—a canteen, a bronze bowl and horn spoon, and two six-foot stakes, each sharpened at one end.

"They are for palisades, when we make camp," Titus explained the stakes. "You will guard all these things closely; if any is lost or stolen, the value will be deducted from your pay. The mill is to grind your wheat; you will receive a bushel a month, which you will make into porridge or bannocks. If you have money, you may supplement your diet as you choose."

"Wine?" I asked.

"Even so, provided you do not get drunk. The punishment for that is fifteen lashes on the bare back. Quintus—" this to the quartermaster's clerk "—he will need also a Marius' mule."

When furnished, this proved to be a stout, forked stick about four feet long, and Titus showed me how to bind the various articles of equipment to it, then carry it over my shoulder.

"One thing more," I said. "My horse. How shall I arrange for him?"

"You cannot keep him," Titus answered. "A foot-soldier has no use for a horse. Quintus, what is to be done?"

"We will buy him for the cavalry," suggested Quintus, "if that suits Durus."

The horse was sent for, inspected, and after some bargaining I received a fair price for him, the money being given me in the form of an order on Flaccus, in Rome. This I enclosed in tablets, with a note requesting that it be paid to Tiberius, and left the whole with Quintus, who assured me that it would be forwarded by the first messenger.

This done, Titus led me to the quarters of his ten, in one of the middle-class houses of the city, where he introduced me to Lucius Fabius, centurion of the sixth century, under whom Titus was decurion, and to seven or eight men who were lounging about, gambling with the *tali,* in the main room of the house. This Fabius, by the way, was a cousin of the centurion of the same name, who was later slain on the wall of Gergovia, during the rebellion of Vercingetorix.

The *tali* are four-sided prisms of wood a few inches in length—different sets vary in size—with the ends and one face slightly convex, and with the numbers I, III, IV and VI marked on the sides. Four are thrown at a time, instead of three, as with the *tesserae,* and the faces resting on the ground are counted, instead of the upper ones. The *tali* is the popular game in the army, as the *tesserae* in the City, and the gamblers invited me to share their sport. I declined, saying that I should prefer to watch and learn the game better—there are complications in the manner of scoring—whereupon one of the gamesters spoke up:

"Let him alone; a brass-man is not likely to have brass."

Now, an *aerarius,* a "brass-man," is the lowest class of Roman citizen, having been deprived of the suffrage for some crime or dishonorable act—for example, bigamy. To be so degraded is a horrible disgrace, and I felt myself grow red at the insult. However, I kept my temper, merely remarking, in a casual tone:

"Even the beggars of the bridges know that a brass-man is not permitted to serve in the army."

My insulter leaped to his feet, snarling:

" 'Beggars of the bridges!' New man, do you bandy words with me?"

He evidently looked for an abject recantation, and was taken aback when I boldly answered:

"Yes."

With that he burst into a tirade of scurrility, pouring epithets of insult on me, lashing himself into a fury. When he had run down:

"No," I said, "I retract. I do not mean to bandy words with you; I have·no such vocabulary of filth; I acknowledge that you are my superior in foulness. It is clear that you have studied the language of obscenity under every branded whip-scoundrel of the Subura, and have completed your education in a slave-prison. Perhaps you yourself are a runaway slave—are your ears pierced? Have you collar-galls on your neck? Let me see them—I dare you to unpin your tunic!" Of course I exaggerated somewhat; his language was not really so bad as all that.

His rage overcame him, so that he could only choke and sputter, and I sneeringly advised him:

"Count ten, or whistle thrice; then you will be able to speak."

The others laughed, and he exploded:

"*Per Deos Immortales,* I will cut your heart out and cook it for my dinner!"

He caught up a sword and rushed at me, and flinging down my equipment I snatched my own blade from the scabbard. His attack was furious, but thanks to Tiberius and Quincunx I was able to guard myself, and called to Fabius:

"What penalty if I slay him?"

"None; he was the aggressor. Still," the centurion added, dryly, "it would be better not to."

"As you please," I answered, and countering a lunge, extended my arm in the good old stop-thrust, Tiberius' favorite, and the most useful trick of all.

My point took the soldier's right arm just above the wrist and ripped it to the elbow; I felt the blade grate on the bone. He dropped his sword, turned white, grasped his wounded arm with the other hand, and swayed on his feet. Throwing down my own sword, I caught him about the waist and helped him to a chair, when the others gathered about and we poured wine into the wound, then pulled the edges together and bandaged the arm tightly, to staunch the streaming blood. He said nothing while this was being done, but sat impassive and silent, merely frowning a little and compressing his lips. When all was finished and the arm adjusted in a sling, and he had taken a drink of wine, he stretched out his left hand to me.

"New man," he said, "you are an admirable swordsman; that counter and thrust came like the lightning of

Jupiter. My name is Manius Cornutus, known in the legions as Bombyx. Shall we be friends?"

I was surprised at this sudden change of manner, but rightly guessed that Bombyx felt no real animosity toward me; that his abuse and attack were merely part of the initiation to which a new recruit was subject. My readiness to fight had brought a result more serious than was common, and all in all it seemed to me that I could well afford to overlook his insulting words.

"Shall we be friends?" he repeated, to which I answered:

"Gladly." And pressed his hand. "My name is Gaius Aemilius Durus. And since I am a new man, it is fitting that I invite you to drink with me. Can wine be purchased near at hand?"

"*Edepol!*" grinned Bombyx. "If you have the brass."

"Better yet; I have some yellow boys."

The men applauded the suggestion, and one of them offering to do the errand, I gave him a gold piece and he went out, presently returning with two kidskins of very passable wine, some small salted fish, and a handful of change. We had several drinks apiece, the others toasting me and commenting favorably on my swordsmanship.

"Oh, well," I passed it off with modesty, "I had a good instructor."

"Who?" inquired Fabius. "If I may ask."

"Tiberius Cornelius Rufus."

"What! Tiberius the Red? Scaevola? * He who was *retiarius* for Dumnorix the *lanista?*"

"The same. Do you know him?"

A roar of laughter went up, and Fabius smiled ruefully.

"*Mehercle!*" he answered. "I met him at Pistorium, when Lucius Catilina died." He pulled down the neck of

* "Lefty."

his tunic and showed a deep scar about two palms long on his chest. "I know him, yes!" He turned to Bombyx, who grinned sheepishly. "The joke is on you, Bombyx," he said. "The joke is unquestionably on you."

"I admit it," Bombyx acknowledged. "Decimus, feel in my purse; I cannot reach it with this disabled arm. You will find some coins there, and I will pay for another skin of wine if you will fetch it." Bombyx, I may here remark, proved on acquaintance to be a cheerful, friendly fellow, and a good soldier. Not a man of transcendent genius, to be sure, but more intelligent and more eager to advance in rank than the average.

The wine was brought, and as we drank it I was urged to tell how I came to study under Tiberius, and how I came to enlist. The men were rough but good-natured, and we had a pleasant talk until dinner-time, when I asked if I might not add some extra delicacy to the meal. This offer was accepted with enthusiasm, and Decimus—as youngest recruit next to myself—was sent off to a cook-shop, whence he brought a huge bowl of stew—meat and vegetables cooked together and well seasoned with garlic. This was devoured with much smacking of lips, and all voted me a right good fellow. When the meal was ended, one of the men brought out his *tibia utricularis,* or bag-pipes, and played some martial airs to which the men sang various camp songs, and after that I was introduced to the *tali,* at which game beginner's luck stood me in such good stead that by the time darkness closed down and we sought our beds I had won back all I had spent on wine and stew, and some ten or twelve *denarii* besides.

"Per Martes!" swore one. "He has tamed the *tali;* they know their master's hand."

This seemed to imply unfairness, and I asked, a trifle sharply:

"Do you mean—"

"*Dii bene vortant!*" he interrupted. "The Gods fore-fend! I mean nothing—nothing whatever. The Gods deliver me from meaning anything when I speak to a pupil of Tiberius the Red!"

The others laughed, and one remarked:

"Gaius is *frenator talorum*—a tamer of the *tali*."

The phrase was greeted with approval, and so I won my nickname; ever after I was known in the legions as Frenator, which means, literally, a tamer of wild beasts, though in time the epithet came to have a more honorable significance, as implying that I could control the men who were under my command.

This giving of nicknames was common in the army; a man who was particularly liked or disliked was sure to have one, and any outstanding characteristic called for some appropriate term. Many of these were so coarse and obscene as to be unfit for gentle ears—the legionaries of Caesar were no sugar-tongued maidens!—but I can give a few.

Bombyx was so called because of his love for fine clothing, since the name means "silkworm." Carnifex, "Executioner"; Lanius, "Butcher"; Nex, "Death by violence"; and Fenisector, "Mower of grass," were named for their effect on the enemy. Flaccus, "Flop-ear"; Scaevola, "Lefty"; Porculus, "Piggy"; Naso, "Big-nose"; Flavulus, "Blondy"; and Coccinulus, "Reddy," were so called from personal characteristics. Cimex, "Bug"; and Maccus, "Buffoon," were named in contempt. One of the less obvious names was that of Arcularius, which means "Maker of jewel-caskets," and this man got the title by his passion for gems; when we looted a town he sought nothing else, and what he took he had set in his armor, so that shield, helmet, scabbard and sword-hilt literally blazed with diamonds, rubies, emeralds, sapphires, and opals.

In addition, the men used an almost incredible amount of slang; I had practically to learn a new language. The *scorpio*, a heavy cross-bow mounted on a pedestal, was named for the stinging insect. The *onager*, throwing heavy rocks from a swinging beam, was so called from the wild ass of Afric, which in flight kicks up stones and dust to blind its pursuers. The hooks on long poles, which in sieges we used to tear down the stones of walls, were called *falces*, that is, "reaping hooks," or "sickles." The soldier detailed to wait on an officer, to polish his armor and do other menial tasks, was known as *capsarius*, that being the name of the slave who carries a schoolboy's books and tablets. *Edepol!* I could write a whole book on the slang of the legionaries, but I must return to my story.

I won back, then, the money I had spent, and was named Frenator. When the question of bed came up, Bombyx declared:

"He sleeps with me. My couch is wide enough for two, and having disabled my arm, Frenator owes me some aid in dressing and undressing." And in truth this was no more than fair. "Besides," he went on, "I like the spirited young devil, and would be friends with him; he will make a good man for the Tenth."

So it was settled, and thenceforth Bombyx and I were *collusores;* the word means literally "playmates," but it is army slang for the closest of friends—men who sleep together, eat together, stand shoulder to shoulder in battle, who defend each other in peril, fight for each other, lie for each other if need be, share one another's blankets, food, loot, and danger; in short, men who are bound to each other by ties of loyalty and affection such as civilians rarely know. Except for an interval of twelve months, while

I was in Britannia, Bombyx and I were together for over a decade; more than once I saved his life, and he, mine; he was shrewd and quick-witted, introducing me quickly to army ways, and in return I taught him to read and write, passed on to him some of what Tiberius had taught me, and helped him on his upward rise from rank to rank. But all this was in the future, and for the present bed was our only thought.

Such was my first encounter with the Men of the Golden Eagle—so called because the standard of our legion was of solid gold—the soldiers who were destined to be my companions in arms until the foul assassination of our great leader, fifteen years later.

Our winter in Vesontio was in the main more comfortable than our summers in the field. On active service we worked hard, marched hard, fought hard, ate sparingly, seldom drank wine, and slept on the ground, taking whatever the Gods saw fit to send in the shape of weather. But in winter quarters we slept in soft beds—and the Gallic beds are vastly superior to the Roman, being equipped with feather mattresses—we kept warm before huge blazing fires, in fireplaces wide enough and high enough for five men to stand upright and abreast within the arch; and as for food and drink, cookshops and wineshops were ever just around the corner. Wine was plentiful, since there were in the city many Roman traders and merchants, and these, as well as the noblemen and wealthy folk among the natives, all used it; the common people have a drink made by fermenting a mash of barley. And it is of interest to note that drunkenness is much more frequent in Gallia than in Italia; we use wine greatly diluted, merely to make our water safe to drink, but the folk of Gallia and Britannia swill their liquor neat, intoxication being the principal amusement of rich and poor alike.

Bombyx was my chief instructor in soldierly duties, but it was Fabius and Arcularius who, being deeper students of affairs, told me what I wished to know of the country and the people.

"The Sequani," said Arcularius, in reply to my questions, "are a manufacturing folk—woollen goods and textiles, mostly, though there is some metal work, and of course, much farming. To handle these things and to supply imported goods, the Roman colony has sprung up. We get along admirably with the latter—common race interests, you know—though naturally we mix little with them; they are only civilians, after all. But with the Sequani it is different.

"Last summer—his first in Gallia—we and Caesar flung back the invading Helvetii, 360,000 strong—"

"That 'we and Caesar' is good!" laughed Fabius.

"Pluto take you! And we drove from Gallia Ariovistus and his Germani. Twelve or thirteen years ago they conquered and colonized much of the country, but last summer we chased them back across the Rhenus River * and set free both the Sequani and the Aedui from oppression and the fear of slavery, besides restoring many towns to their true owners.

"But the Sequani are not grateful. They see in the friendship of the Aedui for Rome a threat to their own supremacy in Gallia Transalpina, and they hate their liberators well-nigh as much as they did their oppressors. Further, they think that this is but the first step to Rome's domination of the whole country—"

"Which in truth it is," Fabius interjected.

"What if it is? Had they the wit to see it, as have the Aedui and the Aquitani, they would realize that Gallia would be better off bound together under Roman civiliza-

* The Rhine.

tion than as a set of savage, wrangling, warring tribes."

"You must admit, though," spoke up Bombyx, "that they have some cause to resent our being here. Add eighteen thousand men to a town of twenty-five thousand, and you strain it to bursting. Nor do the citizens like sleeping in attics and stables while we use their beds, or being forced to wait on us and run our errands. You can hardly blame them."

"It is the price they pay for our aid. And at least Labienus punishes rape and robbery by death. These barbarians are a thankless lot!"

"True enough," Bombyx admitted. "But they did not ask our help. And you must grant that there is a good deal of undetected violence, and much arrogance. It is beneath the dignity of the Tenth to brawl and swagger in the streets, insulting women and pushing citizens off the footpaths into the mud, but the other legions have no such scruples. Small wonder that the burghers scowl and spit as we pass, and pray their gods to send a pestilence on us."

For all of Bombyx' claims, which indeed were true enough, the Tenth, as I came to know, were far from being little woolly lambs; men who face violent death every day for months at a stretch are not apt to be gentle, are not apt to give ear to every squawk of a woman or outcry of a burgher who has lost a few gold pieces. So although the citizens did not hate us as venomously as they did the other legions, still they did not take us to their bosoms. And to inflame their hatred was the fact that though seldom going so far as actual outrage, the soldiers none the less made free with the wives and daughters of the burghers; the women-folk did not hate us as did the men. Only three legionaries—none of them from the Tenth— were crucified that winter, but both then and in later years there were a good many black-haired children born in the country of the blond Gauls.

"And let me warn you now, Frenator," went on Bombyx, "never walk down a narrow alley alone after dark."

"Why not?" I demanded. "My hand can keep my head."

"Oh, we all know you are a wizard with a sword," Arcularius commented, sarcastically, "but no man can guard against a blow from behind. Many of these natives are quite handy with a dagger, and it takes but a few minutes to cut a hole in the ice of a river, big enough to thrust a man through."

"He speaks truth, Frenator," Fabius confirmed. "Watch behind as well as in front; even if your life is naught to you, it is something to Caesar."

"It is plenty to me," I answered, dryly. "I will take your advice to heart."

"Best not go abroad alone at any time," Fabius added. "These Gauls are hot of temper and somewhat lacking in discretion; often they act before thinking."

"Without thinking, you mean," snorted Arcularius. "I doubt if many of them have aught to think with."

This last was hardly fair. Rash and impulsive though the Celtae are, and so jealous that they are incapable of concerted action, none the less they are no fools except in politics, and in craftsmanship they equal if not surpass the folk of Italia. Not at all bad folk, if one allows for their national failings.

Like Caesar, Labienus believed that idleness breeds mischief, and though we had a good deal of time to ourselves, he saw to it that we got enough exercise to keep us fit. Every day, rain or shine, snow, sleet, or frost, the army assembled at the gate in heavy marching order, about ninety pounds of armor and equipment to a man, and marched eight or ten miles out of town and as many back. To be sure, this was less than the twenty-four miles a day which would be our regular march when campaigning, but it was plenty, and *per Martes*, how we came to hate that road! The eternal sickening sameness of it! We knew every bend, every tree, shrub, and rock as I knew my own bedroom on Palatinus, and we loathed them all.

Sometimes the lieutenant-general varied our drill with practice in making camp, when certain men went ahead under experienced centurions and laid out the stakes and lines, and we, coming up, dug the fosse, erected the wall, planted our palisade of stakes, dug wells and latrines, and set up the leather tents. Of course we would have to do this every day when on active service, but that did not make us like it during winter quarters. And for sheer, unmitigated torture, let me recommend digging in frozen ground when the hands are numb with cold and every blow of the spade sends darts of pain tingling to the shoulders. Then having finished our Sisyphean task; we struck camp, packed up the tents, and marched home, cursing at every step of the way, too wretched even to sing. I have seen war-hardened veterans, the toughest of men, tramping along a frozen road, gritting their teeth while the tears streamed down their cheeks from the agony of the biting cold. Happily, we made these practice camps only three or four times during the winter; had it been oftener, I think there would have been a mutiny.

"So help me Jupiter," said Titus, on one such occasion, "if Labienus does this to us again I shall bite my veins and howl, like a mad wolf! The fires of Phlegethon would be pleasant after this cold."

Once a week, instead of a march we had manoeuvres, when we tramped only a mile or so, then at the trumpet signals left the road, deployed in line of battle, charged, retreated, took various formations, and went through all the operations that might be required in warfare. This was more interesting, and there was no little rivalry among the legions as to which should make the best showing—rather, the second best, since it was a foregone conclusion that the Tenth was first of all.

It was during these manoeuvres that I won my first promotion, for Titus came on duty still drunk from a carouse of the night before, and Crastinus promptly awarded him fifteen lashes on the bare back, then reduced him to the ranks, naming me temporary decurion in his place. I had observed the manner of doing things, and was able to inspire my men to carry on with a snap and drive, so I retained my new rank for a fortnight's trial, at the end of which time the appointment was approved by Labienus and was made permanent. According to custom, I bought my ten a couple of skins of wine, and made them a speech of exhortation in which I declared my intention of having the best ten in the whole army.

"And be warned," I concluded, "for laggards will have to deal with me. Off duty, I am your friend and companion, to drink with you, play with you, sing with you, gamble with you, eat with you. On duty, I am no longer Frenator your companion, but Gaius Durus your officer, the Imperator's mouthpiece, to transmit his will to you. So be warned! Let your obedience continue prompt and soldierly, or you will find me stern, even as Caesar is stern and harsh to those who fail."

Some of them felt that I spoke too large words for so young an officer, but I considered it well to establish my attitude at the start. And through several things I managed to keep the good will of the men, one circumstance being the support I had from Titus and Bombyx. Titus, to my intense relief, showed no resentment over his demotion, taking it as a matter of course, and Bombyx, now returned to duty, openly rejoiced in my new rank.

Bombyx, by the way, furnished us a trifle of amusement. Excused from the practice marches and manoeuvres on account of his disabled arm, he sat snug at home before the fire while we tramped through mud or snow or slush, or dug in the rock-hard earth. Then when we came in tired and frozen, cursing Labienus, Gallia, and our own folly in enlisting, he would greet us with mock sympathy and tell us all the pleasant things which had happened during the day. Naturally, he made this last as long as possible, till one afternoon Fabius returned to find him beating the owner of the house where we were quartered, the man having refused some trifling service. A vivacious discussion followed, Bombyx trying to prove that he was unfit for duty, until Fabius won the argument with the words:

"Very well; you are disabled. You may tell Labienus so to-morrow."

Next morning Bombyx turned out in full marching kit. Fortunately, the wound in his arm healed without serious results.

So, with the backing of Titus and Bombyx, and with an occasional hint from Fabius, I was able to handle my men, the more since I mixed commendation and reproof judiciously, always giving the former publicly, the latter in private—a trick I learned from Tiberius' treatment of his slaves. My social position and education helped, also; troopers are inclined at first to resent a patrician or an *eques* in the ranks, but if he shows himself a good fellow, and does not assume airs, he gains a certain prestige because of the very fact that he is from a higher class— always provided, of course, that he deserves respect.

Also, I gained some additional respect through the fact that I never told, or cared to listen to, any foul stories, or used foul language. It is a strange thing, but true, that the very men who delight most in such tales respect a man who does not. Why this should be, I cannot say, but I have proved it so.

Further, Tiberius had once remarked to me: "More flies are caught with honey than with vinegar," so I leaned more heavily on praise than on reproof, and when using the latter tried ever to couch it in the form of a suggestion for improvement, assuming that the man wanted to do his best, but had erred in judgment.

Once only did I have a case of flagrant disobedience; then, instead of reporting it to Fabius and getting the man a public lashing, as was my right, I apparently passed it over without notice. I saw the man grin furtively, and caught disapproving looks on the faces of the others, but nothing more was said until that night in quarters, when, after dinner and a few songs, I casually inquired:

"Fabius, have we any wooden swords about the place?"

"Surely," was the reply. "Do you want them?"

"If you will be so good."

Bombyx was sent to get them, and smiled slightly as he went; I believe he had an inkling of what was coming. When he returned, I explained:

"Porculus and I had a slight difference of opinion to-day, and are going to settle it now. Porculus, will you take one of these swords?"

He did so, and I proceeded to give him a sound beating, using both point and edge, so that his ribs and arms were well ploughed, and his shoulders and head were black and blue. In fact, by the time I finished with him he might better have had his fifteen or twenty lashes. But I have always considered the lash degrading and humiliating— Caesar used it as little as possible—and by my method the offender escaped public humiliation, had the satisfaction of fighting back, got his beating just the same, and in addition was reminded that my superiority was not merely a question of arbitrary rank. And to cap it all, there was a tradition in the Tenth that when a joke was on a man and his companions laughed at him, he too must laugh or be despised for a sorehead. So when the others laughed at Porculus, he had to do likewise, and the very act helped him to retain a good frame of mind. On the whole, the plan worked well, and Porculus became one of my best men, though always inclined to overeat and grow fat.

It would be tedious to my readers, and to myself as well, to relate in detail the campaigns of the next two summers; has not the Imperator himself done this far better than anyone else can do? What other Roman pen can hope to rival the terse, orderly, vigorous, and withal musical language of his wonderful treatise *De Bello Gallico?* Let me say merely that though I worked under him heart and soul, bore a share in his campaigns, including the terrible Civil War, came to regard him with an adoration not less than that I bestowed on the Gods Themselves, and even gained some honor in his eyes, it was not until many years afterward, when Gaius Caesar was dead and his grandnephew Octavianus ruled over the Republic, that I saw in full the gigantic plan which animated that mighty genius under whom I first studied the sciences of war and statesmanship.

To most folk the war in Gallia Transalpina was but one of conquest, undertaken to refill Caesar's depleted purse; Tiberius saw farther, and realized that the Imperator was assembling and welding into a unit an army which would follow him through the impending Civil War. And going a step beyond Tiberius, I came to understand the proconsul's further purpose of erecting a bulwark in the form of a loyal Gallic state between Italia and the savage tribes of Germania who constantly threatened our fertile plains and stately cities.

But Caesar's great plan, to which all these were merely subsidiary, of aiding the regeneration of the Republic by allowing it to expand northward into the wide-flung agricultural lands of the Aquitani, the Celtae, and the Belgae, that our burgesses might there find homes of a nature to encourage and develop the sturdy Roman virtues of their ancestors—that vast conception was beyond me, as it was beyond any save the giant brain that conceived it, that brain which dared to alter and bend to its will the course of history, the destiny of nations.

To me, then, the following summers were ones of making ready, and I strove to take my part in the work in such fashion as to aid this preparation so far as might be. I talked of this with no one; indeed, broadly speaking, I knew none whom I thought capable of grasping the idea, for to all my associates the Roman state was one which had stood since Trojan Aeneas first landed on Lavinia's coast, and which would stand while yet the world itself endured. In all the army I found only one man who could foresee the fated breaking down of the Republic, the dire war which Lachesis was even then weaving into the texture of our lives. That man was Gaius Volusenus, one of the few of Caesar's tribunes who were of any worth, in whose company I scouted the coast of Britannia—but I will tell of that in due order.

To Fabius I did once disclose a little of my purpose, when he and I met in a wineshop of Cenabum, while wintering in that city. Coming in while I was there, he sat down by me, and as he sipped his wine he remarked:

"You are coming on, Frenator. I can see that you are studying the art of controlling men, and of tactics as well.

Continue thus, and you should go high in the army."

My studies were not merely in the hope of advancement, but for a loftier purpose. However, I did not think it best to tell him so, and only answered:

"I am studying strategy also, to the top of my powers."

"Indeed! And how?"

"Why, after a battle, I try to see the Imperator's reasons for his orders—to analyse them and see why he did thus and so. And when a battle impends, I try to plan what I should do in his place, how I would place the legions, what orders I would give. Then after the fight I try to see why the Imperator's plans differed from mine."

Fabius smiled and nodded.

"Excellent!" he said. "Do they ever agree?"

"Sometimes," I answered, with modesty. "And it is no small satisfaction when they do."

"I should imagine so. Yes, you will go high, Frenator; you are studying under the best master in the world. I have fought under no less a general than Pompeius Magnus, and I know whereof I speak. Would that I had your background, your education, to profit by my opportunities," he added, a trifle sadly.

"No reason why you should not profit as much as I can. You are sixth centurion of the Tenth, and Caesar is quick to recognize and to promote a good man."

But he shook his head.

"Brains run in families, my Frenator, like curly hair and brown eyes. My own ancestors were peasants of Etruria. I know my limitations. First centurion of the legion, perhaps, but no higher. But I shall live to see you lieutenant-general, like Titurius Sabinus and Labienus."

"Well," I laughed, "when I am lieutenant-general I will make you first centurion."

Matching my humor, he smiled and raised his cup.

"I drink to your promise," he said. "I will hold you to it."

"As the Gods see me," I rejoined, and drank.

The time was to come when I should recall these words, but I was unable to make them good: by then the shears of Atropos had cut short the thread of Fabius' life, and he lay in an unmarked grave in Gallia Transalpina. But his estimate of Caesar was confirmed at Pharsalus, when Pompeius, superior to our Imperator in numbers, food, arms, equipment—in everything save genius and the devotion of his men—was driven in such utter rout as the world has never known.

My habit of looking ahead, of developing my ingenuity, bore fruit in the shape of a second promotion, in the summer of the year DCLXXXXVIII A. U. C.* The previous autumn, the lieutenant-general Publius Crassus was sent into the country of the Veneti, who occupied the coastal region northward from the mouth of the Liger River.† He induced the natives to give hostages to Caesar, but when during the winter Roman officers went into that country to arrange for a grain supply, the Veneti arrested them and held them as counter-hostages. Then, with the coming of spring, the coast tribes from the Liger to the Rhenus Rivers burst into revolt against Caesar, counting on aid from the Belgae and the Germani.

Titus Labienus was sent with the cavalry to the Rhenus, to hold the Germani in check, and Quintus Titurius Sabinus—the lieutenant-general who was afterward most treacherously slain by the Nervii and the Eburones under Ambiorix, as Mandorix the Aeduan has told in his memoirs —went north with three legions to keep the Venelli, the Curiosolites, and the Lexovii from joining forces with the

* 56 B. C.
† The Loire.

Veneti. Caesar gave charge of the fleet to Decimus Brutus the Younger, and himself made all speed with the land forces to the country of the Veneti.

Doubtless the fate which overtook the Veneti was predestined by the Parcae, and was necessary to Caesar's plans, but I have always regretted it, for they were one of the most powerful and most civilized tribes of Gallia Transalpina. Their strategy was what might have been expected of an intelligent maritime folk, for their strongholds were built on promontories thrusting out into the ocean and were well defended by the usual wall on the land, where, further, the approach was often inundated at high tide, thus making siege works difficult. And when one of the towns, after a siege and a brave resistance, was on the point of being taken, the folk calmly embarked themselves and their goods on vessels which they brought up to the water-gate, and off they sailed to another town. Thus it early became apparent that short of devastating the entire coast we could never subdue them unless we could get control of the ocean as well as the land.

For a long time this seemed impossible, since the Veneti were expert mariners, trading along the coast, to the remotest parts of Britannia, and even to the far-off land of the Hyperboreans, so their vessels were built to withstand the tides and tempests of the great open sea—very different from our ships, which navigate the tideless waters of the Mare Internum, and in the event of a storm can generally find a sheltered harbor. We surpassed them in speed and oarsmanship, it is true, for their vessels were propelled by huge leather sails, but when it came to conflict theirs were so tall and so stoutly built that we could neither attack them with missiles, nor board, nor injure them by ramming. After a number of unsuccessful engagements it became clear that we were not likely to win much honor or profit in this campaign, but I had an idea which, though I myself say it, turned the tide in our favor.

I did not go to Fabius with my suggestion; he was a good man, to be sure, but was never receptive to new ideas, and would only have pooh-poohed me. Instead, I went direct to Crastinus, who listened with attention, then ordered a small boat to set the two of us ashore. We walked straight to the camp, where the decurion on guard at the Porta Praetoria passed us in and told us we would find Caesar in the Praetorium, the main tent which houses the commander-in-chief and his staff.

"He and his generals are planning the attack on this pestilent, flea-bitten town," he said. "And what good will come of it? The natives will simply depart by sea as we enter by land. Tell me, Crastinus, why does not the fleet do something? You and Brutus and your biremes are about as useful as a worn-out slave, exposed to die on the island in Tiber."

"Will you kindly oblige me," pleasantly returned Crastinus, "by getting your belly ripped open in the next assault?"

Whereat the decurion laughed and waved us on.

Giving our names, we were admitted to the Imperator's presence, and found him and his staff discussing various maps and plans. Mamurra, I recall, was pointing out that it would be necessary to build dikes to keep out the sea from the town's approach ere a ramp could be built from which to attack the walls. Caesar looked up as we drew near and saluted, then returned our salute and asked:

"Well, my Crastinus, what is it?"

"This decurion of mine has an idea that he wishes to submit, Imperator."

Caesar turned his eyes on me.

"Well, Frenator?" he inquired. He had seen me once, a

year and a half before, yet knew me instantly and even called me by my nickname. *Mehercle,* what a memory that man had!

I was much embarrassed at speaking to him face to face, and began to doubt the worth of my notion. Still, I answered with apparent boldness:

"It is this, Imperator. We can do no good, as matters stand, against the ships of the Veneti. Their decks are too high for us to reach with missiles or boarding-bridges, and they are too strongly built for our rams to injure their oaken planks."

"All very true. What then?"

"So when we attack, they sail serenely on with our galleys clinging to them like dogs harrying a bear, but doing far less damage."

Several of the officers laughed outright, and a smile twitched the corners of Caesar's mouth.

"An apt simile," he commented. "Well?"

"But if we could cripple their sails, then, having no oars, they could not escape us, and we could grapple them, use ladders, and swarm over them as the dogs do when they have pulled the bear down. So my idea is to have the artificers make up a number of hooks on long poles, similar to the *falces murales* which we use in tearing down the stones of a wall, but more deeply curved and with the inner edge made very sharp. Have three or four of these on each galley, and when we come up with the barbarians, let the men hook the ropes which fasten their yards to the masts. Then the *hortator* sets the stroke, the oarsmen give way, the ropes are cut, down drop the yards, and the barbarian vessel comes perforce to a halt."

The faces of all the officers were keen with interest. and Caesar acknowledged:

"It might serve. What think you, Mamurra?"

The chief engineer's broad, coarse face lit up with delight, and he slapped his huge thigh.

"An excellent plan, Imperator, excellent. It will work, it will work. *Per Martes*, this youth has some good in him!"

Caesar nodded agreement.

"How long will it take to make the hooks?"

Mamurra did a little mental arithmetic.

"Four to each galley . . . three hundred and forty-four . . . six days, Imperator."

"It will take us only four days to storm this town. Still, we can hold back our land operations. See to it, then." He turned to me. "If your plan succeeds, my Frenator, there will be a reward."

"Under favor," I returned, saluting, "it was not suggested for the sake of a reward, but for the army—and for you, Imperator."

A faint smile flickered for an instant on his lips, then:

"Caesar thanks you. None the less, there will be a reward. You may go."

And Crastinus and I saluted and withdrew.

The hooks worked to perfection. The men hailed them with delight, nicknamed them "maritime reaping-hooks" and "Frenator's sickles," and put them to excellent use. On the appointed day, as about the fourth hour the Veneti took flight in their tall ships, we ranged alongside, caught and tore loose the yards, and down came the great leather sails in crumpled masses, spreading over the forward decks and burying passengers and crew under their ponderous folds. Then while the barbarians were in confusion and dismay we grappled them close, set scaling-ladders, and shouting our war-cry of "Venus Victrix! Venus Victrix!" went up and over the bulwarks to meet them hand to hand.

From then on it was a test of skill and courage, with our army looking on from the high ramparts of the town, so that no meritorious act could escape notice. The Veneti fought us bravely, fought till the rocking decks were slippery with blood and piled high with bodies, while the terror-stricken women and children screamed their fright and called upon their Gods to save them from our vengeance. Shouted oaths and curses mingled with shrieks and groans of agony and with the clash of arms, and ever the cry of "Venus Victrix!" rose above the tumult as we forced the warriors back or struck them down. The battle lasted until sunset—about eight hours in all—and in the end we were victors, taking two hundred and twenty of the tall ships and, with those who surrendered later, nearly fifty thousand captives. We were aided, to be sure, by a flat calm which fell during the afternoon and prevented the escape of any of the barbarian vessels, but in the main it was the hooks that brought us victory.

Caesar was exceedingly clement in all his conquests, preferring to bind the conquered tribes to him with chains of friendship, but this revolt, after oaths of fidelity had been given, was so flagrant that he felt the Gauls needed a sharp lesson. Even so, he was merciful, for instead of slaying the entire tribe, as the law of nations entitled him to do, he merely punished them by ordering the six hundred senators to be put to death and by selling the remainder of the men, women, and children into slavery.

A spear was set up, and the tribune Drusus conducted the auction, selling the prisoners in batches to the slave-dealers who always followed the army. Herded like cattle, under guard of the *mangones* * and their whip-armed hirelings, the wretched victims were marched south, body after body driven off, the men grimly silent, the women and children wailing their misery to the sky.

* Slave-dealers.

I have always found something pitiful in this sale of captives, in dragging the miserable folk from their loved homes, in ruthlessly separating husband and wife, mother and child. Doubtless, though, it is a necessary evil; the world's work could not be done without slaves, and this is the principal way to get them. At length the last dust-cloud faded from sight, and the nation of the Veneti was utterly wiped out of existence, as a warning to all who would rebel against Rome.

A few days later Crastinus sent for me. When I reported, he informed me:

"Frenator, the captives brought an average of a hundred and eleven *denarii* * apiece, which, after deducting the officers' portion, brings each soldier's share to a hundred and twenty-seven. Caesar has decreed that in addition to your two shares as decurion, you are to have ten shares for your suggestion of the hooks, making twelve shares—fifteen hundred and twenty-four *denarii* in all."

Nearly seven years' pay—liberal enough!

"How did it come that they brought such a tremendous price?" I asked. For a hundred and eleven *denarii* for captives sold in the field was almost unheard-of.

Crastinus laughed.

"They are strong, healthy, and intelligent, and have not far to march. And so help me Mercury! I have never known a man so clever as Drusus in working up the bidding. He swept the *mangones* off their feet with enthusiasm, and I heard more than one lament his own folly in being carried away.

"There is more, though, for your ear. Since Lucius Fabius is slain, his loss is your profit; you are promoted to be first centurion of the sixth cohort—that is, sixth

* $19.43.

centurion of the legion—in his stead. I suggested this, and the Imperator, who has had his eye on you for some time, saw fit to approve it."

It was amazing news that Caesar had been watching me, but I learned afterward that he knew accurately the capabilities of every man in the entire army. A centurion of the Tenth within less than two years after enlisting! I admit that I felt a thrill of pride—as who would not?

"Still further," Crastinus pursued, "Caesar bids you name what additional reward you would ask; he promises to grant it, provided only that it be reasonable." Then as I hesitated for fear of seeming greedy: "Speak up."

Thus encouraged, I said:

"I would have Bombyx for my first decurion. He is a good man."

"This reward is for you, not for someone else. Besides, it is your right to promote whomever you see fit. Ask something for yourself."

I thought for a moment, then replied:

"I would be permitted to thank the Imperator in person."

Crastinus smiled.

"It is granted; I will answer for it, and procure you an interview. And now let me welcome you to the centurions of the Tenth. Continue as you have begun, my Frenator, and you should go far." And he gripped my hand heartily. "Congratulations, Centurion."

He dismissed me, and I went to find Bombyx and tell him the news. *Edepol*, who would not serve under such a man as Gaius Caesar? Well might he claim descent from Aeneas of Ilium, and through him from the Goddess.*

---

* The Julian gens claimed to be descended from Aeneas of Troy, who, according to the legend, was a son of Venus. Hence the war-cry of Caesar's men: "Venus the Conqueror!"

Stern in discipline and impatient of folly he might be, but he was tolerant of honest ignorance and generous to reward, and I resolved anew to serve him well and truly, to the fullest of my powers, with all my heart and soul. Little did I guess that in a trifle more than a year I should be serving under another leader, the chieftain of a savage tribe in the far-off Cassiterides!

CHAPTER V

*Of the Bridge Across the Rhenus River; of the Fire-Raft;
and How I Was Taken Captive in Britannia*

THE destruction of the Veneti completed the pacification of Gallia Transalpina—or so we thought at the time—and when the Imperator joined us in spring of the following year there seemed little for him to do save administer the government.

"From now on," remarked Porculus, one evening, "life should be one grand, sweet song. Little work, little fighting, and plenty of loot. For myself, I am glad to be here."

Bombyx and Arcularius burst into laughter, and the rest of us chuckled.

"Porculus the Epicurean!" jeered Bombyx. "How little you know your Imperator!"

"Or the Gauls," added Titus. "Doubt not that there will be ample fighting; what Caesar does not invent, the barbarians will force on him. Kiss your dreams of idleness farewell, my Porculus."

Titus spoke truly; we had work enough to satisfy the most eager. First of all, certain Germanic tribes began making trouble. The Usipetes and the Tencteri, harassed by their neighbors the Suebi, decided to emigrate rather than continue their futile efforts at resistance. The Suebi, I might say, are the most warlike of all the Germanic tribes, giving little attention to agriculture, and spending most of their time in hunting and fighting. They are strong in numbers, and can put a hundred thousand warriors into the field at once; therefore, since they live chiefly on milk, cattle, and game, it follows that they need large territories to support their people. Also, to guard against surprise attacks, they devastate the country for many miles around their borders, and as a result are often engaged in wars of conquest. From this constant practice, from the fact that they are large men, and from their mode of life, which makes them hardy fighters, they are the terror of neighboring tribes.

The Usipetes and the Tencteri, then, forced their way across the Rhenûs River despite the resistance of the Menapii, making their way even to the borders of the Condrusi and the Eburones. Thus it became necessary for Caesar to drive them back, but after prolonged negotiations, and while still at truce, the Germani treacherously attacked our cavalry and slew a number of them, among whom were the gallant *eques* Piso the Aquitanian and his brother, two of our most devoted allies. Angered at this treason, the Imperator fell upon the Germani unawares and slew or put to flight the entire horde of nearly half a million men, women, and children, scattering them to the winds and driving them back to their own country. For this massacre he was severely reprobated by his enemies in the Roman Senate, Marcus Cato—moral and righteous, but like all his family a pig-headed fool—even proposing that the Imperator should be delivered to the Germani to deal with as a criminal. Such folly makes me boil! However, Caesar gave it no attention, but went his way, and I, who was there, say that the massacre was necessary if the Roman rule was to survive in Gallia Transalpina.

The Suebi, meanwhile, were harassing the Ubii, the only Germanic tribe which was friendly to Rome, and these latter sent to Caesar to ask aid. The Imperator, never being one to desert an ally, decided to cross the Rhenus River, but on account of the width and swiftness of the stream, and the probability that the farther bank would be defended, he thought best to do so by bridge rather than by boats. So he chose a spot where a nearby forest offered ample material, and set Mamurra and his artificers to work.

To render strict justice, though Mamurra was an abominable scoundrel, it must be admitted that he was a competent engineer. He put the whole army to felling, trimming, and hauling trees, and began by constructing great rafts on which were high scaffolds. Then timbers a foot and a half in diameter were coupled together in pairs, each pair being of a length suited to the depth of the stream and having the lower ends pointed. Working from the scaffolds, men with rammers drove these pairs into the bed of the river, so that a double line of pairs extended right across the stream, these lines being eight paces apart at the water level, and slanting toward each other. As each double pair was set, a timber two feet in diameter was laid across the topmost braces, filling the space between the uprights and joining the pairs, and from each of these horizontal timbers diagonal braces led to the upstream and downstream piles. Further braces were slanted from the river-bed against the downstream piles, the final effect being that the rush of the stream tended to bind the whole structure more firmly together. Then beams were laid from timber to timber, with smaller sticks on top, and trampled earth gave the whole a smooth-surfaced roadway eighteen feet wide. Altogether, it was a magnificent engineering feat, not the least admirable part being the speed with which it was done, for though the river was three hundred paces wide at this point the bridge was complete and ready for use ten days after it was begun. But one of the Imperator's greatest points of strength lay in the fact that he demanded speed in every undertaking.

Naturally the Germani annoyed us as much as possible, so that as the work neared completion we had to shelter our workmen behind mantlets, for protection against arrows. Our Numidian and Cretan archers replied to the barbarians, as did also the Balearic slingers, but since we could mass only a few at the end of the bridge and on rafts, and since the natives were well protected, we did little harm. The *tormenta*,* to be sure, helped us not a little, their power being sufficient to hurl rocks and heavy arrows well across the stream. The barbarians also floated heavy rafts and flat stone-laden barges down the river, that the shock of their striking might loosen the piles. Mamurra guarded against these floating rams by driving clumps of piles above the bridge, to take the impact and swing the rafts and barges gently between the supports. Then some crafty native devised a new scheme, covering large rafts with green hides, building great heaps of fuel on them, and sending the flaming masses down to set the bridge on fire.

We were able to fend off most of these fiery rafts, and by wetting down the bridge, by protecting it with green hides, and by flinging water on the fires, to keep them from doing any damage; but one such raft, in spite of all our efforts, came near accomplishing its purpose. It was an exceptionally large one, was built up to a great height with pine and other resinous woods, well soaked with tar and oil, and as it came floating swiftly down with the current the raging flames leaped ten times the height of a man above the water, great clouds of black smoke rolled down

* A generic term for all forms of artillery, including catapults, onagers, scorpions, and ballistas.

to us, and we clearly heard the roar and crackle of the fire, borne on the wind.

The end of the bridge was then about three-quarters of the way to the Germanic shore, and the barbarian arrows were reaching us handsomely. Mamurra was standing in the lee of a mantlet, directing the work, and when he saw this fire-raft bearing down on us he swore aloud:

"Per Deos Immortales!" Then: "Buckets, men, buckets! Wet down the bridge—here comes trouble!"

Seizing the leather buckets with ropes attached, which lay always handy, the men drew up great quantities of water and drenched the woodwork, while at the same time those who had charge of the hides hung them about the piles or fastened them under the roadway so as to protect the beams when the raft passed under. So rapidly, yet in such orderly fashion, were these things done that all might have been well had not the raft, by evil fortune, caught one of the protecting groups of piles, swung around, and through some freak of the current jammed between those piles and the supports of the bridge.

With the raft thus hung up, nothing could be done. So fierce was the heat that men could not approach near enough to push the raft away with poles or to throw water on the fire, and the woodwork of the bridge was steaming; presently it would crisp and crackle, then burst into flames, and some if not all of our work would be to do over. Above the roar of the fire we could hear the natives on the farther bank shrieking their uncouth yells of triumph, and Mamurra's broad face was a fine, rich purple as, fists clenched and feet wide apart, he cursed the raft, the fire, the Germani, and the Fates. I saw the Imperator hurrying toward us, the purple cloak which marked his rank streaming from his shoulders—but what could he do? Plainly, Fortuna was against us this time. But I had thought of this possibility, and shouted to my men:

"Bombyx! Decimus! Scaevola! Titus! Arcularius!" I called by name ten whom I knew to be expert swimmers, and as they sprang forward I commanded: "Strip—take one *pilum* each—follow me! Balbus—" this to my trumpeter "—take your *bucina* and give us the signal for concerted action."

Balbus was quick-witted and caught the idea instantly, and before the Imperator reached us we were naked, each man had his javelin, and I leaped from the bridge, the ten following as one. Mamurra saw what we were about, and leaving off cursing, he had the men redouble their efforts to keep the bridge wet.

Swimming as much as possible under water, to avoid the heat, we drew near the raft, at length coming to a sand-bar which, by favor of the Gods, lay in the stream under where the raft was. I had counted on this bar from the first; the water was only about three feet deep over it, so that we would be partly shielded from the fire, yet could have footing from which to thrust against the raft; and since the flames rose into the air, the heat would not be so intense at water level as on the bridge, wherefore we could get nearer our object.

There was no need to give orders; my men knew what to do, and placing the points of our javelins against the raft, and taking our time from Balbus' trumpet, we shoved in concert—again—yet again. No result, and by now the water was dried from our heads and arms, and we felt the scorch of the flames.

"Halt!" I cried. "Duck yourselves." Wetting our heads and shoulders, we bent once more to the attack, and this time I felt the raft give a trifle. "Stay with it, men!" I shouted. "Hard! Get your backs into it!"

We should have used poles, not javelins, for with this

effort the iron points buckled, leaving us with only the shafts, and bringing us within four feet of the fire. And, *per Martes*, how hot that fire was! It was terrific! I felt the hair crisping on my head, felt my eyebrows and lashes swept away by the heat, felt the scorch of the flames on my head and shoulders. The tears started to my eyes, and I bent my head to shield my vision. I heard Bombyx on my right cursing savagely, and on my left Arcularius swore aloud as a spark landed on his neck.

"Duck again!" I cried, and we did so. "Now all together! Push—push hard! Once more! Now all together!"

Again and again, with the rhythmic trumpet note blaring above the roar of the flames, we surged against the raft, and at length it swung free, turned slowly about, and floated off down stream, passing harmlessly under the soaked bridge, while shouts of triumph from our men and yells and curses from the barbarians greeted our success.

Arrows and slingstones hissed into the water around us, but fortunately none struck their mark, and ropes were quickly thrown from the bridge. When my ten had been hauled up, I followed, to come face to face with Caesar.

"Well done, Frenator!" he commended me. "Admirably done! Are you much burned?"

"It is nothing, Imperator," I answered, saluting. As a matter of fact, my head and arms and shoulders were a mass of blisters, and I was in agony, but I would not admit it. "Nothing serious," I repeated, whereat he smiled.

"Next to a brave man, I love a good liar," he said. "But I have sent for dressings."

And indeed, even then three soldiers came running

with butter and soft cloths.* While our wounds were being smeared and bandaged, Mamurra came pushing through the crowd.

"The Gods have you in Their keeping, Frenator!" he boomed. "You have saved my bridge. If it had burned—" He made as if to fling his arms about my neck, and involuntarily I dodged. The Imperator stopped him with a word.

"Halt!" he snapped. "Frenator is in no shape for caresses. Give over, Mamurra." He turned to me. "You and your men go to your tents and rest until your burns are healed; you are relieved from duty until then. This shall not be forgotten; see that my secretary has the names of your ten." A smile flickered on his lips. "You have earned a new title of honor. Henceforth you shall be known as *Calvi*—The Bald Ones." And in truth we were one and all as hairless as eggs.

A shout of laughter went up, and the nickname was repeated from mouth to mouth; in some cases it stuck, or was intentionally adopted, and long after retiring from the army Bombyx was known in the City as Manius Cornutus Calvus. Scaevola, too, kept it for a cognomen, as did also Arcularius.

Caesar dismissed us with a wave of his hand, but as we turned to leave he stopped me.

"One word, my Gaius," he said, a friendly note in his voice. "Did you know that sand-bar was there?"

"Certainly, Imperator."

"You counted on it?"

"Of course."

"I understand. You try to foresee events and be prepared for them?"

"I try to, always, Imperator. I had thought that a raft

* The Romans used butter as a dressing for wounds, but not as food.

might catch there, and had planned what I would do."

He nodded, but made no further comment than:

"You have done well. See to it that your burns are properly cared for, as well as those of your men. You may go."

Saluting, I left, and as I went I heard Mamurra's rough voice driving the men back to work.

Swathed in bandages from waist to crown and to finger-tips, my ten were waiting for me at the bridgehead, eager to hear what Caesar had to say.

"Will there be a reward?" inquired Porculus, hope-fully, but I disappointed him by saying:

"Probably not; it was in the line of duty. Still, it will be remembered, and will count in our favor when promotions are given out."

"It seems," he grumbled, "as though there should be a few *denarii* in it for us."

I shrugged my shoulders, then winced.

"You are lucky to be alive," I told him.

"And to have had a sound lesson," chimed in Bombyx. "*Mehercle,* if the flames of Tartarean Phlegethon are as hot as those we felt on our own trifling river, I mean to be my mother's good little boy from now on!"

"You should be thankful, Porculus," spoke up another. "You lost at least five or six pounds of useless suet; I heard it frying out of you and sizzling when it struck the water."

So, laughing and joking at the pain, we made our way to the camp, where I for one was glad to retire to my tent and enjoy my burns in solitude.

The bridge was completed long before our skins were healed, but we accompanied the army into Germania, rid-ing in the baggage-carts and exchanging jests and laugh-ter with the trudging soldiers.

"Edepol!" vowed Bombyx, "It is worth a few burns to ride at ease and watch our fellows doing their twenty-four miles a day, all hung with armor and equipment, and digging like moles at the march's end."

"I must try to get me a few slight scorches," said Titus, "next time Labienus has us in winter quarters."

"Get a sword through the arm," Bombyx advised. "It is less painful, and one gets more waiting on. Frenator, here, will accommodate you with the stop-thrust he learned from Tiberius the Red. Eh, Frenator?"

"Any time," I cheerfully agreed. "Of course, there is always the chance of a mistake, and that the sword may go through your belly."

"Thanks," said Titus, dryly. "I will stick to the fire."

"If only," spoke up Arcularius, "we can continue to sit here and watch the fighting, it will be as good as a seat at the arena."

"Well for Arcularius that he will not be fighting," jeered Porculus. "Let the Germani catch sight of his gem collection, and it would be *pollice verso* * for him."

"I have kept my gems and my head so far," snapped Arcularius.

"Yes, with assistance of myself and Scaevola, who are your mates in the line of battle."

"Any time I ask you for aid—" began Arcularius, with heat, but I stopped him. The men were edgy in the temper from pain, and it would have been a simple matter for teasing to grow into quarreling.

However, the longed-for treat was not in store; there was no fighting. The Usipetes, Tencteri, and Sugambri fled before us, and we had to content ourselves with burning their villages and outlying farmsteads, and harvesting their grain for our own use. From their territory we

* "With turned thumb"; the signal for the death of a defeated gladiator.

marched to that of the Ubii, who fled with their old men, their women, and their children, taking refuge in the depths of the forests. We destroyed some towns here, then after eighteen days without a bit of honest fighting, we retraced our steps across the Rhenus River, collected the garrison we had left at the bridgehead, burned the bridge, and marched straight to Portus Itius on the sea-coast.

The Imperator was so generally right that I must take this opportunity of correcting a slight mistake in his *De Bello Gallico*, even though it is no more than an unimportant slip of the pen. He says that he "tore down the bridge," but he would never have taken the time for this when fire would do the work so much more quickly and easily. As a matter of fact, the bridge was burned, to the great wrath of the Germani, who had hoped to use it for another invasion of Gallia.

By this time our injuries were mostly well, though we were still hairless. Arcularius had some trouble, for he caught cold in his burns and they festered, leaving him, in the end, badly scarred. The rest of us, not so unlucky, were back on duty before we reached the coast, where we made camp outside the town, observing that the fleet used in the campaign against the Veneti lay at anchor in the harbor. As first centurion of his legion, Crastinus was admitted to Caesar's councils, and the morning after our arrival I asked if he might tell me what this concentration of ships portended.

"It is no secret," he replied. "The Imperator means to invade Britannia. The Britanni have been sending aid to their allies and relatives in Gallia, and have furnished sanctuary to the fleeing chiefs of those tribes that we have conquered. Caesar means to put a stop to this. There is in Britannia a colony of the Atrebates, and Commius, who is chieftain of the Gallic Atrebates, has much honor among those beyond the sea, as well as at home. He is wise, brave, and discreet, besides being loyal to Rome, and Caesar has sent him to win the allegiance of the Britannic colony, and, if he can, of other tribes as well. If he succeeds—and perchance if he does not—the Imperator will lead an expedition to that country."

I whistled in surprise.

"It is late in the season for that," I pointed out. "The equinoctial storms will be on us ere long."

Crastinus spread his hands and shrugged.

"I do not imagine," he explained, "that he wishes to stay there long. It will be, I suspect, largely an exploring trip, to spy out the land, gain some knowledge of the harbors, of the Britannic mode of warfare, of the strength of the tribes, and such matters. With, of course, a certain punitive element. Then next year will come the real expedition of conquest."

"I should think these things could be learned from traders."

"One would think so, yes. But it has proved impossible. Caesar has questioned many of them, and they contradict one another—and themselves—continually."

At this point a decurion interrupted us, saying:

"Frenator, Caesar wishes to see you at once in the Praetorium."

Bidding Crastinus a hasty farewell, I went immediately to the general's tent, where I found the Imperator deep in converse with a tribune. I saluted and stood at attention, but Caesar bade me relax.

"Here is your man," he told the officer. "Volusenus, this is Gaius Durus, commonly called Frenator."

"I know him well," Volusenus acknowledged, nodding to

me. "We are old acquaintances." He commanded one of the cohorts of the Tenth, though not the one which included my century.

"All the better," rejoined Caesar. "Frenator, Volusenus is sent on a scouting expedition to Britannia, to find a suitable harbor for our landing. I wish you to accompany him and aid him in every way, keeping your eyes open and noting all that is to be seen. You have some decurion who can take charge of your century in your absence? You will not be gone more than a few days."

"Bombyx—Manius Cornutus—can do it, Imperator."

"Give him your orders, then. From now on until you return you are under command of Volusenus."

He dismissed us, and the tribune led me aside, saying:

"A galley is prepared for us, and will leave at midnight. You will be ready?" Theoretically, a tribune outranks a centurion, but practically a centurion of the Tenth—and especially one so high in rank as sixth in the legion—carries as much weight as any officer below lieutenant-general, so Volusenus put his command in the form of a question.

"Of course," I replied.

"Very well," he acknowledged. "Till then."

From Portus Itius to the nearest point of Britannia is perhaps thirty-five miles, and Volusenus told the captain of the galley to set a slow stroke.

"No need to arrive before full daylight," he said. "The first hour will do."

So an easy stroke of six or eight miles an hour was decided on, and Volusenus and I sat in chairs on deck and talked, our conversation punctuated by the thump of the *hortator's* mallets on the block as he set the stroke, by the "clack-clack" of oars in oarlocks, and by the thud and splash of the waves against our vessel's sides. For an hour or more we spoke of such various matters as war, religion, love, philosophy, gambling, money, slavery, and the like, and in the main I found the tribune's ideas to agree with mine. Then suddenly he shot a question at me.

"What think you, Frenator, of our Caesar? You have served under him for some time, and should have an opinion."

The abruptness of this took me somewhat aback, and I did not reply at once. But after some thought, I answered:

"I honestly believe him to be one of the world's great men of genius; I am prepared to credit that he is descended from a Goddess and a hero. Everything proves it; his gigantic and infallible memory; his ability to make men follow—and adore—him; his power of imposing his will on others; his marvellous strategy in battle; his foreknowledge of coming events—everything. I take him to be a demi-god."

Volusenus thought this over, then:

"Ye-es. Yes, in general, I agree. But he has done some ungodlike things; has taken advantage, used trickery. Look at his treatment of the Usipetes and the Tencteri—massacring them right and left, without distinction of age or sex. Look at his treatment of the Veneti—a whole tribe wiped out of existence, and not a savage tribe either, but one of fairly high culture. And it is well known that he bought his consulship outright, by means of bribes. Such things revolt me, I admit."

"*Edepol!*" I ejaculated. "One must fight fire with fire. The Germani were up to their necks in treason against us, and deserved exactly what they received. The Veneti —well, I regret that as much as you do, but the tribes of Gallia needed a sharp lesson, and the Veneti had revolted after professing friendship. As for buying the consulship

—*mehercle!* how else could he get it, politics in Rome being what they are? He needed it to further his plans, and when did office ever go by merit, save perchance the consulship of Marcus Cicero?"

"You believe, then, that he has plans beyond the conquest of Gallia Transalpina?"

I laughed.

"Do not you?" I countered. "Would a man of his genius be content with a mere proconsulship?"

Volusenus smiled at this, replying:

"I perceive, my Frenator, that you are given to thought and to analysis. What, then. do you take his plans to be?"

I outlined what Tiberius had said, and what had occurred to my own mind, Volusenus listening carefully. When I had made an end:

"You may be right," he admitted. "For myself, I have long foreseen a break in the Triumvirate. Crassus is weak and greedy, and Pompeius grows too large for his shoes. Deluded and led by the nose by that Egyptian astrologer of his—"

"I think he is a Chaldean," I interrupted.

"Chaldean or Egyptian, he is at all events a charlatan—"

"You do not believe in astrology?"

"Pfui!" snorted the tribune. "Do you?"

"I have never thought much about it," I confessed. "I have merely accepted it as taught. Many wise men give credence to the art. But go on."

"So the Magnus, being flattered and toadied to by Cato, Lentulus, Scipio, Ahenobarbus, and the rest of the Optimates, thinks himself the greatest man in the Republic. The time is coming when he will no longer brook Caesar's equality—"

"*Dii Immortales,* what an awakening is in store for

him! He will be forced to brook Caesar's superiority."

"Perhaps," Volusenus nodded. "In any case, there will be a civil war."

"So I think, also. And when that time comes I mean to be on Caesar's side."

"And I too, my Frenator," said the tribune. "Demi-god or no, he is the best leader we have to-day. He may prove the savior of the Republic."

It was a clear, though moonless night about the Ides of Sextilis,* and by daybreak we were nearing the coast; a low dawn-mist hung over the water, hiding the land from our sight, but the whisper of breakers on the shore gave ample warning, despite the fact that the surf here is far from what it is on the rocks of Gallia and Hispania. With the rising of the sun, this fog thinned, shredded out, and lifted into the upper air, and slowly, gradually, there emerged to view over our prow a range of cliffs of the most intense, dazzling whiteness. Two or three hundred feet above us they towered, and we on the galley stared, for all that their brilliance under the morning sun fairly hurt our eyes to look upon. Volusenus drew a long breath.

"Those must be the famous White Cliffs of Britannia," he said, "that Pytheas saw in his voyage of discovery *Mehercle!* I have never seen the like."

"Nor will you ever see it elsewhere," spoke the captain of the galley, behind us. "I have sailed along both shores of the Mare Internum from the Pillars of Hercules to the coast of Phoenicia, and I have sailed the outer ocean north from the Pillars to the Land of the Hyperboreans, but nowhere is there aught to equal this; it is unique."

These cliffs are backed, we found later, by a range of wooded heights that sweep in rising undulations to the sky-line, their green forests alternating with grain-fields

* August 13.

and orchards, but in any case it was obviously impossible to land here, so the tribune quickly decided to push on.

Breakfast was eaten, then Volusenus ordered the captain of the galley to run westward along the coast, which we did for some hours, finding no spot that promised well for a landing. There were many small inlets, but none big enough to shelter the fleet, and everywhere the ground behind them was high, broken, and wooded—impossible for our cavalry, and easily defended by guerrillas. We came, indeed, to a broad, tide-washed flat which might have served,* but here again uplands furnished a chance for defence, and we both were well enough acquainted with Caesar's way to know that he never bade his men charge uphill when it could possibly be avoided. We saw no natives whatever—doubtless plenty of them watched us from hiding—and about noon Volusenus bade the captain turn eastward again. Sunset brought us back to the cliffs we had seen in the morning, and anchoring off a shelving beach at their southern end, we cooked and ate our evening meal, set watches, and went to sleep.

"No luck so far," commented the tribune, as we wrapped our cloaks about us and lay down on the deck. "Well, Fortuna may favor us to-morrow. Good-night, my Frenator."

"Good-night," I replied, and was instantly asleep. That was another blessing of my new life; when a *homo bellus* in Rome I was apt to lie awake for long stretches, or to sleep uneasily, disturbed by dreams, unless, indeed, I went to bed drunk. Now, with the abounding health which comes from hard work and simple food, I slept quickly and soundly; as Bombyx once said of himself: "When I lie down to slumber I simply die until the trumpets sound."

---

* Romney Marsh, at that time open to the sea.

An hour or so after setting out on the following morning, we came to a bay which the galley's captain—an experienced sailor of the Venelli, by name Dubnoreix—said was Portus Dubris.* There was a considerable town here, with a number of trading vessels lying at anchor within the port, and a good deal of flurry and excitement showed itself at sight of a Roman war-galley. However, we did not disturb them, nor they us, and after an examination of the place we continued on our way.

"It is where the traders from Massilia and from Gallia land their wares," Dubnoreix informed us. "A good harbor, roomy and sheltered, and with good holding-ground. It should do your business nicely."

"Yes," agreed Volusenus, with dry sarcasm, "in more ways than one. Did you notice that range of wooded hills which would make an excellent lurking-place for the cavalry, and a fine starting-point for their charge? The cavalry of the Britanni, I mean." I laughed, and Dubnoreix seemed taken aback. I do not believe, though, that he meant any treason; I think he was honestly trying to be helpful, and merely did not understand a soldier's problems. "Round this foreland," continued Volusenus, "and swing north along the coast till we see what offers."

Within an hour's travel, the hills ran down into wooded flats, then into an open beach that extended for nearly ten miles, with no heights to be seen as far inland as the eye could reach, but only a moderate slope to higher ground.

"This is the spot," exclaimed the tribune, with satisfaction. "A gently sloping beach of shingle, and flat ground where the cavalry can ride down the beaten enemy after the legions have thrown them into confusion. I wish," he added, thoughtfully, "that we might land and capture a

* Dover.

few natives, so as to learn something of the population, the water supply, and such matters."

"Give me a few tens of men, and I will go scouting," I offered. Volusenus considered this, but shook his head.

"It is too perilous," he refused. "Beyond question we have been watched, and you might very well be snapped up or slain. And if you were taken prisoner, the natives would have someone to give them information, instead of their giving it to us."

"If you think—" I began, hotly, but he laughed.

"Nay, my Frenator, I was but teasing," he calmed me. "I know you would reveal nothing, even under torture. However, we cannot risk losing you; we must do the best we can from the deck of the vessel."

We continued northward, examining the shore with care, and finally sailed completely around an island which the natives call the Isle of Fires,* from the watch-fires which are there kept ready to light on the approach of an enemy. We found other possible landing-places, but none so good as the first, and Dubnoreix assured us that it was vain to proceed farther. Pointing westward, he said:

"That is the estuary of the Tamesis River,† on which is Londinium, ‡ the chief town of the Cantii. You will find naught there to serve your turn."

"We will take your word for it," said Volusenus. "What think you, Frenator?"

"Well," I considered, "the beach that we saw is favorable enough, and Caesar will want to take the shortest route, what with the transports and all. Why ask him to sail another twenty or thirty miles, braving these villain-

---

* Thanet, which in Caesar's time was entirely surrounded by water.
† The Thames.
‡ London

ous tidal currents that rush back and forth along this coast twice a day?"

"Exactly," Volusenus approved. "I think our task is done; we may as well return to Portus Itius."

"Would it not be well," I suggested, "to go back to our beach and take soundings, to make sure that the holding-ground is good, and that there are no reefs or quicksands?"

"Admirable!" the tribune exclaimed. "You hear, Dubnoreix?"

The captain nodded, saying casually:

"That beach is in the territory of the Cantii."

"What of it? Are they especially fierce or crafty?"

"Nothing," answered Dubnoreix, with a shake of the head. "I merely offered a remark. No, they are about like all the Britanni—none of them cowards, nor have they been greatly enervated by civilization, though they are less savage than the Germani."

"We can handle them," returned Volusenus, with confidence. "Southward, then, to get our soundings."

On the fourth day after sailing, we were back in Portus Itius, and I accompanied the tribune to the Praetorium, for though I was not first centurion, yet as a special scout I had access to the Imperator's tent. Caesar listened to Volusenus' report, asked a few questions, and seemed a trifle disappointed at learning nothing of the interior, but approved the tribune's refusal to set me ashore.

"You did well to offer, Frenator," he said, "but it would have been too great a risk. However, I am pleased with you both; you have done excellently well. Caesar thanks you. You may retire."

We saluted and withdrew, glowing within at having won the Imperator's commendation and thanks.

The preparations were quickly made, and on the eighth day before the Kalends of September, in the year DCLXXXXIX A. U. C.,* we set sail for Britannia. The Tenth and Seventh Legions went, with about five hundred native cavalry and a number of archers from Numidia and Crete, and with Balearic slingers, something under ten thousand men in all. The archers, slingers, and artillerymen went on the galleys, the legionaries on the transports, of which latter there were about eighty. Since the transports, being of native build, were propelled by sails, they necessarily made slower time than the long ships, which were driven by oars, but in spite of this all set out together save for the cavalry, which, being slow in embarking, did not reach Britannia till the fourth day after we did.

The embarkation was quickly and efficiently carried out, and we sailed at midnight; it was five days before the full moon, so moonset came at that hour, but light was less important to us than the tide, which was full an hour before sunset. Of course, in those latitudes there is no true night during the summer, but a sort of dusk; still, for complete insurance each vessel carried a lantern rigged either at the masthead or on a lofty pole. *Per Martes*, we looked like a fleet of fireflies as we set out from Portus Itius to invade this new land!

Head winds kept us back, so it was about the fourth hour when we in the galleys anchored off the White Cliffs to await the arrival of the transports, which did not come up until the ninth hour. Meanwhile Caesar gave explanations and instructions to his lieutenant-generals and tribunes on the long ships, and these orders were quickly transmitted to the centurions on the transports as the latter arrived. Then, the tidal stream having turned

* August 25, 55 B. C.

eastward, Caesar's galley hoisted signals commanding us all to proceed to the landing-place Volusenus and I had chosen.*

On the cliffs and high ground above us we could see the war-chariots of the Cantii, some two thousand of them, with a driver and a fighting-man in each, rushing in a frantic, madly galloping stream over the rugged ground to head us off from the beach. And so vigorous were the horses, and so skilful the drivers, that they arrived long before us; when we ran the vessels aground they were waiting for us, drawn up in line well beyond high water mark.

The *esseda,* or war-chariots, of the Britanni are low, two-wheeled open vehicles, drawn by two horses—practically the same as the *bigae* used for racing in the Circus—the drivers controlling their steeds by reins and voice. With a full-armed warrior and a driver standing in each chariot, the driver will urge his horses into the press of battle, when the warrior discharges javelin and arrows, then leaps down to fight on foot, while the charioteer retires a little way, coming in again to pick up his fighting-man if that one is hard beset or wounded. And now we had proof that Volusenus' galley had been watched, for the Cantii had spent the intervening days in rallying their men and in training the horses to enter the water, that they might come to hand-grips while we, disembarking, were at a disadvantage. The transports were broad-beamed ships, tall and sturdily built, but not designed for unloading troops, for they drew several feet of water, and as they grounded on the shingle, and the men sprang full-armed from their prows, our legionaries found themselves

* On the first invasion of Britain, Caesar landed on the coast of Kent, between the present sites of Walmer and Deal; on the second, a few miles north of this, between Deal and Sandwich.

shoulder-deep in the salt sea, the waves breaking over their heads and buffeting them to and fro. Then with shrill, harsh cries and thunder of galloping hoofs and rumbling wheels, the warriors of the Cantii charged furiously down upon us.

Like the Germani and the Belgae, the Britannic warriors are huge men, tall of stature and broad of shoulder, with fair skins, yellow or tawny or red hair which grows long and floats loose on the wind, and with long, flowing mustaches. Unlike their relatives on the Continent, they dye themselves before battle with a bluish dye, and they are much more given to ornamenting their armor than we are; their bronze shields, corselets, and helmets are inlaid with gold, coral, and enamel of various colors, so that altogether their charge, a mile in length—for our transports were strung out along the beach—was at once beautiful and terrifying.

On they came, gaining speed as they swept down the slope, the men yelling their uncouth war-cries, calling invocations to their Gods, brandishing their spears. On and on, the horses with tossing manes and flying hoofs, till with a tremendous whirl and splash the triple line of chariots and horses tore into the water, the men hurled their spears and shot their arrows, then all wheeled and rushed back up the beach to turn and charge again.

Hampered by shields on their left arms and *pila* in their right hands, taken aback by this strange mode of warfare, our men were thrown into confusion, and those still on the ships hesitated to leap into the water. Again the Cantii charged, though this time, being undisciplined, they were not in formation; it was every man for himself. The legionaries struggled as best they could toward land, defending themselves bravely, but unable to hurl their *pila* and scarce able to withstand the charge. Many were wounded and some were slain, and these last, weighted down by the heavy armor, sank, so that the men in the water trod on the bodies of dead comrades. Shouts and groans and cries mingled with the clang of weapons and the rolling thunder of the charge, and now our men were in dire confusion, bewildered and panic-struck, ready to break and flee—to what refuge?

Suddenly, on the transport next to us I saw the Golden Eagle lifted high, saw Crastinus, sword in hand, poised on the bulwark, heard him shout full-voiced:

"Leap down, soldiers, unless you wish to betray your Eagle to the foe! I at least will do my duty by my country and my Imperator!" And with these words he plunged into the surf.

"Per Deos Immortales!" I cried. "Shall Crastinus die alone? Sixth Century, follow me!" And I too leaped into the water.

This turned the tide of battle. The first and sixth centuries followed as one man, the others came after, and the first centurion of the Seventh Legion, shouting:

"Remember how we fought the Nervii!" carried his men with him.

We struggled to firm footing, then as the chariots again came thundering down we hurled our deadly *pila*.

"At the horses!" I shouted, and the cry was passed along the line: "At the horses! At the horses!"

We stopped the charge. As the heavy javelins pierced their breasts the horses screamed aloud, reared, plunged, fell, were dragged along, threw the whole charge into disorder. The warriors sprang down to meet us hand to hand, and with a glad roar of "Venus Victrix! Venus Victrix!" the legions drove at them.

The barbarians were brave and sturdy fighters. Not giving back, they met us foot to foot and breast to breast, and since we could not form our ordered line of battle the fight broke into a thousand duels. I cannot describe it —who can tell what happens in a mêlée? I have a confused recollection of brilliant armor; blue bodies; yellow hair; overturned chariots; kicking, screaming, plunging horses; shouts and curses and wild yells; faces contorted with rage or pain; and man after man confronting me, only to fall away as the good Roman sword bit hard.

At length I found myself facing two gigantic warriors, and as I opened the guard of one with a feint and drove my steel deep into his body the other stepped behind me. I tried to turn to face him, but my sword stuck in the body of the dead man, and the instant's delay was my undoing. The second man's blade crashed down on my helmet, lightning flamed before my eyes, then all was dark. I vaguely felt myself fall forward, put out my hands to catch myself, and knew nothing more.

CHAPTER VI

Of My Captivity Among the Britanni; and the Flight from Londinium

WHEN I came back to life I had been stripped of my armor and was bound hand and foot, with my knees drawn up to my chin and my wrists and ankles lashed together. I lay on my back in a war-chariot, and was fastened so I could not fall out as the chariot bumped and bounced at full speed over rough ground. The position was intensely uncomfortable, my head ached with a savageness exceeding anything wine had ever brought, and an effort to ease myself gained me only a kick in the ribs from the driver, with a gruff sentence which—not knowing the language—I took for a warning to lie still. I obeyed, and presently the smoother going told me that we had come to a road.

An hour's travel brought us to a town which I afterward learned was Durovernum,* where I was dragged from the chariot and thrust into a rude hut; my bonds were cut, and food and water were brought me. Three or four men took part in this business, but it was dusk, so I could see little, and in any case I was too sick and dizzy to notice much, or even to eat. I took a long drink from the earthen jug, then dropped on a pile of straw in one corner of the hut, where I lay and suffered most miserably for some hours, till at length Morpheus took pity and laid His kindly fingers on my eyes.

* Canterbury.

In the morning an elderly but not unattractive woman brought me milk, boiled meat, and a jug of some sharp, acid drink with a marked flavor of vinegar. This last would be unpleasant to a pure Roman taste, but to me, accustomed as I was to *posca*, it was not disagreeable; further, it proved invigorating, so that I was able to eat, and shortly felt much better. In time I came to relish this native beverage, which is made by fermenting the juice of apples, and is, I believe, a more wholesome drink than wine; at all events, the folk who use it are largely free from many intestinal disorders which afflict the folk of Italia, notably that terrible disease of the bowels which slays its victims within a few short hours.

Left to myself once more, I examined the hut, which was circular, about four paces in diameter, and had been made by digging a pit some three feet deep in the earth, then building a wall of wattle-and-daub around this and roofing the whole with thatch. It had no window and but one doorway, a flight of steps cut in the earth leading up to the latter, while the only other opening was a small hole in the conical roof, to allow smoke to escape. The ashes of a fire in the center of the packed earthen floor indicated the purpose of this hole, as did also a layer of soot on the ceiling, blackest at the peak of the roof.

I have described the hut thus particularly because it was typical of the village and country dwellings which I saw in Britannia, as well as of the poorer class of town houses. These huts varied in size, of course, and some had wooden or stone floors, but in general they were much alike. Chieftains and wealthy noblemen lived in stone or frame houses of great richness and elegance—as such things go in that country—and of great size, for they not uncommonly housed two or three thousand clients and slaves; but farmers, artisans, and petty tradesmen inhabited these huts, the entire family huddling together in one room like pigs in a sty.

Wondering if there might not be a chance to escape, I mounted the steps, but had barely reached the doorway when the points of two lances jammed against my stomach and a growled command proved that I was well guarded. Returning, I sat down on the straw and gave myself over to meditation. It was clear enough what had happened—clear, too, that I was a prisoner, though what disposition would be made of me I could not guess. Something unpleasant, of course; captivity in the hands of barbarians was never a joke, and the fact of my not having been killed at once showed that I was kept for some special purpose. However, there was nothing to do save make the best of it, hope for a rescue, and watch for an opportunity to get away.

No one visited me through the daylight hours, but in the evening four men came to look me over, one of them carrying a torch. Three were warriors, men in the prime of life, wearing bright-colored tunics, tight woollen breeches, and sandals which were cross-gartered to the knee. Also, they carried bronze armor which, where not enameled in fanciful designs of red and blue and green, was polished until it shone in the glare of the torch like ruddy gold. The fourth man was elderly, of placid mien, and had long white hair and a white beard which flowed to his waist; from this, as from his long white robe and from the deference paid him by the others, I took him to be a Druid, one of the priests of the Celtic and Britannic religion.

The four examined me carefully, talked among themselves, asked me a few questions to which I shook my head, and finally the Druid nodded and made some remark, of which I caught the word "Londinium," then they turned to go. I spoke to them in Latin, and they listened attentively but made no answer, so I tried them with the few Celtic words Britannicus had taught me and with what I had picked up in Gallia. They seemed surprised, and glanced from one to another, but still did not reply, and at length departed.

Next morning the three warriors came back, tied my hands behind me, and hobbled my ankles so that I could take only a short step, then motioned me to leave the hut. Resistance would have been foolish, so I submitted calmly to all this, doing as they indicated. Looking around when once outside, I found myself in what seemed a fair-sized town, with several hundred persons grouped for a look at the stranger. For the most part the men were silent, but the women screamed, shook their fists, and spat on me, the children imitating them; the men took no part in this, but neither did they make any attempt to stop it. Of course I simply ignored these demonstrations; it was not for a Roman *eques* and a centurion of Caesar to notice such barbarism.

A springless, two-wheeled cart drawn by one horse stood near, and into this I was hoisted none too gently, and dumped on a pile of straw. The driver walked beside the horse, the three warriors took positions beside the cart as guards, and we started off. My bonds cut my wrists and ankles, and before long the jarring and jolting made me sick at my stomach, but there was nothing to do save endure in silence, which I accordingly did. We marched all day, with occasional halts for rest, and at night stopped at a small village, where I was untied, lodged in a hut precisely like the other, and fed.

The next day and the next were the same, though the pine, heather, and gorse which I had automatically noted during the chariot ride gave way, as we moved inland, to green forests of noble oak, elm, ash, and maple trees, to apple orchards where the fruit hung heavy on the boughs, or to rolling uplands of ripe grain. I noted, and confirmed by later observation, that this part of the country was as populous and as well cultivated as Italia or the more thickly settled parts of Gallia Transalpina. The Great Forest of Anderida, and the Great Plain of Sorbiodunum,* as well as a few smaller moors, were wild, but elsewhere towns and hamlets were frequent, fair-sized cities were not unknown, and between the settlements farm joined farm to cover the arable land in thick profusion. This was no desert island, in truth, but one teeming with a virile and industrious population.

Wherever we went, I was an object of much interest, the folk peering eagerly at me and jabbering in their outlandish tongue, while the women shook their fists and spat on me or struck me, and the children either did likewise or else gazed intently but half fearfully, as I have seen our own Roman children stare wide-eyed at a caged lion or tiger.

Late in the afternoon of the third day we came to a wide stream, over which we were ferried in a large, flat-bottomed boat that easily carried both cart and horses, and so we entered a city as large as or larger than Vesontio, where, after passing through a number of streets, I was imprisoned in a hut that was similar to the others, but was built on the ground level, having a wooden door and a stone-flagged floor. For furniture I had a table and chair and a low cot, with a fairly decent mattress replacing the usual pile of straw.

The day after my arrival I was inspected again, the

* Salisbury Plain. Sorbiodunum was the name of Old Sarum, a very ancient Celtic town which was abandoned in the 13th century A. D. Its traces still exist about three miles north of the present town of Salisbury.

same three warriors bringing another Druid to look at me. This one was much younger than the first, scarcely more than forty or forty-five years of age, with hair and beard still yellow as grain. Also, he was more intelligent looking than the other, and definitely handsome; he would have been a striking man in any company.

After some talk, the warriors withdrew, leaving us two alone, and the idea came to me that I might leap on the Druid, strangle him, and make my escape in his clothes. He must have read the thought on my face, for he casually opened the folds of his robe to show me a long bronze dagger hanging from his inner girdle, then wrapped the gown about him again and sat down, motioning me to seat myself on the cot. Then, to my utter amazement, he addressed me in Greek, asking my name. I was so astonished that I could not answer, but merely gaped at him.

"Oh," he smiled, "there are educated men among us; give the barbarian credit for something, Roman. My Latin is of the hit-or-miss variety, but I studied under Pythagoras in Athenae. Your name?"

"Gaius Aemilius Durus," I managed to reply.

"Patrician, *eques,* or plebeian?"

"An *eques.*"

"An officer of Caesar's?"

"Sixth centurion of the Tenth Legion." I said this with some pride, but he did not appear to notice my feeling.

"How many men has Caesar with him?"

"I do not know."

"Roughly?"

"Roughly, twenty thousand." It is nearly always well to exaggerate one's strength when talking with an enemy. "Perhaps twenty-five thousand," I added.

"What is his purpose in coming to Britannia?"

I shrugged my shoulders.

"Caesar does not confide his plans to his centurions. I cannot say, beyond that it is friendly."

"Friendly!" exclaimed the Druid, in an ironic tone. "With a hundred ships and twenty thousand armed men!"

"He feared that his intentions might be misunderstood —as in truth the Cantii mistook them—and he naturally wished to protect himself. From the reception he got, I should say it was well that he took precautions."

"Then you know nothing of his purpose?"

"Nothing, beyond that he means to bring culture and the arts of civilization to rude peoples, that they may profit thereby."

"As the Celtae have done?" he sneered. "A philanthropist, in very truth!"

"At least," I pointed out, "the Aquitani and the Aedui have benefited, as well as the other tribes that are friendly to Rome. And Caesar drove the Germanic oppressor from the country of the Sequani."

"Freedom is better than golden chains, Roman. And how of the Veneti?"

"They paid the penalty of treason."

"Why was Commius of the Atrebates sent to Britannia?"

"To bring his people into friendship with Rome. Did he succeed?"

"He was arrested as a traitor, and is now held in prison." He reflected for a few moments, then rose to go.

"May I ask a question?" I inquired, and he replied, with courtesy:

"To be sure. Though of course I will not guarantee to answer."

"How did the fight go?"

"The one in which you were taken? The Cantii were dispersed. However, they were no more than what might be called a flying squadron, and little was expected of them. The Catuvellauni and the Trinovantes are now gathering, under Caswallon, and Caesar will shortly be driven from our land—unless, indeed, he stays here forever, under six feet of earth."

I had my own opinion as to this, but judged it politic to keep it to myself, and asked:

"In what town am I?"

"In Londinium, the chief town of the Cantii, on the Tamesis River." I recalled hearing Dubnoreix mention this name, and so got some idea of my whereabouts.

"Were any other Romans captured?"

"No, you are the only one."

"I am an officer; can I look for exchange?"

He bent on me a not unkindly look, with something of compassion in it.

"I regret," he told me, "that I can hold out no hopes in that direction. It is important to our people to have a victim for sacrifice, from whom they may draw omens and so decide what course to follow with regard to Rome."

"And I am to be this sacrifice?"

"What fitter one could be offered?"

This appeared conclusive, but curiosity urged me on, and I pursued:

"How are the omens taken?"

"After purification with water, the victim is stripped naked, laid face upward on the Stone of Sacrifice, and held down by four Druids, while with a sharp knife the Chief Druid removes his entrails. From their aspect, the augury is read."

"I thought that, like the Druids of the Continent, you burned your victims in wicker cages?"

"That is at the quinquennial Festival of Keridwen, at

which time the neophytes are received into the Druidical clan. Ten years of study as Ovate, ten as Bard—during these twenty years one learns history, philosophy, religion, astronomy, geometry, natural science, and the oral traditions of our people—and then comes initiation. There are various ceremonies, and one of the novices, chosen by lot, is sacrificed in the way you mention. But at the yearly festivals the victims are criminals or captives, and the augury is taken as I describe."

"It seems to me," I commented, reflectively, "that I would hardly choose a profession that requires twenty years of study, and carries the chance of death by torture ere one is accepted."

He smiled superior.

"You yourself face death a hundred times a year for a reward that is trivial beside what a successful Druid recives." After all, this was true. "Is there anything else I can do for you? You shall have any indulgence that does not imperil your safekeeping."

"No, I think not. Food and shelter—wine, perhaps?" He nodded. "And, of course, liberty." Here he smiled and shook his head. "Well, then—oh, yes! How shall I be slain?"

"I have just told you; by removal of your entrails."

"No, but shall I not be put to death first?"

"By no means! Were you dead when eviscerated, the augury would be worthless."

This sounded unpleasant enough, in all conscience! My prediction, it appeared, was sound. I made one more effort.

"Will you not send word to Caesar, that he may ransom or exchange me?"

"Certainly not. He has no captives of importance, and we do not want his gold."

So there it was; I was at the end of my tether. Still, I was curious to know how long I had to live.

"When will this take place?" I asked.

"At the annual Feast of Samain, on the first day of the ninth month." * Nine weeks—none too long. "Have you any other questions?" he inquired, and I shook my head.

"None," I replied. "Thank you."

"Let me say that I am sorry," he remarked. "For all you are an enemy, you seem a personable youth, and I regret the necessity. Still, the Gods must be served. I can at least promise that you will be eviscerated gently."

"Thank you again!"

"No need to be sarcastic," he returned. "I assure you there is a vast difference in the way it is done. If the Druids favor you, you will hardly feel the pain." He held out his hand to me. "I am not subject to the insular prejudices of the ignorant," he went on, "and I can recognize a good man when I see one. My name is Tanarus. Can we not be friends—for nine weeks?"

There might be some profit in having a friend among the natives, so I swallowed my contempt for a barbarian and shook hands, when he went away, leaving me to contemplate my situation. It was none too rosy; a trifle more than two months, and then a horrible death. Well, be not downcast, Frenator; much can happen in two months. Escape, rescue—oh, many things! But, *perpol,* never in my wildest dreams could I have imagined what actually did occur.

Meanwhile, I was not badly treated. My food was good, though I found it hard to get accustomed to flesh once more; after three years of grain, meat was singularly flat and tasteless. This surprised me greatly, but I have

* November. The Roman year began March 1.

since learned that it is the usual experience; an eater of vegetable food finds meat insipid. My quarters were comfortable enough, and—happiest of blessings—free from vermin. On the whole, things might easily have been much worse.

I was closely guarded at all times, both by day and by night, two stout warriors with lances watching the door, two more the window, and another two patrolling the circuit of the hut; twelve different men took turn about at this. The ones who brought me to Londinium must have returned home, for I did not see them again. The townsfolk seemed to regard me as a free show, coming singly or in groups, at all hours of the day, to peer in at window or door, and to gaze with attentive interest at everything I did. I tried to talk with them, but got little or no response; they simply stared and giggled when I used my Celtic phrases on them. The guards did not try to stop these exhibitions—indeed, one of them, gathering a crowd, used to deliver what I took to be lectures on this strange animal—but at least they drove away the children when the little pests threw stones or mud or garbage at me. However, in a fortnight or so the novelty wore off, and the curiosity-seekers came less often.

Tanarus came to visit me every day or so, and we had many pleasant talks, he being highly intelligent, better educated than I was, and a broad-minded philosopher; apart from the fact that he relieved the monotony of my life, I enjoyed his conversation. Nor was I long in coming to feel a grudging admiration for him; barbarian he might be, yet he was an attractive one. I asked him why he, a man of education and ability, was content to remain in this barbarous country, among ignorant savages, and he grinned as he explained:

"Oh, they are not so bad, when you know them; they

have their good traits. Besides, here I am a person of importance, having much honor, whereas in Rome or Alexandria I should be nobody. And it is better to be a big frog in a small puddle than a little frog in a big puddle."

"You might at least come to be a medium-sized frog."

He laughed and made an indifferent gesture.

"This place contents me as well as another; I do not especially crave wealth and luxury. After all, the mind is the real kingdom."

I suggested the possibility of my escaping.

"A quick death from a lance would at least be more pleasant than what you foretell for me," I remarked.

"Where would you go? You could no more avoid notice in Britannia than could Polyphemus the Cyclops—'a marvelous monster; not like a man who lives by bread, but rather like a woody peak of the high hills.' As for a quick death, your guards have orders to thrust at your legs." So that discussion was closed.

Once, while talking of religion, I asked him if he truly believed in the faith of his people. He gave me a sidewise glance, and smiled.

"Do you believe in war?" he countered.

"I regard it as a necessary evil, springing from ignorance," I replied. "Were all men wise and intelligent, none would be selfish or greedy, and there would be no war."

"It is much the same with religion, Gaius. Were all men wise and intelligent, there would be no need of religion. But people must believe in something, and war is your profession, religion mine."

"Do you not believe in the Gods?"

"I believe in one God, omniscient, omnipotent, and wholly good, Who rules this world by immutable natural laws. I do not believe in a host of jealous, capricious deities, who can be influenced by petition and bribery to alter the course of nature; who stick their meddling fingers into every human pie; and who send good or evil fortune through caprice or spite." His manner was utterly contemptuous.

The thought was new to me, and I turned it over in my mind; it was the first time I had heard our religion presented in that light, though his statement was by no means fair to our Roman Gods.

"Your people believe in the transmigration of souls," I pursued. "Do not you?"

"Bah! An old wives' tale!"

"At least you believe in the immortality of the soul?"

He plucked a small twig from the fire which burned on the hearth, and held it up.

"This," he said, "may represent the living man." He blew out the tiny flame, and a thread of blue-gray smoke curled upward from the stick. "The soul may linger for a short time about its former habitation, even as this smoke lingers. After that—" he tossed the stick back into the fire and brushed his hands "—after that, nothing."

"It seems to me," I offered, "that you are guilty of a certain hypocrisy if you profess in public what you deny in private. What if I should denounce you, and publish what you have just said?"

He chuckled in amusement.

"You are welcome to do so. How far would a barbarian from Scythia, Dacia, or Britannia get if he accused the Flamen Dialis, the Priest of Jupiter, of heresy? As for the hypocrisy, I do not see it that way, Gaius. My people need guidance; they must believe something; and we Druids lead them for their own good. We execute justice, adjudicate disputes, punish evil-doers, guide the folk as best we

can to the better way. For my beliefs, the folk are not
ripe for them—they are too strong meat. Would you give
a two-edged sword to a babe for a toy?"

"Do all the Druids believe as you do?"

"Zeus Pater! About one in a hundred; there are all
grades of intelligence among us. Many—especially in the
remoter districts—are as blindly superstitious as the common folk. They believe most firmly in a pantheon of gods
and goddesses; in sacrifices of propitiation; in omens; in
beneficent and maleficent spirits; in elves and fairies; in
sprites and demons; in ghosts, witches, and giants; and—
supreme folly!—in magic and in taboos. No, we who have
laid off the faith of children and taken on that of men,
we are a small minority."

I must admit that Tanarus' faith—or lack thereof—
was a trifle strong for me also; I could not throw over-
board the lessons of my childhood, could not dismiss
Jupiter and Minerva, Mercury and Mars, Venus, Ceres,
and Bacchus—and above all, Vesta and the Lares of the
hearth—into thin air. Still, he taught me much, and set
me thinking, so that in the end I profited greatly by
these discussions.

Tanarus stubbornly refused to give me any news of
Caesar, whence I inferred the Imperator's success; if the
Britanni had driven the Romans off, they would be glad
to boast of it. Therefore I continued to live in hope, and
to look forward from day to day, expecting an invasion of
Londinium, and my rescue.

After about a month, I was taken out daily for air and
exercise, Tanarus having observed that I grew pale and
thin.

"We must have you in good condition for the Feast of
Samain," he remarked, and gave orders to that end. In
spite of—or perhaps because of—his lofty faith, there was

a quality of dispassionate, cold-blooded indifference about him that surpassed anything a *lanista* or a slave-dealer could ever show.

So each afternoon two ropes about twenty feet long were tied around my waist, the other ends about the waists of two of my guards, and I had a couple of hours' brisk walk and run in the open air. It was to my own interest to keep in good shape, and besides, I found a certain pleasure—which some might deem childish—in working the guards to the limit of their strength. So I used to take most of my exercise in running, and since I was to some extent a privileged person, they dared not deny me, but had to keep up. And being in better training than they were, I brought them in puffing and blowing, their mouths hanging open, then when they dropped exhausted at the door of the hut I would laugh at them. Foolish of me, perhaps, but I considered that in the circumstances I was entitled to some little amusement. And I must admit that they took it like sportsmen; so far from being angry, they laughed with me, grinning and shaking their shaggy heads as though it were the best joke in the world. But, indeed, the folk of Britannia love a practical jest, even when it is pointed at themselves.

Walking about the city and its environs, I learned that Londinium was a town much like Vesontio. A somewhat larger proportion of wattle-and-daub huts, and the chief industry was not textiles but enamel work—in which these barbarians excel our Roman artisans—and the manufacture of household and toilet articles such as kitchen utensils, mirrors, combs, hairpins, brooches, cosmetic jars, and the like. These things are mostly of bronze, for the native craftsmen are highly skilled in metal work and use a mixture of copper and tin, in varying proportions, for many purposes where we use pottery; they seem to know little of clay. The mirrors are for the most part of polished steel, little silver being used; and strangely enough, though the Britannic workmen produced the finest and most beautiful defensive armor I have ever seen, most of the weapons were imported from the Continent. It will be clear that I spent some of my hours in the open before the booths of traders and merchants, nor do I feel that it was time wasted; I learned much, and got an insight into the character of the folk.

The citizens whom I met on my walks at first regarded me with hostility, and scowled or spat at me, but little by little they came to look on me with indifference, and even in the case of some of the maidens, with not unfriendly interest; one in particular, whom I often saw, seemed to regard me with eyes of pity, as though deploring the fate reserved for so goodly a man. My guards allowed me to stop and chat as I wished with the young women, and I seized the opportunity to learn something of their language, though I was hardly fluent, and the maids giggled often at my mistakes, nor could I understand them unless they took pains to speak slowly and distinctly.

At length, about a week before the date set for the Feast of Samain, a strange Druid came to give me my daily inspection. According to the custom established by Tanarus, he entered the hut alone, and as he approached I automatically noticed that he was about my height, though narrower in the shoulders, and that his hair and beard were scarce longer than mine, which had grown during captivity; also, they were a dark chestnut color, and by night would pass for black. Suddenly it flashed through my mind that here was my hoped-for chance.

When he drew near I rose and dashed my fist against the angle of his jaw, then as without a sound he fell unconscious, I tore open his robe, snatched the heavy dag-

ger from his belt, and drove it through his heart, leaving
the weapon in the wound to prevent the effusion of blood.
I doubt if I could have done all this had it been Tanarus,
but with a stranger I had no compunction—after all, it
was his life or mine. Next I stripped off his robe and
wrapped it around me, taking also his belt and scabbard,
then withdrew the dagger, cleansed it on his tunic, and
sheathed it. And while thus occupied I kept up a mumbled
conversation in Greek, in two voices, to mislead the
guards if they chanced to be listening.

There was no sound to indicate that the watchmen suspected anything wrong, and my heart beat high; it is an
axiom as true as any of Euclides that Fortuna favors the
bold, and it might be that She would aid me. I kept up my
pretended conversation while I propped the dead Druid
in my chair lest one of the guards peep in, and continued
it until the shades of night were fully down. Then boldly
leaving the hut, I saluted the guards—*edepol*, they noticed nothing!—and set off down the street, making for
the Tamesis River. I had, if all went well, some nine or
ten hours' start before the hue and cry would be out after
me; my absence would hardly be discovered until my
breakfast was brought, and even then the pursuers would
not know which way to go. I chuckled to myself as I pic-
tured the consternation which would follow when the
Druid was found stark and cold, and the prisoner gone.
Of course, by slaying him I had irrevocably sealed my
fate if I were retaken, but that was of little moment; I was
doomed in any case unless I could reach my friends.

There were few persons abroad, and none suspected me,
so I reached the river unmolested, then stripped off the
Druid's robe, cast it into the water, and started across.
The stream was swollen by the equinoctial rains, and before I had waded ten paces I was carried off my feet and

swept away. However, all Romans can swim, and I better
than most, so I managed to struggle across, though, being
taken a quarter of a mile or so by the current, I had some
ado to find the road when I got to land. But I reached it
at length and struck east, guiding myself by the stars. I
took the courier's gait, walking fifty paces and running
fifty, and resting ten minutes in every hour; for a long
pull this is the quickest foot-pace known.

Of course, while on the way to Londinium I had made
mental notes of the route—something Crastinus had
taught me to do when in strange country—and I counted
on covering the seventy miles to Caesar's camp in twelve
hours or less. Then I should be safe; wherever the Imperator might be now, he would unquestionably have left
a camp and a garrison to protect his ships.

Mehercle, but the night-breeze in my wet garments was
cold! Still, the exercise soon warmed me and dried my
clothing, and ere long I was sweating comfortably. By the
best of luck, there was moon enough to let me see the
path with reasonable clearness even in the woods, and all
night long I hurried forward, stopping occasionally to
drink from some brook, then on again, blessing the hard
training of the past three years. The old-time Gaius Durus
would have lost his way or fallen exhausted and footsore
ere making a tenth of the distance.

I passed silent farmhouses, standing amid stacks of har-
vested grain; in the deep woods my feet rustled through
fallen leaves; many times I heard the long-drawn "whoo-
oo . . . whoo-oo" of a hunting owl or the booming of
bitterns; and twice there came to my ears the dismal,
blood-chilling howl of a lonely wolf. Coming to a narrow
stream, I surprised an otter fishing, and the beast slipped
into the water, looking much like a swimming snake as
he fled upstream. Several times the road led through small

towns, and I passed boldly on, for the houses were dark, and I knew that anyone who happened to be awake would only shudder and pull the clothes over his head, taking my footsteps for those of a demon or an evil spirit—what human being would choose the dark hours of peril for a journey? And chuckling at the superstition of these barbarians, I pressed on my way.

Durovernum I skirted perforce, since that was a walled city, and even if I could have passed the gates there was a strong chance of meeting the watchmen going their rounds; they did this in some of the cities of Gallia Transalpina, and in Londinium, so probably here also. But that did not delay me much, and striking into the road once more, I hurried east, urging myself to the full—there would be ample time to rest. And when the moon had sunk below the horizon, and Ursa Parrhasis,* swinging round, told that dawn was near, I knew that I should make it.

But Fortuna is a tricksy dame, fond of a jest; she loves to hold out the promise of success, then snatch it from one's eager grasp, even as the cool water and fruits forever flee the parched lips of Tantalus. So she betrayed me after all.

My plan was a good one, my effort brave; they must have succeeded but for one thing; when in the morning hours I topped a rise and saw on another hill in the distance the camp that was my goal, it lay empty and deserted. Uneasy but still hopeful, I hastened to it and mounting the *vallum* swept the shore with my eyes. North and south, as far as I could see, the coast lay bare and empty of ships, and my heart sank—the Imperator had gone!

Then I knew despair. Alone in a hostile land, friend-

* The Great Dipper.

less, with no hope of ransom or rescue, a victim doomed to sacrifice, every man's hand against me, pursuers hot on my trail, and behind me the unpardonáble crime, I was utterly and irretrievably lost. *Vae mihi,* never again should I mount the slopes of Palatinus, never again grasp the hand of Tiberius, my friend! Before me the Stone of Sacrifice—nay, better to drive the dagger through my heart, and with that intent I seized the hilt, half drew the weapon from its sheath.

But it was the tradition of the Tenth never to give up, but to carry on while life remained, long after all hope was gone. It was a tradition which had brought us through many a desperate pass, and as it came to my mind my hand loosened and fell from the dagger. Carry on, Frenator! Never give up—Fortuna still favors the bold!

I made up my mind to search for means of crossing the Channel; perhaps I could find some fisherman or trader whom threat or persuasion would induce to set me across. Or failing that, I might steal one of the foolish little coracles of wicker and leather which the Britanni use; to dare the Channel in one, especially at this time of year, would doubtless mean drowning, but at least it was a chance, and certain death lay behind. So I set off along the shore in the direction of Portus Dubris, judging that I was more likely to find what I sought there than to the north.

I had covered perhaps two miles when I heard behind me the bay of a hound and a wild halloo of triumph, and looking back I saw six huntsmen coming at full gallop on their horses, with three great gray Molossian hounds on leash. Evidently my flight had been discovered sooner than I expected, and my bed had given the dogs my scent. At the time, I saw nothing unusual in this pursuit on horseback, but I learned afterward that it was most exceptional; the Britanni seldom bestride their horses, which are too small to carry a big man well. But these were huntsmen, not warriors.

Well, no use either to run or to fight; I cast my dagger on the ground and surrendered tamely—it was the only thing to do. My captors were anything but gentle; they wrenched my arms in binding my wrists, beat and kicked me until I was black and blue from head to foot, then put a rope around my neck and held the other end while they let the horses rest and themselves lay down on the sand. The dogs tried their best to get at me, whining with eagerness and disappointment, but at least they were not permitted to tear me, which I had expected they would do.

Presently one of the men rose, took the horses, and rode down to Portus Dubris for fresh beasts; when he returned I was kicked to my feet, the hunters mounted, and we set off for Londinium, I being led by the rope around my neck. It may be imagined that after traveling seventy miles in a little over twelve hours I had small stomach for the return journey, but my wishes in the matter were not asked; I could walk or be dragged by the neck, as I chose. I made the entire distance on foot, being vastly stimulated by frequent doses of essence of elm which my back and shoulders received, and at length, utterly exhausted, with arms numb from the bonds, with blistered feet that made each step a new and special agony, and aching all over from blows, I was thrust back into my hut to wait the coming of the Feast of Samain. But at least I could console myself with the thought that I had not permitted my face to express pain, nor had one groan or whimper escaped me.

Twenty-four hours later I was sufficiently rested to rise and greet Tanarus, and to my amazement he expressed great sympathy. I had expected him to be enraged at my slaying of his colleague, but his feeling seemed to be all for me.

"By Hermes, Gaius," he said, "it was a fine attempt you made; I love you for it! Bold, quick-witted, and altogether admirable, and I regret your failure."

"In that case," I joked, "and if your affection is sincere, why not help me escape? It is not yet too late."

He smilingly waved the suggestion aside.

"The affection is sincere enough, Roman, though perchance none of the deepest. But we must have favorable omens, and we need you to impress the common folk."

"Oh, then I am destined to produce a favorable omen?" I was a trifle sarcastic. "How can you be so sure?"

"Are you a child, Gaius, to ask such a question?" he reproved me. "Who takes the augury? The Druids, or the people?"

In spite of myself, I grinned.

"Tanarus," I said, affectionately, "you are a damned hypocrite."

"But in a good cause," he chuckled. "As for helping you to escape—well, it was not I who ordered out the dogs and gave them your scent."

"I thought you would be furious at me. And I am glad you are not."

"For stabbing Lugotorix? Pooh! He was a man of no particular account. Popular with the herd, and a well-meaning soul, but negligible of intellect. Still you have done yourself no good by it—none whatever."

I shrugged my shoulders.

"I can die only once," I said.

"True," he acknowledged. "Most true. But you can die with much more elaboration than was originally planned. It remains to be seen whether the first idea will be adhered to, or the Council of Druids will feel that your sacrilege demànds a fuller expiation. At least you can count on me to do my best for you. I love a daring man!"

"Thanks," I returned. "In any case, I can bear my fate like a Roman; Mucius Scaevola has set us a standard for all time."

"I am sure you will," he agreed, heartily. "I am sure of it; your captors were vastly disgusted that they could not draw an acknowledgment of pain from you. Now rest well; day after to-morrow we set out for the Standing Stones,* where the Feast of Samain is held."

* Stonehenge.

CHAPTER VII

Of the Sacrifice at the Standing Stones; and Brighde of the Dumnonii

TWO days after my recapture, I was roused before dawn by a stir, a hum in the city, with tramping, chattering crowds that passed my hut from daybreak on. About the fourth hour, my guards came in and bound me hand and foot, then carried me out and with little formality dumped me into a cart, where they tied me fast.

All that day and the next, and for five days, we journeyed slowly westward, passing crowds of folk of both sexes and all ages, and of all conditions—peasants, artisans, traders, merchants, poor beggars, wealthy noblemen with their retinues, fishermen, miners, Druids—every conceivable class, all pushing west afoot or in wagons, to celebrate the annual Feast of Samain, one of the two great religious festivals of their people. Perhaps ten thousand went from Londinium, more swelling the tide at every crossroad until the highway was thronged as far as the eye could see, till it was bright with gay clothes and lively with the clack of tongues.

Occasionally, mounting a rise, I could look back and watch the crowd, like a vast parti-colored serpent, undulating uphill and down; or as we threaded the outskirts of the Great Forest of Anderida, that stretches from the highroad southward to the sea, I noted the shifting, weaving patches of color as the yellow sun, pouring through the half-naked trees, threw the long procession into bright relief or deep, contrasting shade. And I marveled at the religious enthusiasm which could move such a horde of folk to leave their homes and journey a hundred miles to attend a ceremony of their faith.

I marveled still more when we reached the Standing Stones, for folk had come in from north and south and west as well as from east, from the whole of Britannia, from Londinium and Durovernum and Portus Dubris of the Cantii; from Verulamium [1] of the Catuvellauni and Camulodunum [2] of the Trinovantes; from Isca [3] of the Dumnonii; from Calleva [4] of the Atrebates; from Lindum [5] and Danum [6] of the Coritavi; from Gobannium of the Silures; and even from far Monapia [8] and the wild land of the Caledoni,[9] and from many a city and town and hamlet whose names I never heard. From farm and orchard, from loom and forge, from mine and quarry and pasture they came pouring in, till there must have been fully a quarter of a million souls camped on the boundless waste of turf and gorse which is the Great Plain of Sorbiodunum.

Some miles out of Londinium we mounted a ridge that the Britanni call "the Back of the Hog," and journeying along this I could look off over the forest, which rolls away to north and south like the vast waves of some mighty ocean, losing itself at length in the dim blue distance. Here and there I saw the silver threads of larger or smaller streams, and occasional spots of lighter hue marked clearings where the natives had laid out farms or hamlets. It was a magnificent view, wilder than the landscapes of Italia, but not less beautiful, and I enjoyed it for some hours, until Tanarus, climbing into the cart, drew my attention to himself. Thereafter he rode with me

[1] St. Albans.   [2] Colchester.   [3] Exeter.   [4] Silchester.   [5] Lincoln.   [6] Doncaster.   [7] Abergavenny.   [8] The Isle of Man.   [9] Scotland.

for most of the way, and we conversed in Greek, which was not understood by the guards.

"I have told them," he said, nodding toward the warriors, "that I am trying to convert you to our faith, that you may die cheerfully and well, thereby insuring a sound augury. Thus I have an excuse to talk with you, of which I must make the most, since I am soon to lose you, and then shall be thrown back on the society of these ignorant ones."

"If you would help me escape," I suggested, "and would go with me to Italia, you might enjoy my society for many years. I should be more than glad to afford you that pleasure, in very truth."

But he merely laughed and shook his head.

"Am I the only sacrifice?" I asked. "The folk we pass look most curiously at me."

"By no means! There will be a score of others, though you are the only one from Londinium. Also, the only outlander, which is why they stare. The others are condemned criminals, so the best augury, and the truest, is expected from you. What a farce it is!" he broke off, in disgust. "As though the Gods declared Their will through the entrails of slaughtered victims! What childish folly! But your Roman haruspices feed the herd on the same delusion—so much so that one of your writers has said that he did not see how two of them could meet and look each other in the face without laughing."

"Our Roman haruspices draw their divinations chiefly from the liver, the seat of life," I remarked. "Nor do they use men, but only animals."

"Man is but another animal," he rejoined. "In any case, it is a ridiculous farce."

"For my part," I commented, dryly, "I see nothing

comic in it whatever. I have read vastly funnier things in the comedies of Plautus and Aristophanes."

He grinned appreciation.

"I love a man who can jest in the face of death, Gaius. But be content; before the ceremony I will give you a drug to eat which will so dull the pain that you will feel hardly anything."

"Some comfort, that, at all events! But what is this place to which we are going? A temple, I take it, like that of Jupiter Optimus Maximus, or of Vesta?"

"Hardly that. A group of huge, dressed stones of unknown age, once a burial-place of chieftains; rather, a monument set up in honor of the dead, for all about are barrows, long or round, where chiefs are buried. This much our tradition tells us, though it is silent as to when or by whom the monument was built. The common folk believe it was erected by magic, or by the Gods, but—" He waved his hand expressively, and I nodded.

"Yes, of course. Go on."

"With the passage of ages, and by an obvious transition of thought, it has become a place of worship, a religious center where the folk of all Britannia gather twice a year; at Samain, and six months later, at Beltane. Samain commemorates the dying year, when the sun dips toward the horizon and the Spirits of the Dead grow in strength; Beltane, the return of the sun, giver of light and warmth and crops. You understand, of course, that I am reciting the popular view; to me it is just so much nonsense."

"I gathered as much," I chuckled. "What are the ceremonies?"

"There are various rites; the festival lasts five days. Prayers and incantations; invocations to the sun; propitiatory sacrifices; religious processions; chants of the

Druids; chants in which the people join, both in chorus and antiphonally; in brief, all sorts of solemn foolery. And on the last day all fires throughout Britannia are extinguished, and the Chief Druid, making fire by friction of wood, relights the Sacred Fire, wherefrom each family receives a brand with which to rekindle their hearth."

"Not unlike our annual rekindling of Vesta's fire," was my comment, and he agreed, saying:

"I think something of that nature is found in all religions; fire is life, and it is natural for ignorant folk to count it holy. To continue, malefactors are denied the fire, which is a dreadful punishment, since they can neither warm themselves nor cook their food; there is naught for them to do but either make submission and atonement, flee the country, or commit suicide.

"You will see it all, my Gaius, and you will see me playing my part as solemnly as any—but you will know that my tongue is in my cheek." An engaging sort of hypocrite, this Tanarus!—I liked him against my better judgment. Yet after all, if I may so express it, there was a basis of sincere altruism to his hypocrisy.

"Nay, I forgot," he resumed. "You will not see it all, for the ceremony of the New Fire comes on the fifth day, and you will be gone by then; the sacrifices are on the fourth. However, you will not miss much."

"It is in my mind," I remarked, dryly, "that I shall miss a great deal."

He laughed and slapped me on the shoulder.

"Always the jester," he responded. "Gaius, I vow I love you like a brother. It will grieve me to see your entrails plucked from your body."

"Not half so much as it will grieve me, Tanarus." And he laughed again, so that the guards turned and looked inquiringly at us.

For all their primitive uncouthness, their lack of finish, the Standing Stones have something majestic and impressive about them. Even I, accustomed to such glorious buildings as the Temple of Jupiter Capitolinus, with its noble columns and gilded statue; and to the Temple and Atrium of Vesta, whose chaste elegance typifies the austere virtue of the Goddess' servants, the one pure spot in all decadent Rome—even I felt the rugged strength and the stern, savage power of the Standing Stones. Small wonder that a rude, barbaric people thrilled to this monument of their mighty ancestors; small wonder that they bowed in awe before this temple of an older time.

Coming to the Standing Stones from Londinium, one approaches up an avenue some miles long and about fifteen paces wide, which is marked by earthen banks six or eight feet high, these banks ending in a low rampart which encloses a circle about sixty paces across. Within this is a circle twenty paces in diameter, of thirty massive, rough-hewn, weathered sandstone rocks, more than thrice the height of a tall man, and perhaps six feet broad and half as thick. These stand on end and support great horizontal stones that are laid from one to another of the vertical ones, to form a continuous lintel. The upright stones are about three or four feet apart, thus making a circular colonnade, the columns and lintels being mortised and tenoned to hold them firm.

Some two paces within this large circle is another like it, but smaller, built of forty stones of a bluish cast, and within this are ten huge vertical stones with lintels, arranged in the form of a horse's hoof. Inside this, again, a horseshoe of nineteen smaller stones with lintels, both of these horseshoes opening toward the avenue, where in the gateway of the rampart is the Stone of Sacrifice.

The Great Altar, a flat rock more than twice as long as

a tall man, lies in the curve of the inner horseshoe, and here it is, Tanarus said, that the Chief Druid rekindles the Sacred Fire, which is never extinguished but at Samain; through the rest of the year it is tended by nineteen virgins. I never learned how it is protected in case of heavy rains, for there is no roof over the altar; unlike that of Vesta, it is open to the sky.

As nearly as I could determine, there is some confusion about the Great Altar and its functions; many of the heathen Gods are worshiped there, though it is primarily sacred to Brighde, Goddess of Fire and Dew. Brighde's virgins are less holy than those of Vesta, however. One of our Vestals who is unfaithful to her vows is, of course, entombed alive, since no man dares to lay violent hands on her; but should one of Brighde's fail in her duty she is put to death like any other malefactor. In general, I never found anyone who could explain the Britannic faith with clarity, and I suspect that the functions of their Gods overlap so that the folk themselves are not altogether clear in their own minds as to what they believe.

Drawing near the Standing Stones, we found the great plain covered far and wide with leather tents, arranged hap-hazard among the gorse and the infrequent copses of trees, and many purveyors of food and drink, as well as of clothing, jewelry, trinkets, and utensils of every kind, had set up booths where they cried their wares. Truly, these folk make a gala occasion of their religious ceremony! Horses, carts, and wagons were dotted all about among the tents, and I saw not a few of the primitive ox-drawn sledges that were used before the invention of wheels, for the pig-headed Britannic peasants cling beyond all sense or reason to the customs of their ancestors.

The smoke of thousands of cooking-fires drifted into the cool, sun-lit sky, the draught-cattle grazed freely on the short turf, and everywhere one saw an intertwining, wavering mass of bright colors as the people moved to and fro, examining the traders' goods and chaffering or buying, or perhaps visiting with acquaintances from other regions, for at these festivals the bitter enmities between the tribes are laid aside and the folk from all Britannia meet in amity—for five days. The men carry weapons for protection while on the journey, but woe betide him who draws sword or dagger while the feast is in progress; he gets short shrift from the Druids, and his family and kin are denied the fire.

A stockade had been built outside the earthen rampart, and I was herded into this, along with fifteen or twenty other victims. We were given food and blankets and were well guarded by armed men, so there was no possible chance of escape, though we were not tied. I looked over my companions, finding none to my liking; as might be expected, they were an ignorant, brutish lot, so I kept to myself. For the most part their faces expressed a sullen acquiescence in their coming fate; three or four stared blankly around in puzzled manner as though not sure what it was all about; and two paced restlessly up and down like caged tigers. But in the main they were stolidly resentful, angry at their evil fortune, yet unable to devise any plan for changing it.

Tanarus stopped in to visit me during the evening, bringing a kidskin of very superior wine, and we sat side by side on my blankets, talking of this and that. I commented on the quality of my fellow-victims, and he, glancing about, agreed.

"Yes, they are clods," he said. "No loss to anyone; like

cattle, they best serve their destiny in serving the demands of their superiors. But you, Gaius, are another matter. *Zeus Pater*, but I regret your fate!"

"You keep coming back to that," I said, a bit irritably, "like a harp with one string. Yet you do nothing practical."

"Frankly," he returned, "I have cudgeled my brain to find a way out . . . if you would accept our religion something might be done. . . ."

I put my head back and laughed aloud.

"A fine one you are, Tanarus, to be preaching apostasy! A glorious teacher of the faith of the Druids! No," I continued, seriously, "I have never been deeply pious, but after all, the Roman Gods are real to me; I cannot accept your Britannic ones."

"You need not actually believe in them," he pointed out, with some eagerness. "It will suffice to say that you do."

This angered me, but I remembered that though educated, he was only a barbarian. So I held my temper, simply commenting:

"It is evident that you have not known many Romans. I could not face the Manes of my ancestors in the Lower World had I denied Jupiter Optimus Maximus and Vesta merely to save my own skin; they would cry out on me for a coward, and no true Roman."

He spread his hands.

"There it is, you see. As for an ordinary escape, it is not to be thought of; even with all the will in the world, I could not compass it." He rose to go. "I must leave you now."

"Do we say farewell?"

"Oh, no. We shall meet again; I have not forgotten my promise of a drug to ease your passing."

It was plain that I had come to the end of my rope, and it seemed strange to reflect that a Roman *eques* and a centurion of the great Imperator was about to be sacrificed to nourish the superstition of a barbarous folk. I myself could not quite grasp it; I knew it with my mind, but it seemed as though I were two individuals, one of whom calmly stood aside and watched the other's fate.

My thoughts went often back to those evenings in Praeneste, when, with Tiberius and Flava Rufus, I dined in the cool and pleasant Alban Hills and listened to the slave-girl reading or to my friends discussing many things —*mehercle,* it seemed another existence! Was I indeed that Gaius Durus? I wondered if Tiberius would ever learn of my death, or if, when the predicted civil war broke out, he would simply miss me and never know what had befallen his friend. Oddly enough, I was not greatly distressed at the thought of what was before me. I regretted it, of course, and would have preferred to die in battle, but I had faced death too often to cringe at the sight, and what mainly grieved me was that now I should not be able to provide for Doris, the charming little Greek girl who had been my *vestiplica.* I was fond of her, and had counted on rescuing her from the hands of Clodius and reëstablishing her in the new home I meant to have. But now she must take her chances with the others. Oh, well, the Fates decide these things to suit Themselves.

I saw nothing whatever of the ceremonies, for not only was the space within the rampart crowded with folk, but as many as could find room stood on the rampart itself, shutting off all view; from our stockade we could not even see the tops of the Standing Stones above the row of heads. We could hear the chanting of the priests, the songs of the multitudes, and the barbaric clangor of the brazen trumpets; but nothing was to be seen except the folk who, missing a view of the ceremonies, came to stare at us and poke us with sticks as though we were caged wild beasts—which, in point of fact, most of us were.

Relieved only by occasional visits from Tanarus, three days passed thus—and I must admit that the waiting was a strain—then on the fourth, soon after sunrise, the crowd began to gather as usual, and the songs and chants commenced. About the third hour, a Druid led a dozen or so armed warriors into the stockade, pointed out one of the victims, and the men dragged the wretch away, he shouting and screaming for mercy, fighting, struggling, and imploring.

"No, no!" he shrieked in despair. "No, no! Not first, not first! Have mercy, have pity! Take someone else—let me wait awhile! Let me wait awhile and I will go quietly—not first, not first. Have pity, in the name of the Gods!" And he wrenched to and fro, fighting desperately to get loose. *Per Martes,* that a man should so degrade himself merely to purchase a few minutes more of life!

However, they paid no attention to either his struggles or his outcries, but took him away, and presently I heard a long, loud blast of the trumpets, and knew it was to cover the shrieks of the dying victim. Then shortly the Druid and the warriors came for another, who at least went quietly. And again the trumpet-blast announced a death on the Stone of Sacrifice. So they went, some walking upright like men, others struggling and screaming, still others flinging themselves down and being dragged by the arms. But one and all they went; there was no ruth nor mercy, nor any pardon for those destined to sacrifice.

When the men came for the twelfth victim, I saw that Tanarus had replaced the other Druid, and bidding the warriors wait, he came over to me.

"I redeem my promise, Gaius," he said in Greek. "You are to go last. Meanwhile—" he handed me a globule the size of the end of my thumb, of some dark, sticky substance "—meanwhile, chew that and swallow it, juice and all."

"My thanks," I responded, putting the stuff into my mouth. "Farewell, Tanarus."

He waved his hand as he turned away, saying:

"This is not the end; I shall be present when you go."

The drug proved to be a gummy mass with a taste which was at once sweet and faintly acrid; not altogether pleasant nor yet wholly disagreeable. For some time after eating it I observed no change whatever in my feelings, and began to wonder if Tanarus had played me some cruel trick—no very gratifying thought, especially since the trumpets did not strike up soon enough for one victim, and I heard his howls for mercy change to a long-drawn shriek of agony that rang out over the great plain till the brazen clamor hastily drowned it.

At length, however, I felt a delicious sort of languor steal over me, accompanied by a tingling in all my limbs and a realization that, after all, this did not matter. It was not like the intoxication of wine, for my brain was perfectly clear and alert, but a sort of rosy glow enveloped the whole world—not a material glow, but a mental one, if I may so express it. There was a delightful sense of well-being, not only for me but for everyone; I was convinced that there was neither sorrow nor distress, neither disease nor pain nor misery, in the life of any living creature. Vaguely I recalled Tanarus' promise that I should feel no pain, and to test it—though it seemed of no real importance—I dug the nails of my right hand into my left forearm, then bit the arm deeply with my teeth. He had told the truth; there was very little sensation left.

Feeling drowsy, I lay down for a nap, but just then they came for me, rousing me up. When the warriors made ready to bind my arms Tanarus stopped them, saying something in their own tongue, then addressing me in Greek.

"I have told them that there is no need to bind you, Gaius," he said. "That you will go quietly. Eh?"

Of course I would—why not? They were good fellows, and I loved them all; why not please them?—nothing mattered much. I smiled and nodded, feeling no inclination to speak, and Tanarus looked sharply at me, then grinned.

"I see the drug has taken effect," was his comment. "Well, we may as well get this over; the Chief Druid waits."

Taking my arms, the warriors urged me out from the stockade and down a long lane of close-packed worshipers, who eyed me curiously as we passed. I smiled pleasantly at them, and a murmur of admiration for my bearing ran through the crowd, and so we came to the Stone of Sacrifice. The folk pressed in as close as they might, but were kept back by a circle of white-clad Druids so there was a clear space four or five yards wide all around the Stone, where stood five Druids, four empty-handed and one, the Chief Druid, holding a bronze knife; he was further distinguished by a magnificent gold breastplate, lavishly adorned with jewels and enamel. From head to foot these five were red as butchers, even their hair and beards being matted with gore, the Stone was red from end to end, and on one side lay a heap of naked, disemboweled carcasses. From the Stone of Sacrifice to the great Altar Stone a lane had been kept open, and I noted vaguely that there were no folk within the inner horseshoe; doubtless that was holy ground.

All this I observed with drowsy indifference, for clouds of sleep weighed heavy on my eyes. Slowly and majestically we marched toward the Stone of Sacrifice, and as we drew near, the circle of Druids struck into a chant which was taken up by the crowd. I could not make out the words, but supposed it to be an invocation to their Gods.

When we were five or six paces from the Stone my eye was caught by a flurry in the crowd to my right, and as I turned my head I saw a girl struggling with two of the Druids, trying to get away from them, and calling out in her own language. A faint impulse stirred me to go to her aid, but it did not move my limbs, and even as the thought came to me she broke away, leaving part of her attire in the Druids' clasp, and raced out to stand in front of me, laying her hand on my arm. My guards moved to thrust her aside, but she said something, Tanarus spoke sharply, and they dropped back; she stood still, gripping my arm.

The five Druids left the Stone of Sacrifice and came striding over to us, the Chief Druid evidently furious with rage, for he scowled like a thundercloud. A colloquy ensued, the Druids apparently trying to persuade the girl to something, but she steadily refused, shaking her head vigorously and repeating the same thing over and over. I could not make out what it was all about, though I caught a few words; "Mine," "My claim," from her, and from the Chief Druid; "Sacrilege," "Impious," "Shameless." He grew more and more angry, waving his bloody knife and seeming about to strike her, but she did not flinch, and one of the others touched him on the arm, saying something, whereat he fell silent, still glowering. This other Druid then spoke at length to Tanarus, who turned to me, using the Greek tongue.

"Gaius," he said, "can you understand me?" Faintly surprised, I nodded. "It is the law," he went on, firmly and incisively, "that when a victim is led to sacrifice, if an unwed maiden claims him in marriage, and he consents, he must be spared to her. This is Brighde, a daughter of the Dumnonii, and she so claims you. Do you consent to marry her?"

By a tremendous effort of will I marshaled my blurred senses and looked at the girl. She was the one whom I had noticed in my walks about Londinium, the one who had gazed on me with pity, and I recalled her, in a distant fashion, as an attractive bit of femininity. But Tanarus' words made little impression on me. Gathering myself together, I asked:

"If I marry her, I shall not be sacrificed?"

"Of course not. Do you consent?"

The drug had me in its grip, and I could neither focus my senses nor make up my mind; all volition was gone, and I was powerless to concentrate my thoughts. The girl looked pleadingly into my eyes, and it seemed a shame to refuse her; on the other hand, it seemed an equal shame to disappoint my good friends of the Britanni, who looked forward to winning the favor of the Gods by sacrificing me. No, it was beyond me to decide.

The Chief Druid growled an angry sentence, but Tanarus stopped him with upraised hand, abruptly shot a question at me in the Britannic tongue, then in Greek said, sharply:

"Nod your head, fool!"

Thus spurred, I nodded, and the Chief Druid, with something that resembled an oath, hurled his knife to the ground, spun on his heel, and marched away, the other four following. Tanarus and my guards turned me about and led me off, Brighde coming with us. They took me,

more and more sleepy, to a tent, where they spread blankets and Tanarus told me to lie down. I had kept up by
a desperate effort of will, but now I let go completely,
slumped on the blankets, and was unconscious almost before I had stretched out. But even as slumber wrapped
me, I fancied I heard Tanarus say something which
sounded like:

"All thanks be to Eros and to His mother Aphrodite!"

I woke to a raging headache, a horrible nausea, a furry
tongue, and a taste in my mouth as though I had eaten a
half-burned horse-blanket. For some time I lay staring at
the leather of the tent, trying to recall what had happened, piecing my recollections together bit by bit, until
I had the whole picture. I turned my head—gently—and
saw sitting beside me Brighde, the girl who had claimed
me; when I moved she rose, brought a jar of water, and
helped me to lift myself to drink, then eased me back on
the blankets. The water soothed my parched throat, but
the motion stimulated the smithy of Vulcan that pounded
in my head—*mehercle,* no drinking-bout had ever left me
half such a wreck! Brighde seemed to sense this, for taking a cloth she wet it in the cool water, wrung it out
loosely, and laid it on my forehead, repeating the act at
intervals, till the hammering within was somewhat abated.
I managed to smile and thank her, and she smiled, then
pointed to me and said: "Gaius," and to herself and said:
"Brighde." I tried to nod, but abandoned the attempt;
my head was still in no condition to be moved.

I lay quiet for an hour or two, thinking things over.
Plainly, I was in a trap of some sort, but just what it was
I could not make out. I had not counted on marriage, especially with a barbarian damsel, however good-looking
she might be, but after all . . . I stole a glance at her;
yes, she was more than good-looking—she might fairly

be called beautiful. Not over eighteen years old, with hair like gleaming yellow silk—the only hair I ever saw which could rival that of Flava Rufus—with blue eyes, clear skin, regular features, and fine teeth; a lovely figure, supple and full of grace, neither too fat nor too thin—yes, beautiful was the word. She saw me looking at her, and smiled, and I smiled in return. Come now, Frenator, it might not be so bad; at the worst, it was vastly better than evisceration, and since she was only a barbarian I need not take the matter too seriously; if a chance came for escape it would not be like deserting a real wife.

While I was meditating, the flap of the tent was lifted and Tanarus entered.

"By Zeus, Hermes, Aesculapius, and all the heathen pantheon!" he greeted me. "Will you sell me a modicum of your luck, dear child of Tyche?* She seems to have you in Her special care, to snatch you from the knife at the last minute, and bestow on you a most charming spouse—one of Her favorite sons, you must be. By Zeus Pater, my Gaius, you will never be nearer death till Proserpina claims a lock of your hair—Charon had his bark moored and waiting for you on the shore of Acheron."

"Tell me more of this," I requested. "I am still far from clear as to what happened. Some intrigue of yours? A plot to free me? *Edepol,* that drug is more than powerful! The numbing effect of wine, and the sense of well-being it conveys, are as naught in comparison. Will you not let me have some to keep at hand in the event of pain, cold, hunger, or other discomfort? The after-effect, I admit, is horrible, but the present—"

Tanarus smiled and shook his head.

* The Greek Goddess of Fortune.

"Use it often," he answered, "and it becomes a necessity; you cannot live without it. And then it destroys you
as surely, as inevitably, as fire or steel. You would become
a thing of no account, craving only the drug, and lost to
honor, to truth, to manhood, to ambition, even as the Lo-
tophagi whom Odysseus met in his wanderings. It is the
fruit of the lotus."

"The lotus? . . . h'm! . . . no, you are right; I do
not want it. Though it can, I think, be a God-sent blessing."

"Most true, my Gaius, most true. A god-sent blessing—
or the most deadly curse of all the Furies. It is no thing
to play with.

"However, what happened to you is simple enough.
No, it was no plot of mine; I admit that this way out
had not occurred to me. But one of the laws of our religion is that if a victim on the way to sacrifice is claimed
in marriage by a virgin, he is released to her. Why, Gaius,
you have a law not unlike that; your Vestals can by a
word pardon and set free a criminal bound for execution."

"They do not, however, marry him, Tanarus. But tell
me, is this sacrifice utterly abrogated, or merely post-
poned?"

He waved his hand.

"Poof! Gone to the winds for all time. As though it
were never planned. You and she will be married this
afternoon, and then you are a full-fledged member of the
tribe of the Dumnonii."

"The Dumnonii?" I frowned in thought. "Somehow,
that name stirs my memory; I have heard it elsewhere."

"Yesterday afternoon I used it to you. By Hermes,
how blurred you were!" I shook my head; the recollection went farther back than that. "Her tribe made war on

the Cantii," he went on, "And being· defeated, gave hostages, which is how your bride comes to be in Londinium. She is a daughter of Tasciovanus, chief of the tribe."

Tasciovanus! The word crystallized my inchoate memories.

"Ask her," I told him, "if she had a brother named Adminius."

Tanarus stared, but the girl's face lit up with interest; she did not understand my words, but she caught the name. Falling on her knees, she gazed eagerly into my eyes, snatched my hand to her bosom, and poured forth a very torrent of words, till the Druid silenced her with lifted hand.

"She says he is indeed her brother," he translated, "and she asks news of his fate."

I told her what I knew of Britannicus—or, to give him his true name, Adminius—and she broke again into questions as Tanarus passed the information along. The Druid laughed.

"You must learn to speak our tongue, Gaius," he chuckled, "or teach her the Roman. I am not going to spend my life interpreting between bride and groom.

"Now are you well enough to rise and go before the altar, to be married? You had better be," he added, significantly. "It would not be well to give Esus—the Chief Druid—any least excuse."

"I am well enough, yes. I seem to recall that he was not pleased, yesterday."

"Pleased! *Zeus Pater!* He has spent the hours since then in chewing up large rocks and spitting out small stones. Well, let us be moving."

He spoke to Brighde, who brought a jar of the native apple brew, and after a long drink I felt much better. Tanarus then led us from the tent, and with an escort of

armed warriors—for I was under guard till after the ceremony—we proceeded to the altar at the heart of the
Standing Stones. It was late in the afternoon, and most of
the folk had started on their homeward journey, but some
hundreds lingered to extract the last possible fraction of
interest from what was to be seen.

The Chief Druid met us—he had cleansed himself and
changed his garments since the day before—and at his
command, translated by Tanarus, Brighde and I joined
our right hands. The other Druids gathered around, and
outside the Standing Stones were grouped the common
folk. The Chief Druid said a few words, then asked some
questions, to which, prompted by Tanarus, I nodded or
shook my head as the case required. The Chief Druid
said something more, then kissed us each on both cheeks
—I had a feeling that he would have preferred to bite
me—and Tanarus said:

"Kiss your bride."

I did so, and the Chief Druid sprinkled water on us,
waved a handful of straw over our heads, and gave me a
burning brand from the fire. He then turned and stalked
away, his very back expressing hate and indignation.
Most of the Druids followed him, only ten or twelve remaining to greet us and to shake hands. Two or three of
them spoke words of welcome in Greek, but most used
their native tongue, and to these I could only nod and
smile.

"Now, Gaius," explained my friend, "you are no longer
a Roman, but a full member of the Dumnonii." I had my
own ideas concerning that, but judged it prudent to keep
silent for the time being. "You are wed to a princess of
the tribe—and, as Aphrodite sees me, no unpleasing one!
—and when the term of her hostageship is up you can return with her to Belerium. Unless, that is, you decide to

settle down among the Cantii, as I hope you will. Meanwhile, you are of the Britanni, free of fire, water, and thatch. To-night you will spend in Brighde's tent, and to-morrow you will return to Londinium.

"And permit me to say that I am more than glad of this end to the affair; I had not looked forward with pleasure to assisting at your sacrifice."

"I can understand the feeling," I rejoined. "I had something of the same, myself. A feeling, so to speak, that I should prefer to be elsewhere."

Laughing, he translated this to the other Druids, who also laughed, then saluted us and turned away.

It was nearing sunset by this time, and Brighde and I returned, no longer under guard, to her tent. A laughing, chattering, applauding crowd accompanied us, but when we came to the tent these left us, and as the flap dropped behind us and we were alone I took my bride gently in my arms. Hers went around my neck, and she broke into a smile as I tipped her head back and smiled down at her. Her arms tightened as I bent my lips to hers . . . not so bad! *Edepol*, not so bad! Far better, at least, than the Stone of Sacrifice.

Brighde and I, with the Cantii, returned to Londinium, where, being well provided with money, she had a house of her own, and lived more like a visitor than like a hostage. The house, of course, was far different from my father's home on Palatinus, and was not even one of the finer stone mansions of the city, but it was distinctly of the better class of frame houses, and was comfortable enough for one who had spent three years under the Eagles. I was treated with the utmost respect by Brighde's fifty or sixty slaves, as well as by her friends, both men and women, who came often to see us, especially after I learned to speak the language and could tell them of my adventures. Part of the prestige I enjoyed came, as nearly as I could tell, from my being one of a more cultured nation, and part from the fact of my having been rescued from the Stone of Sacrifice; the folk appeared to believe that this denoted the special favor of their Gods, and looked up to me accordingly.

My wife proved to be as charming as I could have wished; bright, cheerful, affectionate, and always considerate of my comfort and wishes, as I was of hers, for even though I did not plan to stay here forever, I might as well make life agreeable while I did remain. She was, I must say, an engaging little minx, though being daughter of a chieftain she was inclined to be a trifle imperious, and owned a bit of a temper, so that early in our experience we clashed a few times. Still, I would not give a snap of my finger for a woman who was utterly meek and submissive, and after she understood that I was master we got along admirably. I quickly grew more than a little fond of her, for she was an excellent sort; not like the better class of Roman maids, to be sure, but very superior for a barbarian, so on the whole I had no cause to regret Terentia Laeca.

Once I asked Brighde, teasingly, whether she rescued me from the Druids out of pity or for love. She was sitting on my lap at the time, and she cocked her bright head impudently at me.

"I think," was her saucy answer, "that it was chiefly with the idea of gaining a skilled warrior for the Dumnonii. And perhaps to some extent in the hope that our children might take after their father and so bring new blood into the tribe, which is somewhat weakened through intermarriage."

I pretended that my feelings were hurt.

"There was no affection in it, then?"

"No-o," she drawled. "Of course not. How could a damsel of the Britanni really love one of the Roman tyrants?"

"Get off my knees," I returned. "Cold-blooded, calculating jade! Shameless hussy! Get away!" And I pushed her—but not too hard.

She flung her arms around my neck and held fast, burying her face on my shoulder, so that her soft hair tickled my cheek.

"Idiot!" she breathed. "I loved you the first time I saw you!"

Whereat I laughed and hugged her tight.

I learned the language rapidly, for there is no instructor equal to a wife who speaks but the one tongue, and our friends never tired of hearing me talk of Rome; naturally, I had little to say of my life in the Tenth, for I saw no use in stirring up local prejudices, and considered that the tale of Caesar's victories among the Celtae and the Belgae would not sit too well on their kinsmen's stomachs. I did tell of the conquest of Ariovistus and of our raiding the lands of the Suebi, for these folk hated the Germani and enjoyed the tale beyond measure; they laughed and clapped their hands like children over it, and made me repeat it whenever they gathered in our home, till I myself grew sick of telling it.

As I came to know them better I gradually raised my opinion of these barbarians. They lack our Roman culture, to be sure, and their warriors are undisciplined, each fighting for himself and not supporting his neighbor, so they could never hope to contend with us, who have learned the lesson of "all for one and one for all"; but on the other hand, they have many excellent qualities. They are more given to drink than the Romans, but less to gambling; marital fidelity is the rule rather than the exception; their public men and their voters absolutely cannot be bribed; theft is rare, and assassination practically unknown except when it accompanies highway robbery. They are excitable and easily moved to anger—more than once I have seen two diners jump from the table, draw swords, and fall to carving each other for some fancied slight—but they do not hold rancor; it is a word and a blow, then they are good friends again. They are brave, and charge well in battle—though raggedly—but they lack the steadfastness of the legion's ordered line; this, though, is less a want of cold courage than a matter of training, as I was later able to prove. They have no arenas or gladiatorial combats such as we have, but their main sport—after drinking—is in fighting gamecocks, and these birds are so esteemed that it is fully as sacrilegious and revolting to them to eat the flesh of one as it would be to us to eat the flesh of a man. In general, they are by no means bad folk, and I came to have many close friends among them.

One of their most conspicuous traits—and a very unpleasant one it is to a person accustomed to the daily baths of the City—is the lack of personal cleanliness, the aversion to water, which they share with their relatives of Gallia Transalpina. One and all, they consider that they have done their full duty by the Gods of Cleanliness if they wash their faces and hands almost daily throughout the year, and their bodies occasionally in summer; as for bathing in cold weather, they regard it with horror, believing it dangerous to health. The natural result is that they are an offense to more delicate nostrils, and one to which I could never accustom myself; I could only endure it.

Some of my most vivid arguments with my wife rose from this circumstance, for, once established in our home in Londinium, I insisted that the slaves prepare a tub of hot water in my bedroom each morning, that I might bathe. The servants thought me a mild lunatic, and Brighde remonstrated violently, saying:

"But, Gaius, you will do yourself an injury; it is well known that bathing in winter is dangerous to the lungs. And if you wash so often you will wash all your strength away."

"It is at all events a slow death," I laughed. "Except for my summers on campaign, I have bathed daily for more than twenty years. As for my strength—well, at least I can still stagger about."

So I continued my diurnal baths, and Brighde her remonstrances, until one morning in December when I lost my temper with her.

"Dii Immortales!" I exploded. "Do not expect me to live with a wife who smells like the Augean stables!"

She flared into anger—I admit the remark was somewhat brutal—and abused me soundly, till I rolled out of bed and caught up a dog-whip that lay on the great chest of clothing.

"You will bathe," I told her, "or you will take a beating. Choose!" And, the whip in my right hand, with my left I snatched the blankets clear of the bed. "Choose!" I repeated, and raised the whip.

Furious, she glared at me and cursed me in language that I never thought she could know, but she saw that I meant business, so she got out of bed and washed from head to foot, while I stood by and supervised the operation, and she wept with rage, and cursed me through her tears. When she had finished and was dry, I put my arm around her, saying:

"Now I am ready to kiss you."

But she slapped me savagely and tore free, nor would she grant me a pleasant word or look all that day.

For several mornings this scene was repeated, until one day the slaves who prepared my morning bath surprised me by bringing two tubs. I looked quizzically at Brighde, who grinned shamefacedly, lowering her head and glancing up at me through her eyelashes.

"I . . . I cannot find that it has injured my health," she admitted. "And I am certainly more of a comfort to myself . . . I have told them to make ready two baths in future." I laughed, tossed aside the dog-whip, and took her in my arms. She hugged me, then with her saucy manner she went on:

"Rome is not altogether evil; at least one good thing may be learned from a Roman. You have made a convert to your weird notion of bathing, my Gaius."

"Stay with me, Carissima," I promised, "and I will teach you still other good Roman customs."

"I like it when you call me 'Carissima,' " she murmured, irrelevantly, and snuggled closer.

So the winter passed not unpleasantly, one of our chief diversions being the study of fencing, for I taught my bride to use a sword in the Roman fashion, partly to keep my own hand in and partly for her benefit. She offered some protest at first, but I insisted.

"One never knows when it may be useful," I told her, "so keep at it."

"Are your Roman maids and matrons taught to handle weapons?" she asked, and I admitted:

"No; but their case is different. They are not living in a half-wild country that is civilized only in the towns; a country where one's hand must keep one's head. The day may come when you will be glad I made you learn."

As usually happens when one takes up the study of fencing, it was not long ere she became interested, and progressed rapidly, growing into a better than mediocre swordsman.

One day shortly before the Kalends of Januarius, Brighde came to me, an anxious look on her face.

"Gaius," she asked, "will you do something for me?"

"Anything, Carissima." This of course was an exaggeration, but a little hyperbole is always acceptable to a woman. "What is it?"

She came and perched on my knee, putting her arm about my shoulders and nestling close.

"You are a great soldier," she said. "Skilled in war, and knowing the discipline of the legions, are you not?"

"*Edepol!*" I laughed. "You remind me of Aesopus' tale of the fox, who with fair words coaxed the cheese from the crow's beak. Well, Mistress Fox? Go on."

"I have a letter from my father Tasciovanus—"

"He can read and write, then?"

"No, foolish one! But he has a scribe."

"I see. Continue."

"And he says, among other things, that the Silures,* a wild and savage tribe to the north of us, have several times crossed the estuary of the Sabrina † and have raided into our lands. His spies tell him that they—the Silures— are planning a general invasion, and they are very fierce and dangerous. Would you not aid him against them?"

"That is what you want of me?"

She nodded, asking:

"Will you do it?"

I was tired of inaction, so the thought of a little fighting was pleasant.

"Gladly," I replied. "Most gladly, Carissima. When does the term of your hostageship expire?"

She hung her head, not meeting my eyes, and played with the brooch that fastened my tunic.

* The Welsh.
† The River Severn.

"That is the point," she answered, in a small voice. "Not for seven months yet. We must run away."

"What!" I was horrified. "Run away? Break the hostageship? It is not to be thought of."

But she laughed and kissed me.

"You are still a Roman at heart, my lover," she teased. "You take the Roman view of hostageship. If they catch us during our flight they will undoubtedly put us to death —that is the chance we take—but if we can get clear away, they are so mercurial that they will simply forget all about it. I know my people, Gaius. You will do it, will you not?" she pleaded.

"Will they not take vengeance on the other hostages? Or on your slaves?"

She shook her pretty head.

"Take vengeance on them for our fault? Never!"

"Can we make it? I suppose so, of course, or you would not suggest it."

"That remains to be seen. If we do it cleverly, yes. Once we reach the Great Forest of Anderida we can leave the highroad and take refuge in the depths of the forest until the hunt has been given up. Are you a good enough woodsman to live in the forest?"

I laughed at that.

"One of Caesar's centurions? *Mehercle!* My men would have mutinied against me, else."

"We shall be safe in the forest . . . from the Cantii, that is; they will never pursue us into that wilderness."

"From the Cantii? What other dangers lurk in the depths of these famous woods?"

"Well . . . robbers . . . wild boar . . . wolves . . . outlaws . . . wildcats . . . that is all."

"Oh, surely not all!" I mocked. "Surely there must be others. What are a few wolves, wild boar, and outlaws

to make such a pother about? Only that, and death riding hotfoot on our trail? Pfui! Can you not conjure up a
few demons of the air, witches, evil spirits, and the like,
to add to the delights of the journey?"

Brighde owned to the full the superstition of her folk.
Her arm tightened about my neck and she glanced fearfully over her shoulder.

"Do not mention them, lover," she whispered. "It is
unlucky . . . sometimes they come when they hear themselves called."

"Silly!" I said, and kissed her.

"But you will go?" she begged. "I know it is a great
thing to ask . . . we cannot take any slaves, nor can we
have guards . . . we must make a dash for it . . . you
will go?"

I thought the matter over. Granting no belief in evil
spirits of the night—my life in the Tenth had taught me
that—I still recognized that the dangers of the journey
were ample. On the other hand, Britannicus—Adminius
—had told me that traders from Massilia came often to
his country, and there might well be a chance to escape.
If I could get to Massilia, it would be an easy matter to
join the Imperator, for which I could see no opportunity
while I remained in the country of the Cantii. And there
would be fighting . . . on the whole. . . .

"Yes, I will go," I told her. "When do we start?"

She flung her other arm about my neck and hugged me
tight, kissing me rapturously.

"My Gaius! I knew you would!" she exclaimed. "My
warrior! To-night, if you can make the arrangements."

I shook my head.

"It is a matter of two or three days—perhaps more. It
must be done craftily, not to spread the news abroad. You
can be ready at any time?"

"Five minutes' notice, to change my clothes, and I am with you."

"I will let you know," I promised.

"And make it soon," she begged. "Soon, soon! I have not seen my home for more than a year, and I am on fire to be gone."

CHAPTER VIII

*Of the Great Forest of Anderida; of the Fight
with the Outlaws; and How I Was Made
War-Chief of the Dumnonii*

FROM Londinium to Isca of the Dumnonii—Caer
Isce, they call it in their barbarous tongue—is a journey of a trifle more than two hundred miles. Left to myself, I would have bought the best pair of horses I could
find, would have ridden them till they fell under me, and
if necessary would have gone on afoot, secure in the
knowledge that with such a start I could not be over-
taken. But though strong and active for a woman,
Brighde was not equal to any such performance, which
called, indeed, for a hardened athlete. All of Caesar's
men were so trained and hardened, especially those of the
Tenth, but it was obviously impossible for a girl to keep
up with me on any such merciless journey, and I must
arrange my plans with her in mind. So I decided that the
best way would be to start about midnight, go as far as
we could before dawn, then turn off the road and lie hidden till the pursuit had gone by and we could safely resume our journey. It would be necessary to follow the
Great Western Highway until we had passed Sorbiodunum, for the Forest of Anderida was so difficult as to
be practically impassable; after the capital of the Belgae
was behind us we could, in a pinch, travel by back roads
paralleling the Highway.

So I made my preparations with care; we should have to elude not only our pursuers, but also the folk of the Seguntiaci—tributaries of the Atrebates—who would return us to Londinium out of friendship for the Cantii; and the Belgae, who would slay us out of enmity to both the Cantii and the Dumnonii. And in addition, there were "outlaws, robbers, wolves, and evil spirits." However, I had no fear of the last, and as for the others, danger has always had a pleasantly stimulating effect on me.

The Forest of Anderida has roughly the form of a broad, flat, irregular triangle, one point reaching up nearly to Londinium. Thence it stretches southeastward to the Channel a little south of Portus Dubris, and covers the rolling country of the southern part of Britannia well-nigh to Uxella of the Durotriges. The northern border runs west from Londinium, swings southwest to pass south of Sorbiodunum, then west again, and meets the Channel just east of Uxella. Thus for seventy or eighty miles the Great Western Highway runs in and out through the northern fringe of the forest, and we should not be out of it until we reached Sorbiodunum; if there were dangers, there was also a perfect place to hide.

I did all my purchasing with caution, to avoid attracting notice. Blankets we could of course take from our bedroom, but I could not steal food from the kitchens without causing talk, so I bought a supply of dried and smoked meat; some hard, unleavened bread; and a small quantity of apples. I also purchased arms and weapons—by great good luck I found a sword from Hispania which was identical with those used in the Legion—and two light axes, of a weight to be used in one hand; to these I added an entrenching spade, and four canteens for water. All these things I bought casually, sauntering from shop to shop, indulging in much gossip, and making the purchases with an air of indifference, as though the transaction were of no moment.

Brighde had no horses—for a self-evident reason, hostages are not allowed to keep any—and I expected to have trouble in getting them, but was pleasantly surprised in this regard. By this time I was fairly well known in the city, the Britanni appeared to like me as well as they could like anyone not of their own race, and the dealer from whom I bought the animals only chaffed me for still preferring the Roman custom of riding horseback to the habit of the Britanni.

The horses were those of the country, small but wiry beasts, well able to pull a chariot or to carry a light burden, but not up to the shock of a cavalry charge or to carrying the weight of a full-armed warrior for long distances. Still, they were the best I could get, and those of our pursuers would be no better. This same dealer furnished a supply of grain for the animals, and I bought one of the leather water-buckets which he had about the place, so we were well equipped with respect to mounts.

Oddly enough, the thing I had most trouble in finding was something which could easily have been got in Rome, namely, flint and steel. The Britanni seldom use it, depending on keeping their fires lit, or in emergency borrowing coals from a neighbor, so the shops did not carry such an outfit. At length, in the shop of Lugotorix the Goldsmith, I discovered a kit which, as the inscription on it showed, had belonged to one of the Seventh, and had probably been looted from his body during the invasion. This I bought, professing to have known the man, and to want it for a memento.

At length I had all I needed, and one evening before dinner told Brighde: "To-night." And I promptly had cause to regret doing so, for she was so transported with

joy that I feared lest she betray our secret to the friends
who were to dine with us.

"Dii Immortales!" I conjured her. "Calm down, calm
down! The folk will know that something is on foot if
you are so gay."

"I know," she acknowledged. "I will be most sedate
when they arrive. But in the meantime—oh, Gaius,
Gaius!" She hugged me and danced away, only to return
and hug me again and again. I had never realized that
home meant so much to her. And I must admit that she
kept her promise, behaving soberly enough in company,
though I caught the flash of a lurking delight in her eye
whenever she turned a glance my way.

Neither Brighde nor I favored the drinking-bouts so
customary with the Britanni, so our party broke up about
the end of the first watch, and I settled myself for a
couple of hours' rest. In the Tenth I had learned the
trick of waking at any desired time, and on rousing at
midnight I found the room half lighted by the remains
of the fire and by a round, though hazy, moon. A full-
armed Britannic warrior stood in front of the window,
and by instinct I rolled quickly out of bed and caught up
my sword, only to be checked by a low laugh and the
words:

"Would you slay your bride, Gaius?"

It was Brighde, dressed in tunic, breeches, and high
boots, and carrying helmet, shield, and sword. Where she
had got the things I did not know, but she made a most
charming soldier, and I took time for a few caresses. At
first she returned them, but, growing impatient, she
pushed me away, saying:

"Enough, enough! Save the rest until we are in my
father's house in Caer Isce."

Taking several blankets from the bed, I made a pack

of our things, armed myself, and together we slipped quietly downstairs and out to the courtyard, avoiding the slaves who slept on floor and benches in the main room and the dining-hall; in winter the comfort of the fires was more welcome to them than the softness of beds. I stopped at the well to fill our canteens, then passed into the stable to bridle our horses and wrap their feet in rags lest they betray us on the flagged courtyard or the frozen streets.

It was dark as the depths of Erebus in the stables, but once outside there was light enough to let us see, and mounting, we set off at a foot-pace for the Tamesis. Dark, silent, and with deserted streets, Londinium was like a city of the dead, and I heard my wife breathing hard as we made our way to the river; she pressed close to me, and in whispers I encouraged her, she saying:

"I do not like it; it is eerie . . . I . . . I am frightened." And I felt her shiver under my arm.

"Silly!" I told her. "It is not silence we need fear. Be frightened, if you will, when we hear a noise. Silence is our guarantee of safety."

"I know . . . but . . ."

"When you have been abroad as many nights as I have, you will know that evil spirits are but a myth."

She drew still closer, glancing fearfully about.

"Oh, Gaius," she begged, in a frightened undertone, "do not call them!"

The Tamesis is fordable only at a point some ten or twelve miles west of Londinium, but the ford might as well have been a thousand miles away, since we could not pass the city gates. And obviously I dared not rouse the ferryman, so there was naught for it but to swim; happily, the stream is here only about a hundred and fifty paces wide. The tide being at ebb, our horses were out of their depth for not more than thirty paces of the distance, but the chill of the water was paralyzing, and I was glad indeed when we reached the Great Western Highway and could warm ourselves with a gallop.

Once on the Highway, I halted long enough to remove the rags from the horses' hoofs, for speed was now our best refuge, and noise was of no consequence; even should dwellers along the road tell the pursuit that we had gone westward, they would be giving out no news—the dullest could easily guess that we would head for Belerium.

During our halt I noted a wide halo around the moon, and thought with disgust that a storm was not far off. Still, bad weather would delay the hunt, so it might be a blessing in disguise. Again on horseback, we urged our mounts to a trot, then as they warmed up we shook them to a canter, and swung off toward Isca of the Dumnonii, to put as many miles as possible between us and Londinium ere our flight was discovered.

Morning dawned cold and unpleasant, the air carrying a raw, bone-aching chill which repeated the halo's promise of snow or rain, and low banks of gray clouds in the direction of the sea gave weight to the prediction. I estimated that we had come between forty and fifty miles, and decided to turn off and make camp in the forest; I was fresh enough, but Brighde, unused to the jar and pound of a horse, and unaccustomed to keeping her balance on his slippery back, was weary and sore. So leaving the road, we turned left into the woods, pushing south with much difficulty until we were about two miles into the wilderness. At length I found what I wanted and called a halt, dismounting and tying the horses, then lifting the girl from her mount; she was so stiff that she would have fallen had she tried to climb down.

The spot was ideal for a camp. A small stream about

ten feet wide and a foot or so deep meandered among the trees, and at some time of flood the waters had cut away a bank so as to leave a terrace twice the height of a man. Between this terrace and the stream lay a flat perhaps twenty paces wide and fifty long, almost bare of trees, and here I chose a site.

With Brighde aiding me, I made a small copy of a Roman camp, complete with ditch and wall and palisade, using saplings which I cut nearby for the palisade; the ditch, of course, was chiefly to carry off any rain which might fall, rather than for defence. In two respects ours differed from a regular camp; there were no true *portae*, or gates, and the palisade was stiffened by having branches twisted in and out among the uprights. I must admit that the wall was not very high—barely enough to hold the palisades—for after all it was not a war camp, but merely a shelter from wild beasts.

I made a sort of wattled gate, which could be fastened with two bars, and toward the rear of the enclosure, but not touching the palisade, we built a rude hut of wattled boughs; the roof we wattled and thatched a foot thick with fallen leaves, weighting them down with branches, for protection against rain. I left the front of the hut, the face toward the north, unwalled, for I planned to keep a fire going there, and the heat would be reflected back from the rear wall to keep us warm. Also, before starting any other work, I cleared a space on the ground and built a wide, low fire there; the earth was not frozen, as it would have been in Gallia Transalpina, but if I could get the ground warmed up it would be more comfortable to lie on.

The camp was about three by six paces inside; large enough to contain the hut and a space for the horses. We had it finished shortly after noon, then cooked and ate our midday meal, and spent the rest of the daylight hours in gathering dry wood, which would burn with little or no smoke. And even in the unlikely event of our smoke being seen above the trees it would be taken— being so thin and so deep in the woods—for the fire of a charcoal burner, whereof there are many within the confines of Anderida. I planned to spend at least a week here, that the hunt might pass, scour the country, and return to Londinium, so time was lacking to gather all the fuel we should need, but we got enough for two or three days, and could get more at any time.

All our preparations made, I fed and watered the horses while Brighde cooked our evening meal, then when we had eaten I blanketed the animals, built up the fire, and rolling in our own blankets, my wife and I lay down to sleep.

During the night I was wakened by Brighde shaking me violently and crying:

"Gaius! Gaius! Rouse up; the wolves are on us!"

"What is it?" I demanded, leaping to my feet, and she repeated, in terrified voice:

"The wolves, the wolves!"

To one who is unaccustomed, or whose nerves are not of the steadiest, the near presence of savage beasts is most alarming, and I could not blame her. For myself, I had confidence in the palisade, so was not frightened, but I was concerned for our horses, which were snorting and plunging about in terror; I had no desire to have them break loose and stampede blindly about the camp, but aside from that, we were as safe as though in my home on Palatinus.

On going out to soothe the horses, I could see a dozen or more pairs of glowing green spots flitting about, and I grinned in satisfaction; the palisade was too high for the anthropophagi to leap and too stout for them to break down. A few firebrands tossed over the wall dispersed the wolves, and I managed to quiet the horses, then returned to calm Brighde, who was trembling with fear. Presently, however, we both slept once more.

Four times during that night I had to go out and quiet our mounts, but after that they seemed to realize that the wolves could not get at them, and I had no further trouble, though we were visited every night during our stay. Through the daylight hours the hungry beasts withdrew deeper into the forest, and we saw nothing of them. And after the first alarm Brighde paid no more attention to them.

So passed three rather dull days of eating, sleeping, and desultory conversation. Brighde and I fenced daily, for the sake of practice, and to pass the time, though having no blunted swords we could not lunge or strike freely—that is, I could not—and it was rather unsatisfactory so far as I was concerned; she benefited by the exercise, and improved her skill, for I may in all modesty say that Tiberius had taught me so well that during my years with Caesar I found but one swordsman who was my equal. That was Mandorix, an Aeduan who enlisted in the Fourteenth while I was in Britannia, and who was with Quintus Cicero when Ambiorix attacked the camp at Aduatuca. Mandorix was a good fellow and an excellent soldier—he was promoted to be a centurion of the Tenth for his share in that marvelous defence—but he was inclined to be a trifle conceited over his skill with weapons. He could never beat me, but neither could I beat him, and I often wished that he might fence with Tiberius Rufus; Tiberius was so far my master, and so incredibly lightning-quick, that he would have taken the conceit out of the Aeduan in short order. I must grant, though, that Mandorix was not offensive about it; he was in general a modest enough youth, and his pride of skill was no more than a harmless vanity.

For the rest, I beguiled the time as best I could in telling over again of my life in the City, to which Brighde never tired of listening, and she recounted memories of her youth, but eventually we ran out of talk and in desperation I carved a set of *tesserae* from wood, marked out a twelve-line board on the earth, and taught her to play the *duodecim scriptae*.* She took to it as a duck to water, and thereafter the hours passed more easily, though without stakes the game is rather insipid.

Some of our time was spent in gathering wood, and on the fifth day an event occurred which broke the monotony with a vengeance. We were chopping boughs, and taking a bundle I carried it to our camp, some fifty or sixty paces distant. As I cast it down I heard Brighde scream:

"Gaius! To me! Rescue, rescue! Gaius!"

The fear in her voice chilled my heart and sent me flying toward the sound, drawing my sword as I ran and cursing myself for leaving her alone; the utter solitude had betrayed me into a false sense of security.

Coming to the spot, I saw her, shield on left arm and sword in right hand, defending herself against five of the most villainous-looking ruffians I had ever laid eyes on; our professional assassins of the Subura were gentlemen by comparison. It was evident that they had known of our presence, had watched me out of sight, and then had fallen on Brighde, hoping to gag her and carry her off ere I could get warning. They were armed with daggers

---

* A game of mingled chance and skill, played with dice and counters, and apparently similar to our modern backgammon.

and cudgels, and doubtless would shortly have overcome her, but she was so wary and so agile, and had fenced so much with me, that the surprise attack failed.

The men had their backs to me, and one of them died before he knew I was at hand. At the same instant my brave girl got home a good Roman thrust which pierced the heart of a second, and he too died on his feet. But unhappily her sword jammed between his ribs, and in falling he wrenched it from her hand, leaving her weaponless. Still, for the moment it did not matter, since my shout of "Venus Victrix!" turned the remaining three to face me.

I took a cudgel blow on my shield, and thrusting low, hamstrung the scoundrel, bringing him down; the second, running in, met my point, with a stiff arm behind it, squarely in the teeth, and he also died. But as I turned to the third, a hidden stone rolled under my foot, a frightful pain shot up my leg, and I fell. With an uncouth shout of triumph, the last man sprang forward, raising his club to dash out my brains, as he might well have done, for my shield was caught under me and for an instant I could not free it. But in that instant Brighde snatched up her axe and threw it. From behind her back, in a full-arm sweep, she brought it, and spinning like a child's pinwheel it flew, to strike the robber midway between the shoulder-blades. By grace of Mars, the edge struck first, shearing through his spine and burying itself to the handle in his back. *Per Martes,* it was a blow that would have slain the stoutest bull in all Mevania's herds—one of the All-Father's own thunderbolts could not have been more deadly! Throwing his arms wide, he pitched forward, to be received on the point of my sword, for I did not then know that he was dead.

Getting to my feet, I looked around, gritting my teeth

and waiting for the pain to pass off. The four dead outlaws were scattered about the little glade, sprawled in the limp, grotesque attitudes of men slain in battle, and no other assailants were to be seen; all was quiet save for the rustle of boughs in the trifling breeze, the panting of Brighde, and the groans of the wounded man as he tried painfully to crawl away. Brighde, her eyes blazing, her face flaming with the lust of fight, tore her blade from the chest of the first man she had slain, and ran toward the one who still lived.

"No, no!" I cried. "Brighde! Stop! Harm him not!" I checked her barely in time, and for a moment she hesitated whether to obey or not, but finally did as I commanded.

By this time the pain in my leg had somewhat abated, and I hobbled over to where the man lay groaning and begging for mercy.

"I want some information from him," I told her. "That is why I bade you spare him."

"Yes, husband," acknowledged Brighde, submissively, the light dying from her face to give way to a look of anxiety, and I smiled approval at her. Stepping to me, she caught my arm. "Are you hurt?" she demanded. "Did he—"

I shook my head.

"It is naught," I reassured her. "A mere twist of the ankle; even now it is passing off. Help me to get this man to camp," I went on, and together we urged, carried, and dragged the wretch to our stockade.

There I tied him hand and foot with strips torn from his garments—*edepol*, but they were filthy, verminous, and stunk to Heaven!—then I asked:

"How many are there in your band, and where are the others camped?"

From under his mat of snarled and tangled hair he glowered at me like some wild beast as he growled:

"It is not for me to answer your questions. Find out for yourself. I will tell you nothing."

"No?" I inquired, sardonically. "I think you will reply quite fully. Let us see."

Stepping to the fire, I took from it a brand that I whirled in the air till it burst into flame, then placed my foot on the brute's neck and pressed the brand against his thigh. Smoke rose from the contact, the stench of burning wool filled my nostrils, then that of roasting flesh, and the man howled and squirmed, but could not get away. A glance at Brighde showed me her face pale, her eyes wide with horror, her jaws and fists clenched tight, and I knew that she was sick—in truth, so was I myself —but what was to be done? I had to know. Before long the man wailed:

"I will tell! Have pity—I will tell!"

"I thought you would," was my answer, as I removed the torch.

He groaned for a moment, then asked:

"If I tell, will you let me go?"

"I make no promises," I returned, "and you are in no position to bargain." And I moved as though to touch him up again.

"No, no!" he howled. "I will answer. Our camp is about a mile downstream from here, and we five were all the band."

"The truth!" I said, sternly, threatening him.

"As the Gods see me, it is so! By Tarvos Trigaranus and by the Horns of Cernunnos I swear it!"

On reflection, I felt that he spoke truly, so with Brighde's aid I got him to his feet and half carried, half dragged him southward deeper into the forest. When a hundred paces or so from our camp, I turned off to the right, and after another hundred paces despatched him with a blow of my dagger; although downstream from our camp, I took no chance of his carcass defiling our water. This may seem cruel, but I could not hold him prisoner, his life was forfeit if I took him to any town, and it was kinder to put an end to him than to leave him, hamstrung, to the mercy of the wolves.

Then Brighde and I scouted carefully along till we found the outlaws' camp, inspection of which proved that the man had told the truth. We discovered nothing of value save about a hundred gold pieces, clumsily hidden under a flat rock, and these we garnered in for our own use, since there was nothing to indicate the rightful owners—who, indeed, were probably long since dead.

On returning to our camp, Brighde fell to weeping, and clung tight to me.

"Nay, Carissima," I soothed her, "you have naught to regret. These men were the scum of all creation; they have deserved death a score of times. And you but struck in self-defence. They are no loss—nay, the world is cleaner for their passing; you have done a worthy act, and there is no need for tears." I patted her on the back. "It was their lives or ours—and for you, a fate worse than death. You are my good, brave girl. *Per Martes,* a legionary of the Tenth could not have fought better!"

"It is not that," she sobbed, shaking her golden head. "At least, not altogether. But the peril . . . when I saw you fall, I thought you were slain . . . oh, Gaius, Gaius!" And she hugged me passionately.

Then I knew that it was merely the reaction from excitement, and would soon pass. Sure enough, in a little while she looked up and smiled through the teardrops, and kissed me, leaving salt tears on my lips.

"I am a fool, I know," she said. "But it is sweet of you not to tell me so."

"Nay," I responded, "it is but natural. I have known seasoned warriors to be taken with a fit of weeping after a battle. Often, too, they are violently sick, from sheer excitement. Your tears are no sign of folly."

"Truly?" she questioned, searching my eyes. "You are not saying that just to comfort me?"

"As the Gods see me," I vowed.

"Then I do not feel so bad," she smiled, and I laughed:

"You have reason to feel extremely proud. Two men slain in such a mêlée is no small triumph for a raw fighter. Oddly enough, the first man I ever slew was a robber also —one of a pair." And to divert her mind I told her of my encounter on the road to Vesontio.

But in truth, I myself was more disturbed than I have ever been in war; in battle one never thinks of one's own peril, but when death swings low to a loved one the matter is vastly different. And I had come to feel a deep affection for this brave, sweet girl—so much so, in fact, that I sometimes toyed with the thought of settling permanently in this wild land. I never held the idea long, for memories of Rome, of Tiberius and Flava, of the Imperator, would rise to call back my wandering mind, but at least the thought was not altogether unpleasant. I had known many women, some of whom professed to love me, but their greedy eyes belied their words, the carmine on their lips could not hide the cruel selfishness of their mouths, and after a short while I turned from them in disgust. But my heart went out to meet the true love bestowed on me by this girl of Britannia, the first unselfish love I had ever had from any woman save my *vestiplica*—and Doris was but a child. No wonder I thought at times of a home in this Island of the North.

The following day the long-promised storm broke, with a mixture of snow and rain, and a chill that searched the marrow of our bones. The trench around our hut carried off the water, and the roof and walls were tight, so Brighde kept dry and I got wet only when feeding and watering the horses; I had taken the obvious precaution of storing our fuel under cover. But for three miserable days we sat and shivered; no fire could dispel the chill that was in the air, nor could blankets keep us warm. I was glad enough when the rain stopped; I was sick of listening to its eternal patter, and though to one accustomed to the sunny warmth of Italia, the climate of Gallia Transalpina is bad enough, that of southwestern Britannia is far worse, with its infernal rain, cold, and fog. How any human being can voluntarily live there passes my comprehension, though I am told that farther inland, and among the hills, it is not so bad.

On the ninth day of our outlawry the storm ceased and the sun came out. Even then the air was raw and chill, but at least it was not raining, and by that time I was so cold and bored and disgusted that I was willing to risk capture for the sake of doing something. We packed our few things, mounted, and rode off, Brighde looking back as we wound our way among the trees.

"Good little camp!" she said, to my amazement. "Dear little camp! I shall always remember it with affection."

For a moment I stared in wonder, then had a flash of insight.

"Because it was there you saved my life?"

She glanced at me from the corners of her eyes, smiled shyly, and nodded.

"Partly," was her answer. "Partly that, and partly because it was there we had our first real honeymoon. Hitherto there have always been others around us, and we have had no real chance to get acquainted. But now I feel that I know you better than ever before."

"And love me better?" I teased.

She wrinkled her nose with the saucy air I loved.

"Oh, you are not so bad—for a Roman," she laughed. "You might be worse. On the whole, there are times when I do not entirely regret having snatched you from the Stone of Sacrifice."

It seemed that we had avoided the hunt, for we were not molested after reaching the highroad, and skirting around Sorbiodunum and various smaller towns we came without further adventure to Isca of the Dumnonii, the weather growing viler, the fogs thicker and more frequent, as we approached Belerium. What a country! Pluto might well condemn a Roman, for his sins, to such a climate. Isca, however, is on a hilltop whence a steep slope runs down to the river, so the fogs are not quite so bad there as in the valley, though they are bad enough, in all conscience. To wake in the morning with the world shut out by a gray wall of mist, with one's garments damp and soggy, and with drops of water beading one's armor —bah! What a life!

I pointed out to Brighde that we had not met any of her dreaded evil spirits, and again she made a face at me; she was not afraid of hobgoblins by daylight.

"Your aspect terrified them and kept them away," she mocked. "No self-respecting demon would confront such a horrible-looking object as you are, with that fortnight's black stubble on your cheeks and chin. No, you need not try to kiss me—" And she pushed me away from her. "I do not wish to be caressed by a porcupine. Come see me when you have shaved."

Whereat I laughed, held her tight, and scrubbed my

cheek against hers, and she slapped me—though not very hard.

In Isca, we rode straight to Brighde's home, where she was received with the wildest delight by her mother Cartismandua and by her younger sisters Epona and Boudicca, as well as by the slaves and clients, who turned out in hundreds to greet her. Adminius was the only son of the family, and he was still in Rome—that is, I supposed he was—and her father was abroad on some affairs or other, so we were received only by the women of the family.

I was amazed to note that none condemned the breaking of the hostageship, but all seemed to feel that Brighde had done a clever thing in running away; decidedly, the notions of the Britanni are not ours.

A messenger was sent flying for Tasciovanus, and presently the chieftain came hurrying to clasp his daughter to his bosom and to weep and laugh over her. I was astounded at his size, for though Brighde was large for a woman, she seemed a doll in his arms; he was more like Polyphemus the Cyclops or Prometheus the Titan than like any human being I had ever seen. A huge man, vast of stature and of limb, with a great red beard spreading fan-wise to his waist, and with red hair curling down on his shoulders. Not altogether unhandsome, though.

All in all, there was tremendous excitement in the house, during which time I stood modestly in the background. At length, the first transports of joy over, Brighde turned in her father's arms and beckoned me forward.

"My husband, Father," she said. "He is of Roman birth, but of the Dumnonii by adoption, and when you know him you will love him as I do. He knew Adminius in Rome."

I understood that my reception by the family—indeed,

by the tribe in general—depended on Tasciovanus' attitude, and the prospect was not encouraging, for he scowled as he looked me over from head to foot.

"By the Horns of Cernunnos, Daughter!" he finally boomed. "How in the name of Brighde your Patroness could you wed this—this shrimp? Are there not goodly men of your own race, that you must choose a dwarf? Or was it under compulsion?" And he frowned threateningly.

Brighde flung away and faced him angrily.

" 'Shrimp!' " she exclaimed, and stamped her foot. " 'Dwarf!' Let me tell you, Gaius is no clumsy, overgrown ox, but in spite of his small stature he is a mighty warrior. He could slay any three men in all Britannia as an appetizer for breakfast!"

"Gently, Carissima, gently," I admonished her. "You are taking in a large territory."

"I do not care!" she flamed. "You could, you could!"

I am of good size for a Roman, being more than five and a half feet tall and scaling some hundred and seventy pounds, but Tasciovanus overtopped me by head and shoulders, and outweighed me by at least a hundred pounds; he was indeed a giant, nor was his weight soft fat. He was hard and muscular, and on a slow lift would probably have shown himself twice as strong as I was.

Now at his daughter's words he put his great head back and bellowed a tremendous, deafening laugh, his vast beard wagging on his mighty chest, his mouth showing like some red-lined cavern; I was reminded of the cave where King Aeolus holds prisoner the winds of all the world. The laugh was taken up by the hundred or more folk who were gathered in the big living-room, and Brighde flushed with anger and stamped again, so that I had to calm her with a hand on her arm.

When the mirth had quieted down, and the echoes of the chieftain's roaring were stilled, he turned to me.

"Well, Roman, so you are a mighty warrior?" he demanded, with sarcasm. His voice might have been heard a mile away. "So! Let us see. Will you fight?"

I raised my eyebrows.

"It is my trade. But with whom?"

"With me, of course. Who else?"

I shrugged my shoulders and shook my head.

"Ha, I thought not! So the Romans are not all brave! Still, I cannot wholly blame you; no man craves certain death."

"It is not that," I answered mildly. "But I have no wish to kill the father of my wife."

A shout of laughter went up from the crowd, and Tasciovanus' face flushed till it matched his beard.

"By Tarvos Trigaranus!" he roared. "For that you shall fight me, whether you will or no. Slaves, my arms!"

Brighde and the other women, with some of the clients, tried to persuade him against it, pointing out that whichever way it went, his daughter must lose either a husband or a father. But he impatiently brushed them aside like so many flies, refusing to listen, and armed himself with helmet, shield, and sword.

"Come on, Roman," he boomed. "Fight, or I will give you to be eaten by my dogs." And he strode from the room, his slaves and clients boiling impetuously after him in a crowding, jostling stream, to get good places from which to see the duel. Brighde's mother and sisters followed, in tears.

"I can do nothing with him when he is like that," sobbed Cartismandua. "Daughter, pray to the Gods for your husband's life . . . he seems a personable youth. . . ."

"It is not for him that I fear," stoutly rejoined Brighde. "But Father is a dead man unless Gaius shows mercy." Cartismandua sighed, shook her head, and wiped her eyes on her kerchief, while the girls sniffed tearfully. "Gaius, do not slay him," Brighde implored. "I know he is rough and overbearing, but after all, he is my father. And he is good at heart. You will not?" she begged.

I cocked an eye at her.

"It is, of course," I remarked dryly, "altogether within the bounds of possibility that he will slay me."

"Pooh!" she said, and squeezed my hand as we stepped out into the sunlit courtyard.

The houses of the Britannic nobles are not built like our Roman ones, but invariably have a single wide hall which runs the length of the structure, and from which the rooms branch off in a manner that always reminds me of a litter of piglets nursing. In the smaller homes this hall is merely a straight corridor, but in the more pretentious ones it forms three sides of a rectangle, the fourth being guarded by a lofty palisade. The rooms are outside the hall, and for defensive reasons have no windows in the outer wall, or at most narrow slits for light and air, too small to admit a man. In the remoter districts one story is the rule, the roofs being of wood or thatch, and sloping toward the court, as our own roofs slope toward the *compluvium*. It is a foolish type of construction for a wild country, since the whole roof must be lined with defenders to keep attackers from setting the house ablaze, but it is traditional—"It has always been the custom," is the answer of the Britanni to any suggestion of change.

Tasciovanus' home was a very large one, as became a chieftain, and here the court was perhaps eighty by a hundred paces, stone-flagged, with a stone-curbed well in the center, and now the space was crowded with eager watchers, not a few having seized points of vantage on the roof and on the well-curb. The news had spread through the household, and what with slaves, clients, and their wives and children, there must have been two thousand spectators on hand. I heard odds of five to one and six to one offered on Tasciovanus, with no takers; at ten to one a few small wagers were laid, and fifteen to one brought forth quite a number. I regretted that I could not so invest the hundred gold pieces we had looted from the robbers, for I considered fifteen to one emphatically false odds; still, in my position it would not have done.

I had not been able to find, in Londinium, a true Roman *scutum,* but the shield I had was not much inferior to that of the legionary, being an oblong with rounded ends, and almost as large as I could wish. Of bronze, it was heavier, though no stronger, than the triple bull's hide of which our shields were made, but it would serve. My sword and helmet were all I desired—perfect in every way; the sword was of best Hispanian steel, beautifully balanced, and true to my hand.

The armor Tasciovanus wore was typical of Britannia, being of polished bronze and ornamented with red and blue and white enamel and with jewels, in a fashion to delight Bombyx or Arcularius. But he eschewed the leaf-shaped, pointed sword which is so often seen among the Britanni, preferring the long, straight, double-edged cutting sword, with rounded point, which is popular in Gallia Transalpina. From this, and from his great size, I inferred that he was little skilled in fence, devoting himself to beating down his opponents by sheer brute strength.

My father-in-law was waiting for me, blade in hand,

and with barbaric craft had taken a position where the sun was at his back. Smiling to myself at the simplicity of the move, I unostentatiously pretended interest in the footing, and manoeuvred around till the light was over my left shoulder. Matters being adjusted to my liking, I drew my sword and faced him, noting with some gratification that the delay had irritated him; if one can get an opponent angry, the advantage lies with him who is cool.

"Are you ready, Roman?" he bellowed, and I answered quietly:

"Ready."

But before our blades crossed, there came an interruption in the form of a mighty splash; one of the watchers had slipped from the well-curb and fallen into the well, a distance of some twenty-five or thirty feet. His calls for aid came muffled to our ears, while the crowd rocked with mirth, jeering and deriding him. Tasciovanus cursed the interference.

"Get a rope and haul him out," he commanded, "or let the fool drown. On guard, Roman!" And whirling up his sword, he rushed me.

The Dumnonian chief was strong as a bull—strong as one of those huge beasts of Afric which have a serpent for a hand—and for so big a man he was marvellously quick and active. But as so often happens, his intelligence did not match his size; further, as I had suspected, he had no least knowledge of fencing—power was the whole of his attack. So as he rushed, I stepped in and jabbed him lightly in the upraised arm, about a third of the way from elbow to wrist. Not hard, but just enough to stop his downward blow and to draw a trickle of blood—the good old stop-thrust once more; how useful that has been to me! He halted, drew back, and stared in amazement at the stain which spread over the sleeve of his tunic, then with a roar of fury he rushed me again.

This time I leaped quickly to my right and stuck out my left foot as he went by, tripping him neatly. As he pitched forward on hands and knees, the sword flying from his grasp, I spanked him sharply on the seat of the breeches with the flat of my blade, drawing from the crowd a howl of laughter that did his temper no good. The mirth was checked as Tasciovanus, cursing furiously, caught up his sword, scrambled to his feet, and charged me again.

Giving back before his rush, I took his blade on my shield, brought his shield up by a feint at his eyes, and again using the flat, smacked him on the inside of the right thigh, over the great artery—a blow which would have been fatal had I used the edge. He stared for an instant, then bellowing like the bull he was, he charged for the fourth time.

And now he got the greatest surprise of all, for, tired of playing with him, I met him fairly, our shields clashing together with a tremendous shock and a clang of metal, and I stopped him in his tracks—for all his gigantic size, he had no notion of how to use his weight. Paralyzed with astonishment, his sword still raised, he gaped at me until a prick of my point on his thigh brought his shield down, when I drove the upper rim of my shield up under his jaw in the trick devised by the Imperator and famous through the army as "Caesar's counter." The giant's teeth smashed together and flew in splinters, his head snapped back, and he pitched forward, unconscious. Catching him in my arms, I eased him to the ground, then stepped to the well and brought water in his helmet to dash on his face, while an excited buzz went up from the folk who had seen their chieftain vanquished.

Cartismandua and her daughters came running to tend him, and at their orders the slaves lifted him and carried him indoors, laying him on a couch in the big living-room. Cartismandua ordered most of the people out, allowing only a few of the clients to remain, and presently Tasciovanus opened his eyes and blinked dazedly around, then as consciousness returned he sat up, shook his head to clear the fog from his brain, swung his feet to the floor, and felt of his broken teeth.

"By Tarvos Trigaranus!" he mumbled. "You are a stout duellist, Son, for all your tiny stature. You are the first man in all my life who has bested me in a fight. You held me at your mercy three several times."

"Four," I said, and after a moment's thought he corrected himself.

"Four, yes. But I do not think your tricks of fence would serve in a mêlée."

"I have been in more than thirty dog-fights," I pointed out, "and am still unscarred."

He fumbled with his teeth, wrenched one out, made a wry face, and spat a mouthful of blood on the floor.

"H'mph!" he snorted. "H'mph!" And he glared at me from under his bushy red eyebrows, working them up and down after the fashion of the manlike apes of Afric. "Well, I withdraw the 'shrimp'; you are a stout warrior." He wiped a smear of blood from his beard and bellowed:

"Slaves! Bring mead! Quickly!"

Men came running with foaming pitchers of the drink, and two beautiful goblets of hammered gold were filled, Tasciovanus taking one and having the other passed to me.

"Son," he said, "I pledge your health. Long life and happiness to you. Drink deep!"

"And to you, Father-in-law," I responded, pouring out

a small libation. "Empty cups!" And we drained the beakers.

They were refilled, and we sipped more slowly, while the women-folk, retiring to a corner of the room, demanded news of Brighde's adventures, listening eagerly as she told of the Feast of Samain—at which none of the family was present, but of which they had heard from neighbors—of our life in Londinium, and of our flight. Tasciovanus was evidently turning something over in his mind, and presently he inquired:

"Son, what may I call you?"

"My name is Gaius Aemilius Durus," I answered. "Of the great Aemilian gens. You may call me Gaius."

He nodded.

"What chance, think you," he pursued, "have the folk of Gallia Transalpina of throwing off the yoke of Rome?"

"None whatever," I told him, frankly. "They are strong, brave, and good fighters, but often I have seen the legions turn to rout more than twenty times their own number."

"Because of your tricks of fence?"

"Not at all. Partly because of the godlike genius and incomparable strategy of the Imperator, and partly because of the perfect discipline of the legions. Oh, well, skill of fence may have something to do with it, but it is partly—largely, perhaps—because the folk of Gallia Transalpina cannot present a unified front to an enemy, but pull hither and yon among themselves. It is destiny— the will of the Gods."

He nodded again, stroking his beard thoughtfully.

"It is a major fault of our race," he admitted. "We are the same in Britannia. But I have heard something of this discipline, Gaius, yes. Are you familiar with it?"

I smiled.

"Being a centurion of the Tenth Legion, which is the finest and best-taught body of soldiers in all the world, I should know somewhat of their training."

"If I make you war-chief of my army, with full power, will you teach it to my men? Your discipline, that is."

I shrugged my shoulders.

"The Gods know whether or not I can. It is no light task to take men who are accustomed to think: 'Each for himself,' and teach them to think: 'All for one and one for all.' It goes deeper than mere training; it is the teaching of our father Quirinus, and is bred in Romans for hundreds of generations; the Roman child draws in that creed with his mother's milk."

"But will you try?"

I considered the proposition. It meant hard work, to be sure, but this would keep me in condition against the time when I might rejoin the Eagles. It would mean commanding men, and I might well practice more of that art; I had learned a great deal in the Tenth, but one can never know too much. It would give me a further insight into the Britannic mind, which might some day prove useful. If the war with the Silures materialized, I should have a chance to practice strategy. On the whole there were many elements of attraction, the greatest of all being that while enjoying a position of responsibility I should be more likely to have a chance of escaping what was, after all, a form of slavery.

"I will try," I agreed, at length. Tasciovanus' face brightened.

"Good!" he exclaimed. "Another goblet to seal the pledge."

Per Bacchum, that mead is heady stuff! A smooth and apparently harmless drink, but insidious as unwatered Caecuban, and potent—! Further, one of these goblets held at least eighteen *cyathi*—a pint and a half. With the third I felt my vision begin to blur, and since it would never do to let these barbarians see me giving signs of unsteadiness—in their eyes the ability to hold vast quantities of liquor is essential to manhood—I asked:

"Father-in-law, I have had a hard fortnight. May I go to rest?"

"To rest! It is barely sundown!"

"Even so, I crave sleep. The Gods know I have had little enough of late."

"But will you not eat, first?"

I shook my head.

"No, this mead is food and drink in one."

"So it is, so it is," he acknowledged. "Well, as you wish. And to-morrow we can start the training."

Calling slaves he bade them conduct me to my room, where I dropped my clothing and rolled into bed. I was barely between the covers when Brighde entered and looked me over.

"I must say, Roman," she commented, sternly, "you did a fine job on my father's teeth. It will be many a long day ere he chews solid food again." A lurking twinkle in her eyes belied the severity of her manner.

"He asked for it, did he not?" I retorted. "And I spared his life when it was forfeit by all the rules."

"Yes," she granted, "you spared his life . . . what are you grinning at, Roman ape?"

"I have found favor in your father's sight, Britannic barbarian," was my answer, "and I am grinning at the thought of a Roman *eques*, a centurion of the Men of the Golden Eagle, holding the post of commander-in-chief of an army of breeches-clad savages in the wild land of the Dumnonii. Now hush your chatter, blonde magpie, and let me sleep, for to-morrow I have work to do."

Whereat she laughed, undressed, and climbed in beside me. My last conscious thought, ere Morpheus touched my eyes, was of Praeneste and Tiberius and Flava Rufus. A long way I had come since then! Centurion, captive, commander-in-chief, and married to the princess of a barbaric tribe. What new surprise, I wondered, had Fortuna in store for me?

CHAPTER IX

*Of the War with the Silures; and the News
Brought by Marcus Ganeum*

IF the Silures meant to attack us—and it appeared certain that they did—there was no time to be lost in making ready. Tasciovanus' spies assured us that the invasion would not come until spring, so we had three or four months, but what are a few months in which to equip and train an army? *Per Martes,* it would tax even the genius of the Imperator to accomplish it in so short a time! It would be easy enough to teach our men to form in line of battle or in line of march, and to go through the evolutions required; I might even give them something more than a rudimentary knowledge of fencing; but to teach them the lesson of self-sacrifice and of mutual aid —that was a far different matter. Still, the effort must be made, and I warned the chieftain to call in his men for training.

"A question of a fortnight to get them here," he confidently told me. "Even from the southernmost tip of Belerium. I will send out messengers at once, and we use the same method as in Gallia to insure prompt obedience."

"The last man to arrive is put to death with torture?"

"Even so. It works to perfection. Each strives not to be the last."

"Obviously," I nodded. "Still, were I the last man, I would not come at all."

"But," objected Tasciovanus, faintly puzzled, "how would you know, until you arrived, that you were going to be the last?"

"Evidently I should know that I was not, if I did not come." I explained this with all the bland innocence I could put into my voice and face.

"But then someone else would be last."

"Not so. If the last man did not come, there could be no last. Is that not clear?"

Like most big men, especially of the Britanni, Tasciovanus was sluggish of wit, and he frowned and mulled over this, then burst out:

"By Epona, it is not clear at all! There must be a last man. Of course there must!"

"Not at all, if the last man does not come. Look at it this way. Suppose a certain man does not answer the summons. You cannot put him to death, can you?"

"Of course not. That is, unless we hunt him down in his home."

"We are speaking of those who answer the call. Well, then, suppose this man who fails to come is the last man; how are you going to put him to death? You admit that you cannot. But then, you say, someone else will be last. Very well; he does not come, either. You see the difficulty? I am amazed that none of the Britanni has ever found this simple way to avoid death by torture; you need an infusion of Roman intelligence in your tribe."

The giant tugged his beard, wrinkled his brow, and bent his head to one side, thinking deeply, till Brighde, present at the interview, burst out laughing.

"Gaius," she said, "stop teasing my father; you are not respectful. Father, do not let him bedevil you; he is merely wrapping you in a sophist's nest, as the *retiarius* snares the *secutor*."

Tasciovanus looked at me and grinned sheepishly; he was at bottom a good-natured soul, though apt to be choleric.

"Were you teasing?" he demanded, to which I nodded and smiled. "By Tarvos Trigaranus, you had me fogged," he admitted. "I know I am not quick-witted. However, Son, fog the Silures as completely, and you are forgiven."

"It should not be difficult, in this rainy country. I will do my utmost."

He looked at me doubtfully.

"Is that a joke?" he asked.

"A feeble one at best," I granted.

Often during the following months I teased him thus, till he never knew whether or not to take me seriously. But secretly he enjoyed it, and I think took pride in having a son-in-law who was not only his master with the sword, but was also more nimble of wit; at least there was no base envy in his rather simple character. And later I was able to give him still further cause to respect me.

The army assembled within the promised time, about twenty-five thousand men in all, each armed according to his own fancy. The first task was to get them equipped alike, and I organized gangs of artificers to make short Roman swords, helmets, javelins, and shields like those of the legions, two by four feet, slightly curved about the long axis, and of triple bull's hide stretched and dried on a wooden frame. There being an insufficiency of bulls, we used the hides of cows and oxen, but the result was much the same. And since nearly all the warriors had more or less skill as craftsmen, and since I drove them hard, the outfitting did not take long.

Meanwhile I was choosing my centurions, two hundred and fifty of the most able and reliable, as nearly as I could judge by going about and mingling with the men.

This called for some diplomacy, as every scion of a noble house wanted to be an officer, but I got around the difficulty in the same way that the Imperator did—by organizing a staff of ornamental tribunes, who followed me about, rejoiced in gaudy armor and showy titles, and ran errands and carried messages, without having any actual responsibility. To be sure, I had a few good men on my personal staff, but then so did Caesar, as witness Gaius Volusenus.

As fast as the arms were ready, I taught my centurions to fence in the Roman manner, then taught them to drill, after which I set each one to teaching his hundred, while I exercised a general supervision over the whole. To my extreme satisfaction, the naive and childlike minds of the Britanni seized on this new fashion of warfare with all the pleasure of an infant receiving a shiny toy, and they fenced, drilled, formed in line, took new formations, advanced, retreated, charged—in short, went through all the evolutions—as eagerly and delightedly as though it were some brand-new game. The idea of fighting on foot seemed especially to please them; they used chariots because the custom had come down from their ancestors, but being men of courage and stout heart, they enjoyed the thought of coming to grips with the enemy.

The chief trouble was to make them give up the habit of dyeing themselves with the villainous blue dye they were accustomed to use when preparing for war. So strongly entrenched was this custom that I was obliged to forbid it under pain of death.

"But it has always been done since immemorial ages!" they remonstrated, this being to the Britannic mind a perfectly valid and conclusive argument.

"Then," I retorted, "it is high time we did otherwise.

And it does not become the dignity of trained warriors to dye themselves like a horde of savages."

I had to have four men executed ere I could break up the custom, but in the end the result was good; our foes, expecting to meet blue warriors, were taken aback on seeing us in our natural skins. Anything different, however trifling, has the value of a surprise.

Before the interest began to flag, I stimulated it by offering prizes, in the form of particularly ornate standards, for the best performances in fencing and in drill, whereupon a hot but good-natured rivalry broke out among the centuries. This rivalry being settled, I gave it a fresh impetus by combining the centuries into cohorts and teaching them to drill thus, then offering new prizes for the cohorts. Finally I amalgamated them into six legions, and announced that field trials would be held, the legion making the best showing to receive a standard of pure gold and to be known by the proud title of the Commander's Own.

It will be noted that I did not use quite the theoretic organization of our Roman legions, but approximated that of Caesar, of a number of smaller, more mobile units, rather than the full legion of six thousand men. Also, I used forty centurions to a legion rather than sixty, for I felt that a good man, with the help of his decurions, could easily manage a full hundred. I might also say that my choice of centurions proved very fortunate; I had to demote only three out of the whole two hundred and fifty.

Of course I took care to organize a baggage-train, and a well-taught force of some twenty-five hundred cavalry, who would be useful for scouting and as a reserve. This last branch of the service provoked great mirth, for the horses of the country are not as a rule taught to carry riders, and few of the men had ever bestridden a mount. Consequently there was much bucking, rearing, and plunging, with not a few runaways, when a horse would go careering madly across country, reins flying about his hoofs, with the rider prone on the animal's back, frantically clasping the beast's neck. We had half a dozen or so broken arms, twice as many fractured collar-bones, and one leg so badly smashed that it had to be amputated. Besides these, one man had his neck broken, and another's skull was crushed when he was flung against a rock, but these were the only casualties except for a plentiful crop of sprains and bruises, and in the end both men and beasts learned their lesson, so that my cavalry was second to none, either Roman or Gallic, so far as training went; as I have said, the horses were too light for the shock of a heavy charge.

I myself was surprised by the rapidity with which all this was accomplished, for by the end of Aprilis, a little over three months, I had a very respectable and well-trained army. To be sure, my success was largely due to the fact that these Britanni are natural warriors, and in some measure to the other fact that they are always eager for a new thing. In this they are like their relatives of Gallia Transalpina, and the characteristic gave me some uneasiness, for men who love a change are not apt to be steadfast. However, I could only do my best, and leave the outcome to Mars and Bellona.

Naturally, I could not tell how my troops would behave in actual conflict—that is, whether or not they would support one another as they should, but I hoped for the best; drill and discipline, with good centurions, are great stiffeners of morale. Besides, the close formation of the Roman line of battle promotes this solidarity much better than the loose, irregular style of fighting from chariots.

And in addition, I took pains to see that friends, relatives, and men from the same districts were grouped in the line; the reason for this is obvious.

I think I may say, without undue conceit, that the men liked me in spite of the severe discipline I maintained and the harsh but just punishments I decreed for a few refractory ones. At all events, they cheered when I showed myself, and the officers treated me with proper respect, though this was perhaps engendered by the tale of my victory over Tasciovanus; none cared to risk the anger of him who had so easily and so contemptuously vanquished their stoutest warrior.

Of course I tried to model myself after Caesar; firm but always just; stern to wanton misconduct but lenient to well-meaning error; quick to reward merit; dignified but kindly; and always thinking at least one jump ahead of the best of the men. It seemed to work, though I realized that among these volatile folk personal popularity was an elusive thing; a whim of the men might readily cost me not only my command but also my life, so fickle and so easily swayed by their emotions are the Britanni.

On the whole, I had an army which looked extremely good, so far as one could tell without actually trying them out in battle, and I began to have notions of conquering the whole of Britannia, bit by bit, and establishing myself as ruler of the entire country.

To be just, it was Brighde who put this idea into my head, one night at dinner, and Tasciovanus supported her.

"It might easily be done, Gaius," he said. "The girl is right. You have an army second to none as fighters, an army which adores you and which is trained in the discipline and tactics of Rome. I cheerfully grant that you are a master leader; my own idea is to charge at the head of my men, letting them follow as they will, but I recognize the superiority of your plan. And as for organization —why, your commissariat train alone is masterly; unheard of in this land. You are beyond question a genius, and there is no reason why, with your brains and our strength, you should not sweep the entire country, defeat the tribes one by one, bring them into harmony, and rule over the whole. And with all Britannia united under one leader, by Tarvos Trigaranus, we could master the world!"

It was an alluring thought, and I toyed with it, meditating deeply, turning my golden goblet in my fingers, and staring into the depths of the amber mead, while Cartismandua and the girls watched me open-eyed, a trifle awed, and the tribunes hung on my words. Of course, my father-in-law's estimate of my ability was exaggerated; I was not the mighty genius he thought me, for my success was not the result of pure invention—I had for the most part only followed what Caesar had taught me. Still, I had originated some things . . . and the man who could follow in Caesar's footsteps . . . At length I sighed and shook my head.

"It will not do," I answered. "It is a pleasant thought, but it will not do. It would bring us into conflict with Rome."

"What of it?" impetuously demanded Brighde. "You are no longer a Roman; your allegiance is to the Dumnonii."

"It is not that," I explained. "But Caesar would devour me as easily as Tarvos devours this scrap of meat." And I tossed a fragment to one of the great dogs, who caught it in midair and swallowed it with one gulp.

"I do not believe it," my wife stoutly affirmed. "You cannot tell me, Gaius, that the brain which could organize and train an army in three short months, as you have done, could not also devise a masterly campaign of strategy."

"You do not know the Imperator, Carissima. He is not a man; he is a demi-god, descended from Aeneas of Ilium, and through him from the Goddess Venus. He is more like the heroes of ancient time; wise as Nestor, crafty as Odysseus, terrible in battle as Achilles. His genius so far transcends that of other men that no comparison is possible. He would out-think, out-manoeuvre, and out-fight me. He would only need to stretch forth his left hand to crush me utterly. No, it will not do."

"He did not achieve much against the Cantii," remarked Camulus, one of my tribunes.

I gave him an indulgent smile.

"That was no more than a scouting expedition," I pointed out. "And at that, he beat the Cantii whenever they stood to face him. It was only flight that saved them from destruction."

Brighde pounded her goblet on the table.

"You make me furious!" she stormed. "You and your Imperator! At least you could try. Or if you will not match yourself against him, then when your famous Imperator finds you ruler of the whole land, with a stout army at your back, well taught in his own discipline, at the very least you could make an honorable peace with him."

I considered this, finding it not without merit.

"It might be done," I conceded. "It might be done . . . we will see . . . it depends on many things. Meanwhile, we have a task before us—to beat the Silures."

"Where will you await their invasion?" Tasciovanus inquired.

"I will not await it at all. The best defence is a quick and sharp attack. We march against them in three days."

"You will invade their country?" The chieftain was incredulous.

"Even so."

"By Tarvos Trigaranus!" he boomed, and caught me a slap on the back that well-nigh loosened the teeth in my jaw. "Son, you are a man after my own heart. Ho, slaves, fill the goblets! A bumper, to be drunk standing—to Gaius Aemilius Durus, of the Dumnonii, health and long life! Bottoms to the sky!"

Springing to their feet, the tribunes shouted the words, drained their goblets, and crashed them, ringing, on the table. Rising, I acknowledged the health, then said:

"To-morrow and the next day we make the final preparations, and at dawn of the third day we march. Spread the word!"

Of course the Druids had to be consulted, auguries must be taken to learn whether or not the date was propitious, and sacrifices must be made to Andate, Goddess of Victory. But the Chief Druid of the Dumnonii was a friend of Tanarus, had studied with him in Graecia and shared his views, and was on the outs with Esus, Chief Druid of Britannia. I had the wit to make friends with him shortly after arriving in Isca, showed him the utmost respect in public and privately laughed with him over the gullibility of the superstitious natives, so that we were on the best possible terms. Therefore a polite hint sufficed, and the omens were quite as I desired.

I had laid my plans with care, and at the appointed time the whistles shrilled—for the sake of custom I retained the barbarian signals rather than the Roman bugles —and the centurions marshaled their troops in line of march. When all was ready, we set forth, the men swinging along, heads up, Marius' mules over their shoulders, proud as any Roman legions, all set to do their twenty-four miles a day and to make camp at the end. Nor do I think I can be blamed if I felt a thrill of pride as I looked over the long line of gleaming helmets and tossing standards, as I listened to the rhythmic tramp of thousands of feet and to the swing and lift and beat of the marching-songs, and reflected that three months before, this well-knit force of trained men had been a loose, undisciplined mob. Truly, the conquest of Britannia might not be such an idle dream.

From Isca to the point where I meant to cross the estuary of the Sabrina is a matter of about forty miles, and I planned to make the distance in two days, pitching camp each night; a fortified camp, not that I feared attack, but for the sake of use and practice. I had chosen this spot for crossing because, although the estuary is here about ten miles wide, and lies open to the sea, there is a good landing-place on the farther shore, while on the hither are woods to furnish ample material for the rafts which I would use. And if I went farther north, where the Sabrina is narrower, that would take me through the land of the Belgae and into that of the Atrebates, and either of those tribes would be prompt indeed to resent an armed invasion of their country. So on reaching the shore, my artificers spent four days in felling trees, making rafts, and shaping oars, and on the seventh day out from Isca we set forth on the water, each raft carrying two hundred men and being propelled by twelve pairs of great sweeps, each oar requiring three men to handle it.

Our crossing was necessarily slow, but by choosing the time with care we made the tide aid us, and crossed in about three hours, our landing being wholly unopposed. We marched inland a few miles, then camped for the night, and on the eighth day set about the business of conquest.

It is not my intention to detail fully our war with the Silures. The country over which we fought is less densely populated than the rest of Britannia—than the southern part, at least—and is harsh and rugged in the extreme, with range after range of rocky hills lying irregularly athwart the land as though tossed there by Titans at play. The people are fierce and most dangerous fighters; rude, filthy, unkempt of hair and of dress, clad mostly in the skins of wild beasts, and armed with long, crooked knives, and their delight is to get in close and fight hand to hand. And I must admit that the sight of a wild-eyed band of them rushing into battle, brandishing their knives, yelling their uncouth cries, and eager for slaughter, is no encouraging spectacle even to one who has been through as many encounters as I had. To make matters worse, anyone who is wounded and left on the scene of battle is foredoomed to a slow and agonizing end, for the Silures take their women to war with them, and after a fight these harridans go over the field, rescue such of their own men as are not too grievously hurt, despatch those who are beyond hope, and in fiendish joy whittle a wounded enemy to bits, as slowly and as painfully as they can. No, I do not feel that I could ever grow fond of the Silures.

Fortunately for us, our enemies knew nothing of organized fighting, nor even of true guerrilla warfare; their sole notion was to assemble as many warriors as possible in one spot, then in a body rush in to slay or be slain. They had not even sense enough to lay an efficient ambush and pick us off at long range with arrows or slingstones, or to roll rocks down the steep hillsides on us—they are men of one idea—and the result was that although they greatly outnumbered us, their loose, irregular charges gained them nothing against our ordered line.

Unlike the Imperator, I found it necessary to stimulate

and encourage my troops by fighting personally in the front rank, but with this example to hold them together, my warriors stood to it like men, keeping their alignment, aiding one another, and executing to perfection the flanking and enveloping movements which made it possible to take our foes on both sides as well as in front. And given more time for training, I believe I should have been able to direct the battle from a point of general supervision, as did Caesar. However, that is mere speculation, and I cannot say for certain.

But though we moved rapidly and struck hard, the Silures were active and mobile, wherefore many of them escaped from each fight, and since they lacked the foresight to assemble all their clans at one place and hurl the entire force against us, it followed that we could not annihilate them at one blow, so the war resolved itself into a long series of minor engagements, in which we wiped out one clan after another. It was hard and grinding work, hunting them through the rugged hills and fastnesses of that wild land, but at length Fortuna favored us, and my scouts brought word that the main body of our foes was camped in a valley some forty miles from us. Making a forced march overnight, we came at dawn within striking distance of them, and dividing my forces, I gave half in charge of one Lugos, son of a noble house, and the most intelligent of my tribunes. He was my chief of cavalry, but for this occasion I promoted him to be a temporary *legatus*, or lieutenant-general.

The scouts were able to show both Lugos and myself paths, about six miles apart, whereby we could descend into the valley, and timing our attack nicely we caught the Silures between our two divisions. Favored by a shrouding mist that filled the valley and concealed our advance, we smote our enemies unaware, just as they were preparing breakfast, and the fight raged furiously until noon, when the last who stood before us was slain. Some few escaped by climbing the steep sides of the valley, but to all intents and purposes we wiped them out, leaving, as nearly as I could judge, between eighty and ninety thousand dead in or beside the river. I tried to spare the women, but my men had seen their slain on other fields, and there was no pity in them—the more since the women, seizing weapons, fought as savagely and as desperately as their husbands and fathers.

So the war came to an end, and with it all fear of an invasion by the Silures; it would be many, many years ere they who survived could build up enough of a population to become dangerous. We burned, of course, the chief towns, Isca of the Silures * and Gobannium, as well as all the hamlets far and wide; we laid waste the land, took the stored grain, and drove off a few thousand head of the shaggy, half-wild cattle; but on the whole there was little material profit in the expedition—we gained naught but safety, for the land was too poor to be worth looting. Still, safety was much, and I was hailed with delight by the army when the last battle was over; their cheers and plaudits were as long and loud as any that we of the legions had ever given the Imperator.

Thereupon we marched back to the Sabrina, recrossed the estuary, and journeyed thence to Isca, where we were received with all the frantic delight that could be shown by a gay and mercurial people to a victorious army who had eased a fear of generations' standing. Garlands of flowers were strung across the streets; bright tapestries flaunted from windows and balconies; the folk met us outside the city and escorted us in with songs; cheering, shouting crowds packed the streets or showered blossoms

* Caerleon.

on us from the roofs; and the whole city gave itself over to a mad holiday.

Shall I be blamed if pride swelled my bosom as I rode through the shouting streets at the head of my army, to be hailed on every side as "Conqueror!" "Deliverer!" and "Son of Teutates!"—Teutates being one of the names by which the Britanni call their God of War? I knew, I think, something of the feelings of the *triumphator* who rides with his victorious troops up the Via Sacra and through the Forum to the mighty Temple of Jupiter Capitolinus. True, this was not Rome, and my triumph was over a barbarous nation, but to these folk I was a hero beyond compare, and as Tanarus said: "It is better to be a large frog in a small puddle than a small frog in a large puddle."

Fires were lighted in the squares, food and drink were brought for the army, which camped outside the walls, and feasts were spread for me and my officers, feasts which would have gorged an army of Cyclops, and at which I was the only guest who stayed even partially sober—one and all, the rest were as drunk as any Bacchanal ever dreamed of being or hoped to be.

I managed to avoid excessive drinking, for I wished to be in condition to greet my wife, who had a most un-Britannic prejudice against intoxication, and my abstinence was well repaid. When Brighde saw me coming home from the feast steady on my legs and clear of speech and of eye, she well-nigh strangled me with her hugs and smothered me with her kisses. Between weeping and laughter she clung rapturously to me, crying out to her mother and sisters:

"Said I not he was a great warrior—a great commander—a very genius? Who else could have destroyed the Silures? Who else could have freed us from the ever-present threat of invasion? Under him we shall conquer all Britannia—oh, Gaius, Gaius! *My* Gaius—mine, mine!"

Cartismandua and the girls greeted me with more restraint, but joyously, and I had to tell them the whole story of our expedition, while they hung on my words and two or three of the bards of Tasciovanus' house listened with eager ears, storing up memories to be woven into songs. Every noble house has its bards, from three to seven or eight, depending on the wealth and importance of its patron, these bards earning a good living by playing their harps and singing at the feasts, even as did Homerus and his colleagues of olden times. With this difference, though; Homerus sang of departed heroes, but the bards of the Island of the North are expected to celebrate the praises of their living patrons, for the childlike minds of the Britanni soak up flattery as a sponge absorbs water. Most of Tasciovanus' bards, to be sure, were industriously getting drunk with the other revellers, but these few had followed me home to get the tale firsthand from my lips; they felt that business should take precedence over pleasure.

When I speak of the noble houses of Britannia or of Gallia it must not be supposed that I am instituting any comparison between them and the great families of Rome. Such a comparison, whether of wealth or of civilization, would be ridiculous, even though we considered such princely houses as those of Diviciacus of the Aedui, Vercingetorix of the Arverni, or Tasciovanus of the Dumnonii. It is true that from their commerce with those who come to buy tin and to sell the products of other lands, the Dumnonii are probably the most civilized of all the tribes of Britannia, but even so, their culture seemed barbaric to one used to the magnificent Forum Romanum and the palatial homes of Mons Palatinus. *Edepol,* in this wild land it is only the Druids—and by no means all of them—who can read and write! It must be admitted, though, that this fact is probably due less to a lack of culture than to the desire of the Druids to keep a tight rein on the common folk; they hold that to reduce their secret knowledge to writing would diffuse it among the people and thus lower their own importance, so all knowledge is a matter of oral transmission. But after all, everything is comparative, and the ruling houses of Britannia yield no whit in pride of wealth or arrogance of birth to the Julii, the Cornelii, the Sergii, or—though I myself say it—the Aemilii.

And it was this pride and arrogance that made serious trouble for me, for about a week after our return to Isca I was told of a cabal which was forming against me in the army. Lugos brought me the news.

"It is Camulus who is fomenting it," he said. "Urged thereto by several things." This Camulus was a self-headed cadet of a noble family in the south of Belerium, a handsome, conceited, foolish, and arrogant youth. "First," Lugos went on, "he has been in love with Brighde since childhood, and counted her his own. This is no secret, and though it is common knowledge that she repulsed him, he did not give up hope—honorable hope, that is—until you appeared.

"This being so, our Camulus has ever dreamed of himself as son-in-law to Tasciovanus, and next in the succession, so of course he hates the man who shattered the delightful vision. Also, he resents your position as commander-in-chief; that, he feels, should go not to a Roman but to a man who is of the Dumnonii by birth."

"Namely, himself," I interjected, and Lugos, smiling, agreed.

"May I add," he went on, "that I do not share this belief? To me, the best commander—"

"You need not tell me," I interrupted. "Your actions are proof."

"My thanks. So," he pursued, "Camulus has stirred up all the discontented; those who were disappointed in their hopes of Silurian loot; and those who are angry because you will not grant them leave to return home and sow their crops. Of course I see your reason for this—that an army, once dispersed, is hard to collect, and that the loot of the Belgian and Atrebatian fields will far outweigh what grain we could raise. But there are many who cannot see it, and they resent your order. And Camulus—"

"I have had trouble with him ere now," I remarked.

"Do I know it!"

"And I have had to reprimand him several times. Doubtless he feels injured, but I had no idea he would go so far as treason. How much of a following has he, Lugos?"

"He is a born demagogue, smooth and persuasive of tongue, and his family has much influence in the south. I should say, as nearly as I can learn, that about seventy of the centurions and a quarter to a third of the troops are for him. Perhaps not actually for him, but inclining that way."

"*Per Martes!* So many? And he has been able to raise this sedition without my suspecting it!"

Lugos grinned.

"If I may be pardoned for saying it, General, you are too trustful. You do not suspect readily enough."

"H'm! How of the tribunes?"

"I believe all save Camulus himself to be loyal."

"And of the cavalry?"

"They are my men," replied Lugos, proudly. "I will answer for their fidelity to you."

Brighde was present at this interview, and she clicked her teeth in anger.

"The proper thing—the necessary thing—" she declared, "is to seize Camulus and put him to death ere he can do more harm."

But Lugos and I both shook our heads.

"It will not do," I assured her, and Lugos echoed my words, adding:

"It would precipitate a mutiny. Camulus' younger brother—indeed, all his family—would resent it, as would the whole of the men from the south. They would rebel at once."

"Beyond which," I pointed out, "Camulus' brother, Lugotorix, is the best of my tribunes, after Lugos, here." Lugos smiled a gratified smile at this; verily, a little butter is a great smoother of human relations! "If I can keep Lugotorix faithful to me," I continued, "I would like to do so."

"He is still faithful," Lugos assured me. "Though," he added, with a faintly ironic smile, "perhaps less from true loyalty than from a touch of envy of his older brother."

"Then what action will you take?" demanded Brighde, and again I shook my head.

"Dii Immortales!" I exclaimed. "Can I say offhand? It needs thought."

"Think fast, then, Gaius; your life is at stake. Is it not, Lugos?"

"That is obvious," I laughed.

"I fear so," the tribune acknowledged. "I fear that Camulus intends to slay the General and Tasciovanus, assume the chieftainship, and seize you, Brighde."

"Let him try it!" she snapped. "He would get a hand's breadth of bronze between his ribs on the wedding night."

A slave came just then to summon us to dinner, and I insisted on Lugos dining with us.

"I depend on you to learn how far this conspiracy has gone," I told him, "and to help me find means of checking it."

"Could you not have Camulus quietly assassinated?" Brighde asked. "Surely there are plenty who would do it. How about you, Lugos?"

"Assassination is not a task for one of gentle birth," the tribune answered. "But if the General wishes, I will pick a quarrel with the traitor and slay him in a duel. I think I could master him."

"And involve your two families in a blood-feud," I said. "Thank you, no. I will fight my own duels." I flung my arm around Brighde's shoulders. "For a sweet little blonde, Carissima, you are amazingly eager for death and destruction. A bloodthirsty little maid, for all your innocent blue eyes."

She snuggled close.

"Only for your sake, Gaius," she remonstrated. "When you are threatened . . ."

"Thank you, Cara," I smiled. "However, my hand has kept my head for some years past, and, Fortuna aiding, will continue to do so." And we proceeded to the banquet-hall.

Neither the Britanni nor the Galli recline at meals, as our custom is, nor do they limit the number of folk at table, as in Rome. The more there are at dinner, the greater the importance of the host, so planks are laid on trestles for a table, the gentry sitting up to it in great armchairs, with the clients and the more important slaves, lower down the board, on benches. They have a curious custom of placing a huge silver salt-cellar at the dividing line, whence the superior folk are said to "sit above the salt," the phrase "below the salt" being used to describe an inferior or dependant; between equals, it is a term of insult.

The size of the hall in Tasciovanus' house may be judged from the fact that there were five such tables, with more than seventy diners at each. The noise of their feeding, with the clash of knives on bronze platters, the loud conversation—each one striving to out-shout his neighbor —the running back and forth of the slaves who served the meal and their calling to one another, all made up a pandemonium which was augmented by the snarling and yapping of a score or more of dogs which fought under the tables for the bones and scraps of meat and bread tossed them by the diners. Torches and cressets flared along the dark-paneled walls, their yellow beams dancing on bronze and gold, and two huge fires blazed at each end of the room, dispelling the dampness that rose from the river. The rushes on the floor—strewn ankle-deep the previous autumn, and by spring reeking with garbage and other filth—had recently been changed, and the aroma of the new ones came pleasantly to the nostrils, so that altogether it was a scene of rude magnificence, rich, ostentatious, and barbaric—far other than the dinners I had enjoyed at Tiberius' villa in the Alban Hills.

Presently, when all were full-fed, the meats and vegetables would give place to mighty tankards of mead and the fermented juice of apples and pears, the bards would tune their harps and sing their songs, and the whole company would get riotously and uproariously drunk as a finale to the day. All, that is, save the women, who would retire when the serious drinking began, and save one adopted son of the Dumnonii, who, being of Roman

birth and used to Roman ways, could stand just about
so much and no more of this riot, and would seize an early
opportunity to slip quietly away. Although I liked the
barbaric drinks well enough as beverages, I felt that my
early years as a "pretty man" had known enough intoxication to last a lifetime.

Being son-in-law to Tasciovanus, I sat at the chieftain's
right hand, and for this occasion had on my right a trader
from Massilia, by name Marcus Ganeum. He was an elderly man, reserved of manner and shrewd of face, who
traded in tin between Belerium and the estuary of the
Liger, shipping the metal overland from the latter place
to Massilia. Also, he had trading vessels dealing in other
goods throughout the Mare Internum. Landing at Ictis,*
he had bargained for a shipload of tin, but some dispute
concerning the business had arisen between him and the
Carnabii, who mine and smelt the metal, cast it into ingots, and sell it. Since the Carnabii are tributaries and
subjects of the Dumnonii, Ganeum had left his vessel in
charge of one of his men, had got him a horse, and had
ridden the hundred and twenty miles to Isca to have the
disagreement adjudicated by Tasciovanus. And, he being
a Roman—or at least of Italia—the chieftain's steward
had in courtesy placed him next to me.

As may be supposed, there was much to talk about, and
under cover of the uproar we carried on a brisk conversation. It did not happen that Ganeum knew any of the
friends I named, but he had seen the Imperator, had
heard of Tiberius Rufus, had dealt by letter with my
father, and was able to give me an account of political

---

* There has been much dispute over the location of Ictis, some writers
claiming it to have been the Isle of Thanet, at the mouth of the Thames,
and others the Isle of Wight. Dr. T. Rice Holmes, however, has pretty
definitely established that it was St. Michael's Mount, near the southern
extremity of Cornwall.

developments in Rome and in Gallia, thus waking in me
the worst fit of homesickness that any human being has
ever known. By what he said, affairs in the City had
grown rapidly worse since I left, Clodius was openly defy-
ing Pompeius, the Senate was divided against itself, anarchy was rampant, and no man could guess what the outcome would be.

I think Brighde sensed my trouble, for several times I
caught her eyes fixed anxiously on me from across the
table, and even the reassuring nod and smile that I managed to send her did not clear the worry from her face.

At length Ganeum said:

"You have heard, I presume, that Caesar is making
ready for another invasion of Britannia?"

"No!" I cried. "Tell me about it." For these words
roused in my memory the sleeping recollections, which
late events had driven to the back of my mind, of my
adored Imperator; of Bombyx, Arcularius, and my other
friends; and of the great days I had known with the Men
of the Golden Eagle. "Tell me about it," I repeated.
"When does he sail? Where land? Is he planning to conquer the entire country?"

Ganeum smiled.

"After all, I can tell you little; as you know, Caesar is
not one to spread his plans broadcast, for the benefit of
all listeners.

"But it is common knowledge that the legions have
been busy all winter in constructing ships, and that vast
quantities of tackle and rigging have been brought from
Iberia to Portus Itius and to the coast towns near the
mouths of the Liger and Sequana Rivers. By the way, do
you know Marcus Cicero, the orator?"

"I have met him; he is much older than I am. Why?"

"His younger brother, Quintus, has joined Caesar and

has been appointed *legatus*. Well, to resume. Dumnorix of the Aedui, who, like his brother Diviciacus the Druid, is an incurable politician, but who, unlike Diviciacus, is hostile to Rome, has been fomenting rebellion in his tribe, and Caesar is having trouble with him."

"The Imperator will manage him, never fear." In' this I spoke true prophecy, for about a month later Dumnorix broke out in open revolt and was slain by Mandorix the Aeduan, whom I have already mentioned. "Go on," I urged, growing more and more eager with Ganeum's words.

"I know little more. Troops are being concentrated at Portus Itius, and it is said that they will set out during the coming month, though just when is not certain. It may be that the Proconsul himself does not know, for Cingetorix and his father-in-law Indutiomarus are struggling for the supremacy of the Treveri, the former being loyal to Rome, the latter hostile, and Caesar dare not leave Gallia Transalpina until their dispute is settled. However, it is thought that the sailing will be some time about the Ides of Quintilis,* so far as one can guess."

"Thanks, Marcus, thanks," I told the trader. "You have brought great news, great!

"Now tell me of your dispute with the Carnabii; I have influence with Tasciovanus, and perchance may be of service to you."

He recounted the difficulty, which was largely a question of price, and I may say here that I was able to persuade Tasciovanus to decide in favor of Ganeum—*perpol,* it was little enough to do for the man who brought news that set me on fire.

Yes, I was on fire. With these tidings I was all Roman once more, my allegiance to the Dumnonii relegated to the

* July 15. Caesar actually sailed on July 6, 54 B. C.

back of my mind as though it had never existed. And to those who may hold me to blame for this, let me point out that I had never sworn any such allegiance; the Druids, Brighde, and the tribesmen had merely assumed that such a tie existed, but I myself had never confirmed it with any oath. Therefore I held myself free to act as I saw fit— observing, of course, the laws of hospitality toward those who had treated me as an honored guest.

When the heavy drinking began, I withdrew as usual— the Dumnonii forgave even sobriety to the man who had conquered the Silures. But my brain was hot and my hands and feet were icy cold, so I knew it would be useless to try to sleep; Morpheus was far from propitious, that night.

Consequently I did not join Brighde, but went for a walk along the heights which overhang the river. The mists had cleared away, and it was a bright and beautiful night toward the end of Junius, the deep blue sky hung with millions of twinkling stars, the air soft and balmy, reminiscent of the Alban Hills, and below me I could trace the gleaming surface of the stream, like a silvery dragon winding along the valley, its beginning and its end both lost in the hazy distance.

But I gave little attention to my surroundings, for one after another, with rush and sweep, vivid images came crowding in to fill my mind. The strong, kindly, high-bred features of the great Imperator . . . the rough, good-natured face of Bombyx . . . the thoughtful eyes of Volusenus . . . Arcularius' gem-studded armor . . . the gross countenances of Labienus and Mamurra . . . the tramp of slogging feet on the march . . . the songs of the legionaries, foul, profane, obscene, blasphemous, but with a wonderful rhythm to lighten the weary miles . . . the deep notes of the brazen-throated *tubae* . . . the Legion's

ordered line . . . the set faces and glowing eyes of my
century . . . the last look to right and left as the *bucinae*
blew the charge . . . the Eagles dancing as the men
charged home . . . the crash of battle joined, and the
fierce exaltation of the fight . . . then the evening chatter of the camp, as the battle was fought over again . . .
the smell of wood-smoke from a thousand fires as the men
prepared their evening meal . . . ah, Jove Optime Max-
ime, should I ever again know these joys? And last of all
. . . Brighde.

Ah, yes, Brighde! For it cannot be denied that my gay,
blue-eyed, flaxen-haired, . saucy, brave, and loving wife
had woven the texture of her life into my own, that the
tendrils of her heart had so wrapped themselves about my
own heart that it would be a wrench and a bitter pang to
leave her. But how take her with me? *Per Martes,* the
camp of the legionaries was no place for a decent woman
—for any woman, since the other kind was not allowed.
Venus be my aid! What could I do? I could not take her—
nor, by Eros and Aphrodite, could I leave her behind! And
sitting down on a jutting rock, I buried my face in my
hands; I had come indeed to the parting of the ways.

To return to the Imperator—or to renounce all thought
of Rome and make my home forever in this wild land?
Either way offered its reward, and either, its bitter sorrow . . . which to do? Minerva, Goddess of Wisdom, aid
me! Suddenly a thought came to my mind; here I had an
army of twenty thousand men, eager to overrun Britannia
—why not take them to the Imperator and grant them
their desire under his leadership? *Per Deos Immortales,*
he would welcome such an auxiliary force, trained in the
discipline of the legions—what general would not?—and
I should have great merit in his eyes—perchance he would
even make me a *legatus*.

Then I remembered the cabal of which Lugos had warned me, and I wondered if the men would go. Some of them certainly would not—Tasciovanus would probably die in an apoplexy of rage at the suggestion—but I felt I could count on my tribunes and on most of the centurions. As for the rank and file, that remained to be seen; at all events, I resolved to try. Brighde could remain with her family, to join me later; the Imperator was first in my thoughts.

On this decision I rose and made my way home, where I found Brighde waiting for me in our room. She asked where I had been, and I told her all that was in my mind, her eyes growing more and more stormy as the tale proceeded. Once she interrupted to ask:

"And how of myself? Am I to be deserted, as Ariadne was deserted by Theseus?"

"Not at all," I replied. "You can stay at home, as you did during the campaign against the Silures, and I can rejoin you at the end of the summer."

"So, indeed?"

"Yes. As I have already pointed out, it is useless for the Britanni to struggle against the Imperator, but by aiding him against the other tribes, the Dumnonii will profit vastly." And I continued, showing the manifold benefits which would accrue to Britannia under Roman rule; the greater wealth; the spread of knowledge and civilization; the greater comfort; the higher standards of living. "And," I concluded, "it is impossible to overestimate the advantage to the Dumnonii should they be the first to earn the proud title of 'Friends of Rome.'"

When I had detailed my plan, she burst out in rage:

"Dis Pater take me to His realm of eternal night if I live with a man who shamefully proposes to betray his country into the hands of a foreign tyrant! Give up this treacherous project, or we are strangers forever. That is my last word; give me news in the morning that your heart is changed, or never speak to me again while the world endures."

I was angry enough to be sarcastic. "Have you been reading Plautus and Aristophanes?" I demanded. "Considering that I am a Roman born, and that I have never yet renounced my allegiance to Rome, or sworn faith to Britannia, your designation of the latter as my country, and of Caesar as a foreign tyrant, bears with it a certain element of comedy."

At that her fury burst all restraint. "A Roman born you are," she blazed, "and a Roman you remain at heart. Brighde my Patroness have pity on me that I ever thought I loved you! Turncoat, traitor, and oppressor, may you die in agony on the field of battle, with none save wolf and raven to hear your cries, nor any to bring water to cool your burning thirst!"

And she stormed from the room, slamming the door behind her with a jar that shook the house.

Slowly and thoughtfully I undressed and got into bed.

CHAPTER X

Of the Rebellion in the Army; and the Disobedience of Brighde

SLEEP was long in coming that night. For hours I lay awake, trying to decide just how I should meet the situation, just what I should do. It seemed to me that it would be best to parade the army, address an exhortation to them after the manner of Caesar—oh, yes, quite after the manner of the Imperator!—and lay the matter before them, inspiring them to march with me to the country of the Cantii. That being settled, there came the question of what I should say. And while I was planning the speech, Morpheus touched my eyelids with His magic fingers.

How long I slept, I cannot tell, but it must have been some hours, for when I woke, a full high moon was laying bars of silver light across my floor. I was roused by a thundering on the door of my room and a voice shouting: "Gaius! General! Open, in the Name of all the Gods! Open! Open!"

I sprang from the bed and grasped my sword, calling: "Who is it?"

"Lugos," came the reply. "Open, General, and let me in!"

I thrust back the bolts, and in rushed the tribune, close followed by two or three of the same class, half a dozen centurions, and Brighde. For an instant I thought that this was an assassination, and I stood on guard, but Lugos dispelled the idea.

"Flee!" he gasped, panting from exertion and beside himself with excitement. "Dress and flee—there is no time to lose!"

Well, if it were to be flight I should need clothes, and if battle, armor. So I caught up my things and began to put them on, while the invaders all tried to explain at once. Presently I saw that the tribune had regained his breath, and I motioned the rest to be silent.

"Now, Lugos," I asked, "what is it?"

He spoke quickly and incisively.

"Camulus has called out his adherents, some five thousand in number, mostly of the Carnabii, and from the southern districts of Belerium. I think he planned to fall on the loyal ones and either kill them in their sleep or force them to join him, but Orgetorix, first centurion of the Commander's Own, was on the alert, had the whistles blown, and formed up the loyal ones in line of battle.

"There was frightful confusion in the camp, with much uproar, and for a time a riot seemed imminent, but Camulus thought better of it and drew off his men. He is marching hither, to seize Tasciovanus by force and un-aware, put him and you to death, and grasp the chieftain-ship. Getting a horse, I passed him by a detour, but he will be here in half an hour, and Tasciovanus, with his slaves and clients, cannot hold this house against five thousand warriors. In the Name of Cernunnos, General, save your-self!"

The idea of saving myself by flight, and leaving my wife, my father-in-law, and the women and children to the tender mercies of the rebellious tribune, did not appeal to me. I was a Roman, yes, but, *per Deos Immortales*, there is a fundamental honor which must be observed even toward barbarians—nay, still more with them than with civilized folk, for the ignorant and unthinking are ever the readiest to misunderstand and to criticize. And besides, it is not in the tradition of either the Aemilii or the Men of the Golden Eagle to run away.

I saw Brighde's eyes fixed anxiously on me, and I smiled reassurance. Then singling out one of the crowd of slaves who by now were pressing around the door:

"Run wake Tasciovanus," I commanded. "Bid him turn out the slaves and clients and make ready to defend the wall for an hour. Speed!" The man dashed off, and turning to Lugos: "Your horse is in the courtyard?" I asked.

"By the well," he answered. "Do you want him?"

"Yes."

Brighde's face grew dark, and she spat the one word: "Coward!" at me. But I lacked time to explain, and went on:

"Do you, Lugos, remain here and aid the defence—"

"May I not go with you, General?" he begged. "It may be that Caesar can find some use for me."

"Do as I bid you!" I snapped, and rushed from the room.

In the courtyard, I bellowed to the gatekeeper to open, and vaulting on the horse's back, I gave full rein. The camp was about two miles from the city gates, and therefore some three miles from Tasciovanus' home, which lay on the river side of the city. The guards made no bones about passing me out, and a hundred yards from the city gates I turned off on a rocky track which was little more than a goat-path. My sturdy little Britannic pony scrambled along at a good pace over the uneven ground, and when half way to the camp I saw, a quarter of a mile to one side, the tossing, bobbing torches of Camulus' raiders. They had forgotten their discipline—rather, Camulus was not able to maintain it—and they streamed along in a disorderly mob. I grinned to myself; so much the better for me.

Reaching the camp, I found a horrible confusion; no guards were at the gates, no sentries on the walls, and within the enclosure men were running wildly and aimlessly about, or standing in knots to argue and dispute at the tops of their voices. Evidently the excitement was too much for their discipline, and the childlike minds of the Britanni had succumbed to the pressure.

I noted with satisfaction, though, that the Commander's Own stood firm in line of battle, their centurions and decurions in place, and Orgetorix out in front, the golden standard firmly clasped in his hand; every man was rigid and at attention, as though waiting the signal to charge, and the torch-bearers held their brands aloft at the proper intervals. As I approached I raised my hand and cried aloud "Good men!" Then to Orgetorix himself: "Well done!"

Taking the silver whistle from my belt, I blew the "Assembly." Again and again I blew, till other whistles through the camp took up the call, and to my inexpressible delight the men heeded the notes, ran for their armor, and fell into line. When all were ranked and all sound was hushed, I urged my horse up a slight eminence and addressed the warriors.

"Men of the Dumnonii!" I cried. "There is treason among us. Camulus has led his men against Tasciovanus, planning to slay the chieftain and me, to seize the chieftainship, and to take my wife for his own. Even now he is besieging the stronghold of Tasciovanus; even now they are fighting at the gates.

"Are you traitors also? Will you permit this foul wrong? Or are you true men? Will you follow me, to stop

Camulus' treason?" Drawing my sword, I brandished it over my head. "By Tarvos Trigaranus, if none goes with me, I go alone! Those who are loyal, those who will follow me, three paces forward!"

The moonlight and torchlight glimmered on shield and helmet as with a roar from thousands of throats and with clashing of javelins on shields the ranks surged forward, then at my lifted hand they fell silent once more.

"Good men!" I shouted. "The Fourth Legion and the cavalry to stay and guard the camp. The others form in line of march and follow me."

The centurions repeated the order, the whistles shrilled, and while the lines re-formed I sprang from my horse, gave him a slap on the flank which sent him cantering off, and placing myself at the head of the troops, I led them out through the *Porta Praetoria* and calling for double time, set off toward the city.

We covered the distance to the city gates at a steady trot, then I slowed to a walk, that we might come fresh to the fighting. Along the main street we flowed like a mighty river, hearing in the distance the uproar of the fight, the confused sound of the attack, seeing in the houses flitting lights, and meeting terrified burghers who ran to and fro about the streets like the foolish insects which in summer skitter back and forth on the smooth surface of a pond.

Presently we were close enough to see the thousands of Camulus assaulting the palisade, to distinguish the shouts and the clash of arms. Torches in the hands of the men and on the neighboring roofs mingled their yellow glare with the cold light of the moon, and their smoke flowed in wafts and billows across the scene. Ladders had been placed, and men were scaling the palisade and leaping down into the courtyard to be received by the defenders, while others fought desperately on the roofs, standing precariously on the slanting thatch or rolling in fierce grapple down the slope to crash on the stones below. Arrows and javelins flew thick, and in one place a bucket-brigade handed water along in leathern pails to extinguish a fire in the thatch. Shouts, cries, clash of weapons, groans, and curses mingled with the shrill screams of women and children to form a pandemonium of noise which the home of Rhadamanthus could not surpass, and ever and again I heard above the uproar the deep voice of Tasciovanus booming encouragement to his defenders.

I shouted an order, the whistles blew a piercing note, and my men opened out in the narrow space about the stronghold. Another blast, and with a roar of "Andate! Andate! Aemilius Victor!" we charged the attackers.

Happily, the men of Camulus were mostly from the south, men of the Carnabii, between whom and the Dumnonii there lay an ancient jealousy. We smote them in the rear, forcing them against the palisade, and for a time there raged a furious mêlée of thrust and cut, stab and slash, of savage and deadly slaughter. But we outnumbered them two to one, and it was the old story of disciplined troops against a mob; my men held to their training, but those of Camulus had thrown the lesson to the winds.

It chanced that Camulus and I met face to face, and he, raging, furious, cast aside all thought of fencing and rushed at me with flailing sword. Coolly I took his blade on my shield, brought his shield up with a feint at his eyes, and drove my sword with an upward thrust into his belly, till the point touched his heart and he died. A cry went up "Camulus is slain!" and panic ran through the ranks of the traitors, so that within half an hour from the time of our first charge the last of them either lay stretched in death upon the ground or was fleeing blindly for the south.

The gates were thrown open, and bidding the centurions bivouac the men in the square outside the palisade, I marched in at the head of my tribunes. Within the courtyard bodies lay scattered thick, and men sprawled in the fantastic poses of death or writhed and groaned in agony on the cold stones. Slaves and clients, both men and women, flitted here and there, despatching the traitors who still breathed, or bringing succor to their own.

Brighde descended on me like a whirlwind, flinging her arms about my neck and crying:

"Gaius, Gaius, forgive me that I called you coward! I should have known—oh, Gaius, you are in truth a gorgeous fighter! Forgive me!" She wore again the armor of our flight, and her right arm was red from swordpoint to shoulder—*per Martes,* she had not stood aloof from the fighting! What a wife for a centurion of the Tenth!

Tasciovanus greeted me with open arms.

"By Tarvos Trigaranus!" he bellowed. "You came in the nick of time—the traitors were about to overwhelm us. Ho, slaves, bring mead!" There is the typical Britannic mind for you—every occasion of joy or grief must have a drink. "It is you for the head-work, Son," he went on. "Not but that you are a grand man of your hands— I should be the last to deny it—but I have never known your like for planning." And he insisted on me and my tribunes drinking with him then and there.

At length I managed to get him calmed down a trifle and led him and the tribunes into the house and to the huge dining-hall for a conference. More mead was brought, and a great babble of tongues ensued, some advising a punitive expedition against the Carnabii, others that we attack the Belgae and the Atrebates—in short, each man putting forth some wild suggestion of his own. Seeing that naught was likely to come of this save the usual barbarian drunkenness, I rose and pounded on the table with my swordhilt, then when their attention was secured I addressed the crowd.

"We are in no position to attack the northern tribes," I said. "We have lost a quarter of our men through the treason of Camulus, and we shall need our full strength against the Belgae. On the other hand, without the loot of the Belgian and Atrebatian fields, we shall need what grain we can raise, for our own support. As for the Carnabii, they have had their lesson; most of their fight-ing-men are destroyed, so that they cannot attack us; we need fear no revolt from the south, so why pursue the re-mainder with vengeance? And for another thing, I have sure knowledge that Caesar is planning another invasion of the lands of the Cantii.

"Now, it would be an incalculable advantage to us to be known as 'Friends of Rome.' Trust me, who know the mighty genius of the Imperator and the irresistible power of the Roman state as well as the resources of Britannia —trust me, I say, that resistance is folly; those who resist will be enslaved as surely as the sun rises in the east, as surely as rain dampens the earth beneath. But how if we show ourselves ready to profit by the culture of Rome? You have seen what Roman discipline, what Roman train-ing, is worth in war. Without that training, could we have destroyed the Silures? And it was our discipline that overwhelmed Camulus—not so much the discipline in fight, though that counted also, as the discipline which held the Commander's Own steadfast when the outbreak began. And believe me, Nobles, Rome is as great in the arts of peace as in those of war.

"Why not profit by the chance the Gods lay open to us? We must have grain, therefore let us disband the army and return the men to their homes to sow and harvest against our needs. But also let us send troops to aid Caesar against the Cantii and the other northern tribes, thereby gaining his goodwill and at the same time cutting down the strength of our Britannic foes. Who among us would not relish a turn with the Cantii and the Catuvellauni? Or have you forgotten the defeat which the Cantii inflicted on the Dumnonii not so long ago?" A growl of anger answered this question.

"Then if you approve," I went on, "I will take the cavalry and the centurions—or such as are loyal—and meet Caesar at Portus Dubris. He will receive us gladly and with honor.

"Well, Nobles, what think you of the plan?"

"I am for it!" shouted Lugos. "Whatever the General says is right with me."

"And I! And I!" chimed in others, but Togodumnus, one of the tribunes, asked:

"How if the Belgae and the Atrebates attack us while our troops are disbanded? They will eat us alive, as Polyphemus ate the comrades of Odysseus."

Edepol, here was a literate barbarian—even though he erred somewhat, for the Cyclops slew the Ithacans ere devouring them. I laughed as I answered:

"Trust me, the northern tribes are going to be too busy this summer to plan any invasion against the Dumnonii."

"Suppose," another offered, "that the Roman invasion fails? We shall have all Britannia against us, and no defenders."

I smiled and shook my head.

"It will not fail," I answered, simply.

More debate followed, to be ended at length by Tasciovanus, who rose in his place, red from head to foot, a bloody kerchief binding his forehead.

"I never thought to see the day," boomed the giant, "when I should be helping a foreign invader of our land. But Gaius is wiser than all of us together; he has traveled more, has seen more lands, is more able in both war and politics, his judgment is better. This he has clearly shown in saving us from the Silures, and again from Camulus and the Carnabii. Whatever Gaius says, that I approve." And he sat down. "Son, when do we march?"

"You do not march at all," I rejoined. "You stay here to maintain order and to rule the land. I and my cavalry start at noon, prepared for a long, hard ride. Lugos, see to it that the men are ready."

Lugos rose and saluted.

"Yes, Imperator," he said.

" 'General,' " I corrected him. "There is but one Imperator."

"Yes, General," he returned. "All will be ready at noon."

"Does Brighde go with you?" inquired Tasciovanus.

"She does not. There is no place for a woman in a Roman camp."

The chieftain stroked his beard thoughtfully.

"It is in my mind," he reflected, aloud, "that there may be some trouble in persuading her to remain at home; she appears to feel some attachment for you. Odd as it may seem," he added.

I grinned at him.

"Father-in-law, you are improving," I complimented him. I thought of my wife's remarks of the night before. "There will be no difficulty in persuading her to stay behind." I pointed to the slitted window, where the eastern sky glowed red with the dawn. We could still hear the voices of the slaves and clients as they moved about the courtyard, clearing up, and the sound of their feet as they brought the wounded under shelter. "The night is gone," I said. "Aurora peers in at us. One last drink, then to get a little rest ere we march."

All sprang to their feet and extended their full goblets toward me.

"To Gaius Aemilius Durus of the Dumnonii!" bellowed Tasciovanus, and he and the others poured the amber mead down their throats, then held out the empty goblets, upside down.

Rising, I acknowledged the toast, saying:

"To you, Nobles, and to the Dumnonii." But as I emptied the goblet I added, silently: "And first of all, to the Imperator."

Some hours later, at the head of my two thousand cavalry, I rode out from Isca of the Dumnonii and struck into the Great Western Highway that leads to Londinium. It was not my plan to go clear to the latter town; I would turn off several miles west of it, skirt south, and so to Portus Dubris, but for most of the distance this was our route.

Our mounts, of course, were but the shaggy little ponies of the country, far different from the great chargers of the Germani or the powerful warhorses of the Sabine Hills, and ridiculous enough they looked with the huge men of the Dumnonii straddling them, the warriors' feet almost trailing on the ground. But though small, the beasts were sturdy and enduring enough to carry their riders a good fifty miles a day, and I counted on reaching our destination in six days at the most.

I noticed, from time to time, a good deal of sly amusement among the troopers, but paid no attention to it, being fully occupied with my own thoughts; in any case, I

would have said nothing, for it is always best not to seem
to notice anything of the sort—it will come out in the end,
and curiosity is undignified in a commander.

I had food for thought in plenty. Aside from the question of how Caesar would greet us—though I had no fears
on that score—there was the further question of whether
or not we should reach the coast before he did, and have
to maintain ourselves in a hostile country until his arrival.
Happily, I had both infantry and cavalry, for my men
could fight as well on foot as on horseback, and since they
were schooled in the Roman discipline I believed we could
make good our stand for some days at least. And of course
we should be fighting from within a fortified camp.

Then there was the matter of Brighde. She had forgiven me, in view of what I did to the traitors, and when
I said good-bye to her she clung about my neck, weeping
and imploring me to take her with me, until I had to
loosen her arms by force and speak sternly to make her
accept my decision. In truth, it was harder for me than
for her, since I did not tell her my plan in full, and she
looked confidently forward to my return within a few
months, whereas I had no definite intention of ever going
back to Isca, and did not know whether or not I should
ever see my wife again. I hoped to send for her to join
me in Rome when the troubles were over, but the Gods
Themselves could not tell when that would be, or what
might happen in the meantime. Aye, it was a wrench, and
a heavy one, but after all a true Roman must be ready to
leave home and family when the Republic has need of
him, and my first allegiance was to Rome and to the Imperator.

Our best safety lay in speed and in taking all possible
precautions, so I urged my men along as rapidly as I
could—my plan was to sweep through the hostile country

before our hereditary foes could gather to attack us—and each night I had the troops make a fortified camp in the correct manner.

Our second day took us past Sorbiodunum, which we left south of us, the going being vastly easier on the Great Plain than in the Forest of Anderida. Our route lay past the Standing Stones, and you may judge what memories they brought back to me! Nay, I could even recognize the very clump of gorse beside which Brighde's tent had been pitched, nor do I think it shame to admit that my throat was dry as we rode past. The nineteen virgins who tend the fire of the Goddess Brighde—Goddess of Fire and Dew—on the altar of the Standing Stones came to the doors of their rude dwellings to gaze curiously at us as we thundered by, and some of my men waved to them, drawing in return a wave of the hand in greeting. *Per Deos Immortales,* I can see our Vestals waving their hands to a troop of guerrillas!—they would not so much as deign to turn their heads to glance our way, nor would they notice so insignificant a worm as a mere soldier. But these barbarians lack the dignity of the sons and daughters of Quirinus.

We did a little better than fifty miles a day, and on the fifth we pitched our camp on the crest of a rolling down which overlooked the shore where Caesar landed on the previous year. The old camp was still there, but I did not use it; it was far too large for my twenty centuries to defend against assault.

Fortuna favored us, it seemed, for about midnight or a trifle after, my sentries roused me with word that an armada was making its way up the Channel. The camp was astir, and hastening to the rampart, I found there practically my whole troop, eagerly watching the hundreds of lanterns which marked the Imperator's fleet.

Excitement ran high, and great was the chatter, but my heart sank within me as I noted that the flood tide, sweeping up the Channel, was carrying the ships far to the north of us. Doubtless Caesar was making to another landing-place—perchance the Isle of Fires or even Londinium—and we should have to fight our way to his side through swarming foes. Well, it could not be helped; such is the fortune of war.

While thus I watched the yellow lanterns and the ships, the latter half-seen in the nocturnal light of that northern country, I felt a hand slipped through my arm. Looking sharply around to see who dared such familiarity, my astonished eyes met those of Brighde.

"Dii Immortales!" I swore in amazement. "How in the Name of Mercury did you get here? Did you fly on the wind?"

Smiling, she squeezed my arm, then wrinkled her nose at me.

"I have been with you all the time—all the way from Isca," she answered. "But you were too wrapped in your own thoughts to see me. Great stupid!"

"All the time? All the way from Isca?"

"All the way from Isca," she repeated, nodding. "I rode with you when you left the city, and have been with the troop ever since. Lugos and Bericus have been watching over me."

"In whose tent have you slept?" I demanded sternly.

Again she made a face at me.

"In my own," she said. "With four trusted men guarding it front and rear . . . are you not glad to see me, Gaius?" she went on, plaintively. "I . . . I flattered myself you would be, in spite of my disobedience. But . . . but . . ." And her eyes filled with tears.

This was too much for me; I caught her in my arms and kissed her.

"Glad!" I cried. *"Mehercle!* Am I glad? My heart was breaking! Though what I am to do with you in camp the Gods alone know."

"I have thought of that," she explained, with eagerness. "See, I am dressed in armor—" true enough, she was "—and I shall be the young brother of your wife until the campaign is ended. The men will keep the secret, and I can pass for a boy. Will it not do, Gaius?" And she gave me an appealing look.

"So that is why the men have been snickering and glancing mischievously my way! Well, well, it may work with the legionaries, but never with Caesar; one look, and he will know you for a girl. There is no deceiving that man."

"But after all, need I face him? You are not obliged to present me to him, are you?"

"No, but he will see you in action sooner or later. However, he is not likely to betray you; the Imperator has a most infinite capacity for silence."

"Then I am to stay?"

"Dii Immortales, what else is there to do, bad girl? Can I send you back to Isca through a country that is roused by our passage? You, alone? *Per Martes,* we may have to fight our own way back!"

"You . . . you are not angry with me, are you?" she pleaded, looking anxiously into my face.

"I should be, for thrusting yourself into peril against my orders . . . but after all, it will be pleasant to have an Amazonian wife riding beside me into battle. I will rename you Penthesilea, I think. And you must have a bodyguard . . . however, I forgive you."

My joy must have shown through the sternness of my manner, for after another look at me she squeezed my arm again and rubbed her cheek against my shoulder.

And so we stood and watched the mighty fleet of Caesar disappear from view up the Channel.

CHAPTER XI

Of the Second Invasion; and How I Returned to Rome

SHORTLY after dawn the tide turned, and to my delight the flotilla came down the Channel with the ebb, landing at a spot some ten miles north of where we put ashore the previous year. This time the Cantii had not gathered to oppose the landing, so I and my troopers were unmolested as we rode north to report to Caesar.

The armada was a tremendous one, far greater than the first, including more than eight hundred ships of various kinds, and transporting about twenty thousand legionaries, two thousand Gallic cavalry, and numerous foreign slingers and archers. This mighty force was in the act of disembarking when we drew near, and at sight of us the well-remembered notes of the bugles summoned the troops to line of battle. But I left my men behind, and with only Lugos and two other tribunes for companions I rode down to where I saw the Golden Eagle gleaming in the noon-day sun.

When I was within a few yards of the line there was a shout, and a man rushed at me.

"Frenator!" he cried. *"Dii Immortales,* it is Frenator!"

Leaping from my horse, I clasped Bombyx in my arms —for it was my *collusor* himself—and we hugged and embraced each other, while sundry old-time friends came running to greet me. Lest any misjudge the discipline of the Tenth, let me say that these were centurions, and might properly leave their places in an emergency; the rank and file stood fast.

We had the gayest of reunions there on the sand, with hand-shaking and questions in plenty, till Volusenus came hurrying to see what it was all about. He too hailed me with evident pleasure, insisting that I go at once to the Imperator.

"It is what I came for," I rejoined. "You may as well let the disembarking proceed; my scouts tell me that the Cantii, who gathered to oppose you, have returned home, dismayed by the size of the fleet." And indeed I had received such a report that very morning.

He glanced toward the Dumnonii, drawn up in battle array some three or four hundred paces distant.

"How of those?" he queried, and I smiled as I answered:

"They are mine, come to offer allegiance to the Imperator. Two thousand well-trained cavalry."

"Yours! *Dii Immortales!* Who are you, then, in this wild land?"

"I am war-chief of the Dumnonii," I explained, and Volusenus swore in amazement, while Bombyx cried:

"Dear child of Fortuna! Said I not he would fall on his feet, like a cat? To my heart again, Frenator!"

"Per Martes, they are welcome," Volusenus exclaimed. "But, my Gaius, come with me."

We found Caesar on the deck of a war-ship, whence he could overlook the work of disembarking, and he also greeted me in friendly manner.

"We thought you were lost, Gaius," he said, kindly, "and give thanks to Fortuna that it is not so. What troops are these?"

"Two thousand of the Dumnonii, Imperator," I answered. "They are trained in the Roman discipline, and can fight either as cavalry or as foot-soldiers. They are come to offer you their allegiance and their aid."

He raised his eyebrows.

"What is your position among them?"

"I am their leader. I am war-chief of the tribe of the Dumnonii."

He turned the blaze of his eyes on me, and I felt as though a javelin had pierced my stomach. His voice was cold as he said:

"I find it difficult to believe that one of my centurions would desert me for what honors a barbarian tribe could offer him."

"Nor did I, Imperator. As Jupiter Optimus Maximus sees me, I did not leave the legions voluntarily."

"Explain."

In a half-dozen sentences I summarized my adventures of the past year, and he nodded acknowledgment. His look and tones were softer as he replied:

"I was loath to think you would be unfaithful to Caesar."

"Never, Imperator!"

He smiled faintly.

"And you trained these men in the discipline of Rome?"

"These and twenty thousand more—I should say fifteen thousand, for an insurrection cost me a quarter of them."

"But you put it down?"

"*Edepol!*"

"You seem to have made excellent use of your time, Gaius," he went on. "But why did you not bring the others as well?"

"It was not possible, Imperator." I gave my reasons, and he nodded again. "They await you when you reach Belerium," I concluded.

"That is in the lap of the Gods; it may not be for this year. But you have done excellently, my Gaius, excellently." I felt my cheeks flush at the warmth of his praise. "Let me see," he went on. "Your old position is filled; Bombyx is centurion in your place. Yet the man who brings us two thousand cavalry, and has made the Dumnonii our friends, must have a reward. H'm! Trebonius commands the Gallic cavalry; suppose I give you command of these you have brought, with the rank of *legatus*. Will that satisfy you?"

Glowing with pleasure, I saluted and replied:

"It is all I had hoped for, and more, Imperator."

"Very well. We must hear your story at length, when leisure offers. Now bring in your men; they are to be enrolled as a separate command. You may go."

Saluting again, I rode off to my troops, my heart full of rejoicing; to be a *legatus,* ranking with Labienus, Cotta, Sabinus, and the others—*mehercle,* who would not be proud? And my men cheered again and again at the news of my promotion; they rejoiced because I was glad, and because they would shine in reflected glory, though Lugos the tribune loyally remarked:

"After all, it is no more than you deserve."

The landing completed, ten cohorts and three hundred cavalry, under Quintus Atrius, were left to protect the fleet, and Caesar marched the rest of us inland three or four miles, in the general direction of Londinium, to make camp on a slight rise of ground. Under orders, I sent about five hundred of my men, commanded by Lugos, to reconnoitre, and they brought in some prisoners who reported that the Cantii, in great numbers, were bivouacked near Durovernum, twelve miles farther on.

The Imperator decided on a surprise attack, allowed us only a few hours' rest, and at midnight led us toward the enemy. We met them at dawn, and after a sharp engagement drove them into the woods west of Durovernum, where they took refuge in a typical Britannic stronghold. This was hardly more than an earthwork with an abatis of logs, and the Seventh Legion, advancing under a *testudo,* filled the ditch with fascines and earth, then speedily drove the natives in flight. By this time it was afternoon, so we made camp and prepared for rest.

As a *legatus,* I was lodged in the Praetorium, the tent of the commander-in-chief, with the other lieutenant-generals and the tribunes, so obviously I could not take Brighde with me. Therefore I arranged for her to have a tent of her own, and I appointed a bodyguard to watch over her day and night. As excuse for this I gave out— through Bombyx and Arcularius—that I had married in Britannia and this was my wife's younger brother, making his first campaign, wherefore I wanted him specially guarded. Most if not all of the legionaries believed the tale, and since Brighde naturally associated but little with the Roman troops, it passed muster.

The morning of the second day, a council of officers was called, at which the Imperator read a letter that struck consternation to our hearts. It was from Atrius, saying that a storm of wind had dashed the ships ashore, that many had collided with one another, and that a large number were destroyed or seriously damaged. This was a calamity indeed, not only for the actual loss and the danger to our communications, but even more for the injury to our prestige, since it necessitated postponing the invasion and returning the whole army at once to the coast. But there was nothing else for it, so back we went,

Caesar hurrying on ahead to see with his own eyes what harm had been wrought.

Many persons have blamed the Imperator for not taking the obvious precaution of drawing his vessels beyond reach of the waves as soon as they were unloaded, but to my way of thinking he was justified. The time he could give to this invasion was limited, every day was of value, and though of course he knew the risk he calmly accepted it, trusting to Fortuna. That she played him false in no way invalidates his judgment; every commander is obliged to take chances that he would prefer to avoid.

The next ten days were ones of most intense activity. About forty of the ships had been totally destroyed, but the rest could be repaired, and Caesar set to work to haul these up beyond the danger mark and to get them in condition for sailing. Galleys were hastened off with letters to Labienus ordering him to despatch gangs of shipwrights to Britannia (he had been left with three legions to keep order in Gallia Transalpina) and the rest of us set about preparing capstans and greased ways to haul the vessels up on dry ground. Mamurra and his artificers dismantled the most seriously damaged ships, using the materials to repair the others, torches and fires were got ready, and the men were told off into shifts of eight hours each, that the work might go on day and night without interruption. Thus after ten days and nights of toil we had all secure, with an earthwork to protect the ships from attack, and the Imperator turned again to the conquest.

During this period he sent one day for me, had a chair set and wine brought, and spent more than two hours in questioning me as to the habits and customs of the Britanni, their religion, the relations between the various tribes, the resources and wealth of the country, its civilization, the size of the island, the climate—in short, everything that could be of interest not only to a general but to a statesman. I realize now, as I did not then, that he was thinking of the land as a place for colonization, but at all events I answered as fully as I could, and later had the satisfaction of seeing my replies incorporated in his letters *De Bello Gallico*. But he must have drawn some of his information from a less reliable source, for in these letters he says that the Britannic wives are accustomed to have several husbands at one time, and I could never have made so ridiculous a statement. Monogamy and monandry are as rigorously practiced in Britannia as in Rome, the barbarians holding, as we do, that the family is the unit of society, and the oldest male in the line of succession is the rightful head thereof.

The Britanni made good use of the ten days' respite. Cassivelaunus had been elected commander-in-chief of their forces, and organized his troops well, joining the Catuvellauni, the Cantii, the Regni—in fact, all the tribes of southeastern Britannia save only the Trinovantes—in a huge confederacy against Rome. The Trinovantes, occupying the country to north and east of Londinium, were at perpetual feud with the Catuvellauni, and sent ambassadors to Caesar to make submission and ask protection from their foes. The ruler of the Trinovantes, a youth named Mandubracius, had fled to Caesar in Gallia Transalpina when Cassivelaunus invaded his lands during the spring of that same year, and Caesar, taking hostages, now sent Mandubracius back to his own country, guaranteeing him protection.

The ships being safe, the Imperator resumed his march toward Londinium, fighting a dozen skirmishes a day with the men of Cassivelaunus, who continually opposed us.

It cannot be denied that they harassed us badly, for the native chieftain made skilful use of the irregular mode of fighting to which his troops were accustomed, and steadfastly refused to meet us in a pitched battle. Since the Roman discipline involves a solid and ordered line, and since the heavy-armed legionary cannot well pursue the light-armed barbarian, it follows that the strike-and-run tactics of the natives caused us much annoyance and considerable loss. Not such total annihilation as the Parthians wrought on Crassus at Carrhae, to be sure, for several reasons; first, they were fewer in number than the Parthians; second, they were less able bowmen; third, we had better cavalry than Crassus had; fourth, the nature of the country favored us more than the sandy desert of Mesopotamia did Crassus; and fifth—and more than all else put together—Caesar was a far greater general than his colleague of the Triumvirate. But even so, they gave us trouble enough, and I and my men had fighting enough to satisfy the greediest, for the brunt of each affair was borne by the cavalry.

At length, however, we had our revenge, for on a certain day the barbarians, elated by success, got out of control, and in spite of all Cassivelaunus could do they pressed home an attack on the legions. Of course that delivered them into our hands, for the line stood firm, Trebonius smote the natives on one flank while I drove in on the other, and we hurled them in utter rout, following so closely that not even the charioteers could find opportunity to turn upon us. We slew thousands of them, and instilled such fear into their hearts that nearly all the allies save the Catuvellauni deserted to their homes, nor did the barbarians ever again meet us save in trifling guerrilla raids.

Cassivelaunus still had about four thousand chariots

and a few horsemen, and with these he harassed us when opportunity offered, but was not able to do more than to annoy us faintly, and we marched on Londinium practically unopposed. Not that Caesar cared aught for Londinium, though; his real purpose was to confirm the Trinovantes in their allegiance and to punish the Catuvellauni—all, of course, subject to his fundamental motive of exploring the country. For this reason he called me to him one day, asking:

"Gaius, I am planning to take Verulamium, the stronghold of Cassivelaunus. Do you know the route thither?"

"Yes, Imperator. That is to say, I have never been there, but I know the road."

"And where the Tamesis may best be crossed?"

"I should know that, Imperator," I smiled, "after the months I spent in that region. The only practicable ford is about ten miles west of Londinium; elsewhere one must cross in boats."

"We have not yet had the full tale of your adventures," he remarked, thoughtfully. "Still, that must wait. Meanwhile, take your cavalry and scout ahead to the ford, to see if we can cross without opposition or if it is defended. You may take your wife with you."

I stared at him.

"My wife!"

"Your brother-in-law, if you prefer," he smiled. "Nay, I will not betray your secret—indeed, I commend your discretion—but though the tale of a brother-in-law may impose on the men, I am not beguiled since I have seen her. I congratulate you, Gaius; she is very beautiful, and seems a woman of spirit."

"Yes, Imperator," I stammered. For all that I had more than half expected this, I was taken aback when it occurred. "Yes, in truth, she is all you say. She—"

"Never mind that, just now. Present her to me when opportunity offers. Meanwhile, guard her well; the men are fond of you and respect you, but my babes are not exactly lamblike where women are concerned."

"I will do my best to guard her, Imperator."

"You will be well advised," he remarked dryly, "to do somewhat better than your best. Listen, Gaius; for her safety bring her to the Praetorium; I will appoint her a tribune, and she will be safer than in the camp. And keep close to her in battle."

"I have already given her a bodyguard, Imperator."

"I am aware of it. Even so, bring her to the Praetorium. In the Name of Vesta, what possessed you to bring her with you to the army?"

"I did not. I strictly forbade her to come. And I told her that the story of her being her own younger brother— that is, of her being my brother-in-law—that is—well, you know what I mean—that it would not deceive you. But she came in spite of me. She is a headstrong piece."

He smiled, and gave one of his rare chuckles.

"What woman is not?" he asked. "But get rid of her as soon as possible; the camp is no place for her."

"I had thought of sending her to Rome, Imperator. I feel sure that Flava Rufus will take charge of her while I am on campaign. And Flava and Tiberius Rufus are well able to protect her."

He nodded again.

"A sound scheme. And I will pass the word to my kinsmen to have an eye on her. She will be safe under the aegis of the Julii—not to mention the Aemilii and the Cornelii. Meanwhile, bring her to me; her commission will be ready. What name does she use as your brother-in-law?"

"Caratacus, Imperator. Her real name is Brighde."

"It is well. You may go."

However, it proved impossible to keep the secret. I never knew who let it out, but shortly after the westward march began, a deputation called on me one day while the evening meal was being prepared. Bombyx, Arcularius, Scaevola, and two other centurions of the Tenth composed it, and though I freely granted them audience they seemed ill at ease, nudging one another and fidgeting even more than was natural when addressing a *legatus*. At length Bombyx was thrust forward as spokesman, and on my urging him he began.

"Frenator . . . General . . . General, I mean . . ." he stammered.

"Well, what is it? Speak up!"

"General," he repeated. Then taking his courage in both hands he blurted out: "It is reported that your wife is with you in the camp. . . ."

Looking back on the situation from the vantage-point of years, I am convinced that I over-estimated the danger of discovery; Caesar's favor, my reputation, and the presence of two thousand of her own tribesmen would in any case have protected Brighde. But it was one of those affairs that are more alarming at the time than in retrospect, and I turned slightly sick at his words. But putting a bold face on it:

"Well?" I asked.

"General, the Tenth esteem you . . . they . . . we hold you in admiration . . . and they have sent us to ask if you will not grant us permission to take her as our patroness. It is said that she rides into battle, and the men feel that with her at our head Fortuna could not fail to attend us. We should be proud! We pray you grant us the favor; those who know her say she is a gallant fighter, in the Roman tradition . . . it would hearten the men vastly. . . ."

Judge if this was a load off my spirit! Protected and guarded by the Men of the Golden Eagle, riding as their patroness, Brighde would be safe beyond any aid I could give—as safe as though in her father's house in Isca. Still, there were objections, and I voiced one.

"But I am no longer of the Tenth. I am with the *auxilia*, the native troops."

"That need not hinder," spoke up Scaevola, as he saw signs of my yielding. "You could march with the *auxilia*, and she with us. *Per Martes*, General, we would guard her as we guard the Golden Eagle!"

"And," Bombyx added, "you will come back to us in time."

I thought it over, then finally conceded:

"It rests with her and with Caesar. The Dumnonii would object to her being taken from them—they would resent it bitterly—but if Caesar will incorporate them with the Tenth, it may be arranged."

"Thank you, General," they chorused. "Will you speak to him?"

I promised, and dismissed them.

On my broaching the matter to the Imperator, he was at first doubtful, but in the end gave his consent.

"It is unusual," he said. "Nay, unheard-of; it has never been done in a Roman army. Still, that is no good reason to refuse; after all, the legends tell us that Penthesilea and her Amazons fought side by side with Hector and Aeneas at the siege of Ilium. Yes, on the whole, I think the plan a good one; she will be safer thus—they will cherish her like the Palladium; like a very goddess—and the moral effect will be great. By all means let it be done."

He chuckled with amusement. "It will give Pompeius and his henchmen something to mull over—a Roman legion led by a girl!"

So Brighde received a full set of Roman-made armor, was mounted on a huge white stallion from Gallia Transalpina, and rode at the head of the Tenth during the rest of the campaign. The men fairly adored her, even changing their war-cry for the time being from "Venus Victrix" to "Venus atque Brighde," and was she a proud girl when first she heard that roar go up from four thousand mighty throats! Nor, I must admit, was I myself ill-pleased.

All this occurred after my return from the reconnoitring expedition, from which I reported to Caesar that the ford of the Tamesis was protected by a row of sharpened stakes that were sunk in the river-bed just below the surface of the water, and that Cassivelaunus was encamped on the northern bank to dispute our passage. However, all this availed the barbarians nothing, for when we came to the ford the Imperator sent the cavalry ahead to force a way, following them with the infantry, and though the tide was at flood and the water so deep that the foot-soldiers barely had their heads above the surface, the attack was made with such dash and spirit that horse and foot reached the farther bank practically together; the Tenth, of course, must needs win the approval of their new patroness, and the other legions, envious of the Tenth's glory, would not be outdone. The barbarians could not withstand this savage charge, and following a half-hearted attempt at resistance, fled in confusion, nor did we again catch sight of them until we reached Verulamium, the capital of the Catuvellauni.

This town was a moderately strong place, reasonably well fortified and further protected by woods and a marsh, but we attacked on two sides at once and carried it in a few hours, slaying many of the barbarians and taking several thousand prisoners, to be carried back to Gallia Transalpina and sold as slaves. Also, the Catuvellauni had concentrated practically all their cattle at this place, and these we drove off, the effect of this victory being the definite end of all resistance.

The Trinovantes sent in the hostages and the grain that Caesar had demanded, and five of their dependent tribes made submission, these being the Segontiaci, the Cenimagni, the Ancalites, the Cassi, and the Bibroci. The slaves and herds, however, were to all intents and purposes the whole of our booty, for Britannia is not a rich country; aside from the tin mines of Belerium and a few iron mines of little importance, it has no natural resources. In time, though, it may repay development as an agricultural land.

During this advance of ours, the Cantii and the Regni, inspired by Cassivelaunus, gathered themselves together and made an attack on our ships, but Atrius beat them off with little trouble, and making a sortie, captured their chief, one Lugotorix. Learning of this, Caesar made a hurried trip to the coast, accompanied only by a few hundred of the Tenth, to assure himself that all was well. Returning, he got back to Verulamium in time to receive the ambassadors of Cassivelaunus; the Britannic chief, disheartened by the failure of the attack on the ships, abandoned all hope and made humble submission. According to his custom, Caesar showed mercy to the vanquished foe, merely imposing a tribute and enjoining on Cassivelaunus that he refrain from harassing the Trinovantes.

So far, only the southeastern part of Britannia was subdued, wherefore Caesar planned to winter in the island and complete the conquest during the following summer. But letters from Labienus informed him that Gallia Transalpina was in a dangerous condition, with many of the tribes, especially in the north, giving evidence of restlessness, so the Imperator commanded a return to the Continent.

On the night before the day we sailed, which was the seventeenth before the Kalends of October,* as the embarkation was taking place, a sudden whim struck me, and leaving the shore I walked two or three hundred paces inland, where from a little rise I could overlook the whole operation. I could safely leave, for Lugos and the centurions were competent to get my cavalry on board without my oversight.

It was an impressive spectacle, with the hundreds of ships anchored in shoal water, the thousands of flickering yellow torches and fires to light the work, and the long lines of men and horses either quietly waiting their turn or, when it came, moving in orderly procession to the place assigned. Of course there was much shouting of commands to and fro, with signals from trumpet or bugle, but there was no jostling, no confusion. As far as the eye could reach along the coast all was order and precision, and I thrilled with admiration of the mighty genius that could so organize and train these thousands of men that he need say but the one word: "Embark," and all would be carried out with perfect smoothness and accuracy.

While I thought thus, I saw a man climbing the slope toward me, and as he drew near I recognized the Imperator; his *paludamentum*, the long cloak which marked his rank, could not disguise that erect, proud figure, or the alert turn of his head. Standing at attention, I saluted, and he returned it with equal smartness, then said:

"Ah, Gaius, we had the same thought, it seems. You came up for a general view of the work?"

* September 15.

"Yes, Imperator."

"A goodly sight, is it not? One to fill the heart with pride at being a Roman, eh?"

"In very truth, yes, Imperator!"

"Your men can handle their task without you?"

"I have trained them to that end as best I could."

He nodded agreement.

"You have done well, my Gaius." And my heart swelled at the approval in his voice. "And you have done well for yourself," he went on, reflectively. "From enlisted man to *legatus* in four years—is it not?—is no small stride. But you have earned it. Yes, it is deserved."

"I had a good teacher, Imperator," I ventured, and he flashed me a smile.

"Well, Gaius, look your fill," he said. "It may chance that you will never see the like again."

"We shall be coming back next year, shall we not?"

He was silent for a time, then answered slowly:

"I do not know . . . I do not know. . . ."

There flashed into my mind what Tiberius had said, and what Marcus Ganeum had told of the disorders in the City, and I understood Caesar's doubt, his hesitation. I turned this over in my thoughts, then, greatly daring—for though a *legatus,* and though loving Caesar, I went in awe of him, as in truth did all his men—I yielded to an impulse.

"Imperator," I said, rather timidly.

"Yes, Gaius?"

"Imperator . . . if it should come to civil war, I and all these—" I waved my hand toward the shore "—will be at your side."

He whirled on me, and I felt the impact of his gaze, almost like a physical shock.

"Who told you aught of civil war?" he demanded, sharply.

"Tiberius Rufus first suggested it, and my own wits confirm it," I answered, holding my ground. "The Senate is at cross-purposes, the party of the Populares is gaining strength, and the rule of the patricians is breaking down, nor is Pompeius Magnus the man to control the anarchy which threatens."

He stared for a moment, then broke into a short laugh.

"Edepol! So you are a statesman as well as a soldier, my Gaius?"

Daring again, I replied:

"I have an excellent example of both before me, Imperator."

He laughed once more, in kindly fashion, then turned to watch the shifting scene below us. For a long time he was silent, then he spoke, slowly and thoughtfully.

"It may come to that in the end," he said. *"Di bene vortant!*—may the Gods forbid! But it is true that the Republic is breaking down, and that anarchy is at hand— nearer than you think, for all your wit. Selfishness, greed, licentiousness, the mad scramble for wealth and power . . . the old Roman virtues are lost . . . nay—" he shook his head slightly "—nay, I cannot believe them gone forever; they are but in abeyance, to be called forth at need . . . to be called forth by a strong man. . . ." He was talking to himself, not to me. "But to seize the power, to attempt the regeneration of the State—I have often thought of it, but, *Dii Immortales,* what a task!"

I thought to myself that he was the one man in all the Republic to undertake that same task, but I did not venture to interrupt.

"I have often thought of it, my Gaius," he went on,

slowly, "and have planned what I would do. And yet . . . and yet . . . to plunge the Republic into civil war, with brother slaying brother, and son, father; Italia bathed in blood; fire and slaughter and rapine; violated hearth and ruined city—the Gods forbid that I should have these things on my soul! And if I fail, to leave a name that men will curse through all the ages . . .

"But on the other hand, anarchy, a slave rebellion, Rome at the mercy of bands of dagger-men, and more than all else, the glorious Republic of Aeneas lying defenceless against the northern tribes . . . and ruin . . .

"Yet if I do not grasp the power, who will? The Magnus? A great general, but a pattern soldier; no statesman, and under the thumb of the Optimates. Marcus Antonius? A warrior but no statesman—a body without a brain. Marcus Cicero? A statesman but no warrior—a brain without a body. Crassus? Lepidus? Clodius? Cato? Ahenobarbus?" He shook his head.

"And if the Gods give me the strength, do They not mean me to use it? But are there Gods? Are They not a figment of our brains, of our imaginations? Do They exist? Or did man invent Them? Did the Gods make man, or man, the Gods? What priest, what philosopher, can surely tell?

"Yet there is no doubt of the ruin that lies in wait for the Republic, of the gulf that yawns before us, even as the one into which Curtius leaped as a sacrifice of Rome's greatest wealth . . . a terrible sacrifice, yet it saved the City . . . perchance the Gods demand another such. . . ."

He fell silent, looking past the busy shore, out over the gently heaving waters of the Channel, and I believe there came to him a prescience, a vision of that dreadful day ten years in the future, when the Ides of Martius saw Pompeius' statue red with the blood of Rome's savior.

At length he heaved a sigh, and turning, laid his hand on my shoulder, gazing deep into my eyes, while I trembled at the honor of his touch.

"Nothing of this to anyone, my Gaius," he said, his voice firm and decisive as usual. "You have beheld Caesar in a moment of weakness; let it be a secret between us two."

I saluted.

"To share a secret with you, Imperator, is honor enough for any man. But I would not call it weakness; it is the bending of the bow that speeds the arrow."

He laughed and slapped me on the shoulder.

"Warrior, statesman, and diplomat," he said. "You should go far, my Gaius; Tiberius Rufus has taught you well.

"Now we must get on board. Say farewell to Britannia; only the Fates can tell whether or not we shall ever see this land again."

Side by side we marched down to the shore, where with a pleasant "Good-night" he left me, going on his flagship while I moved on to where the Tenth awaited me.

Little remains to tell. Some weeks later Brighde and I rode with Caesar to Gallia Cisalpina, where he halted at Ravenna, while she and I went on to Rome. Before we parted, the Imperator asked me to forego my vengeance against Clodius.

"He is useful to me," said Caesar, "and I will give you letters to him that will insure you against whatever enmity he may feel." Of course I agreed—who could refuse the Imperator when he asked a favor?—and a truce was patched up between Clodius and myself, though I never liked the man. Admitting that he had great personal charm

—even I felt it to some extent—he was an abominable scoundrel, and I rejoiced when Milo's dagger-men slew him.

In Rome, Tiberius greeted me with delight, and Flava took Brighde to her heart. From time to time I had sent Tiberius my share from the sale of slaves or plunder, and he had invested this money to such good advantage that now I found myself not rich, indeed, but comfortably well off, and able to buy back my father's house on Palatinus and most of my former City slaves. It was not until after Octavianus assumed the power that I regained my country estate, and by then the farm slaves were too widely scattered to be found. However, there was not the personal feeling toward them that there was for the *familia* of the City, whereof Doris, Pericles, and Carinthus were the first to return. It was my whim to have them purchased by a dealer and brought to my home in ignorance of their new master, and their delight on learning the circumstances was pathetic; indeed, we four wept together for very joy. Also, not telling either Brighde or him what I meant to do, I bought Adminius from Dumnorix, and took him to my house, letting him and Brighde meet all unexpectedly; he had heard no word from her since he was kidnaped. To see their happiness at the reunion was worth the years I had spent in foreign lands.

I manumitted Adminius and sent him back to Belerium, where he continued my discipline in the army, and extended the rule of his people to subdue the Durotriges and the Atrebates (this was after the death of Commius, the Atrebatian chief) and to wrest part of their lands from the Belgae. I never saw either him or Tasciovanus again, though we corresponded two or three times a year, traders carrying our letters, and thus I heard that the chieftain died full of years and of honor, content in the presence and ability of his son, and glorying in the latter's conquests.

Lugos served under me with honor and distinction, going through the rebellion of Vercingetorix, and fell, fighting bravely, at the siege of Massilia, during the Civil War. He was as dear to me as any of my comrades of the Tenth, and I had at least the comfort of being with him when he died, of receiving his last words, and of ordering special honors for him. Bombyx and Arcularius survived the hazards of war, the former now being—of all things in this world!—a bookseller in the City. Arcularius married a girl of the Aedui, and is a farmer in Gallia Transalpina; I have heard that his wife is the envy of her friends for the jewelry that she wears on holidays and public occasions.

Shortly after the accession of Caesar to the Dictatorship, I had a visit from my friend Tanarus; he was on his way to Alexandria, having been driven from Britannia by the adherents of the Chief Druid. I understand that he gained much repute in the Egyptian city as a philosopher, and died greatly respected and mourned; his views on religious matters were not too advanced for the Alexandrines, whatever they may have been for the Britanni.

In March of the year following our return to Rome, Brighde bore me a son, Gaius Iulius Aemilius Durus, and later another, Tiberius Rufus Aemilius Durus. Still later, two daughters, Flava and Brighde, who with their brothers and mother passed safely through the frightful years of the Civil War, when Tiberius and I rode side by side at Pharsalus, where the legions of Caesar drove the Optimates of Pompeius in utter rout and made our adored Imperator master of the world. Safely, too, they came through the still more dreadful time of anarchy which followed Caesar's death, and now, in the Golden Age of

Augustus, they and their mother, with our grandchildren, sit about me on the terrace of my villa at Baiae, where they can look out over the blue water of the Mare Tyrrhenum and hearken with eager ears while Tiberius Rufus and I talk over the adventures of our youth, or can listen while Doris reads aloud what I have written on this scroll.

"It is difficult," says one, when the tale ends, "to imagine Grandmother riding in armor with the Tenth Legion, or fighting with outlaws in the Great Forest of Anderida."

My wife smiles at me, and I press her hand.

"None the less, she did," I reply. "For all that your grandmother was born and grew to womanhood in the Island of the North, she has all the courage, all the virtues, of a true Roman matron. See to it that you are worthy of her."

Author's Note

Some writers have questioned the accuracy of Mommsen's belief that Gaius Julius Caesar foresaw the approach of the Civil War and deliberately planned his life through many years in order to be ready for the part he was destined to play in that crucial struggle and during the following time of Rome's regeneration. However this may be, no doubt can exist that he realized the breaking-down of the Republic, and that his conquest of Gaul and his invasions of Britain were largely motivated by a desire to rebuild the greatness of Rome by restoring, through colonization of those territories, a class of free, land-loving, patriotic burgesses to take the place of those dispossessed and driven to the cities when their farms were amalgamated into vast private estates operated with slave labor.

Many persons have regarded the invasions of Britain as a failure, and if we assume that they were undertaken for the purpose of conquest, this is undoubtedly true. But it is difficult to understand how anyone can read Caesar's own narrative and fail to see that he intended the first invasion as hardly more than a scouting expedition, the second as a voyage of exploration with some punitive features. And considered thus, the invasions were beyond question a success; Caesar put an end to the aid which the Gauls were receiving from across the Channel, and at the same time pointed the way to later rulers, whose colonization of Britain proved immensely valuable to Rome.

As is—or should be—the case in all stories of this kind, the facts of history have been followed as closely as possible. The main events are true, and the incidents are characteristic of the people and the time; the personal adventures of the non-historical actors are fictitious. There is no record that Gaius Aemilius Durus ever lived, and it is certain that no British tribe aided Caesar in the invasion of the land; but there is nothing in the events narrated which is inconsistent with historical possibility, and I believe that the character of Gaius Durus may be accepted as typically Roman.

In vividness of romantic adventure, lofty altruism, and magnitude of genius, the life of Gaius Julius Caesar remains without parallel in the history of the world. It has been a great source of pleasure to me to deal, however lightly, with an altruism and a genius that could, for the benefit of Caesar's countrymen, open a new land, and do it simply as a minor incident of a career. I hope that this tale may in some measure contribute to a better understanding of "the strongest personality that has ever lived," and that it may, as Dr. Rice Holmes says, help to secure a better fate for the *Commentaries* than "to serve as a mere whetstone for gerund-grinders."

PAUL L. ANDERSON

East Orange, N. J.